Dead Man's Bluff

Debbie Burke

Tawny Lindholm Thriller Book 4

Tawny Lindholm Thrillers With A Heart by Debbie Burke
Instrument of the Devil
Stalking Midas
Eyes in the Sky
Dead Man's Bluff

Cover Design by Brian Hoffman
Copyright © 2020 Debbie Burke
Media Management LLC
P.O. Box 8502
Kalispell, MT 59904

ISBN: 979-8-6478-3840-7

Acknowledgements

My wonderful critique group and smart beta readers make writing more fun than work. Many thanks to: Betty, Debbie E. Phyllis, Bec, Marie, Ann, Holly, Kiki, Dita, Patti, Clare, and Leslie. And to Tom Kuffel for ever-patient technical assistance. Also Brian Hoffman, whose artistic talent is only exceeded by his generosity.

Jamie Gane and Gina Carpenter graciously shared prosthetic information.

Special thanks to Sue Purvis for search dog insights.

To Tom, who's always there and always giving.

For Jessica who loves dogs and who loves to read.

Table of Contents

Chapter 1 – How to Show a Girl a Good Time

Tawny Lindholm struggled to hold a heavy sheet of plywood against the frame of a picture window as intermittent gusts of wind tried to tear it from her hands. Her lover and boss, Tillman Rosenbaum, quickly tacked nails into the top, anchoring the wood enough that Tawny could let go. While he nailed off the four corners, she leaned against the trunk of a foxtail palm and plucked another large splinter from her hand, one of many that had pierced her skin during the past hour of boarding up windows. She flexed aching fingers, arthritis reminding her that she was fifty-one.

Tillman straightened to his towering six-foot-seven and tested the strength of the barrier. "That takes care of the windows. But, hell, Hurricane Irma's probably going to tear the roof off so why bother?" He wrapped an arm around her and they entered the single-story cinderblock bungalow. He shoved the door closed against a fresh blast of wind and rammed the deadbolt into place.

They stood side by side in front of the air conditioner, letting it cool the sweat dripping from their faces after working in ninety-five-degree heat.

Tawny held her auburn french braid away from her sticky neck and peered up at the dark-haired, lanky lawyer. "You really know how to show a girl a good time. Bring me to Florida with a hurricane on the way."

A half-smile played across his face. "Can't think of anyone I'd rather ride out a storm with." His jaw jutted. "But about this vacation…it's more work than boarding up windows."

She searched his dark, intense eyes for the secret she'd suspected he was keeping from her. Tillman had a disconcerting habit of dragging her into difficult situations—first with his estranged father, then with his troubled teenage children—without telling her until it was too late to back out. She heaved a sigh. "Not again, Tillman."

He lifted one broad shoulder. "Smoky needs my help. Can't stay away from the sports book. He's a helluva coach but he keeps losing jobs because of gambling. The problem goes way back to when I graduated high school. That's why he asked me to come down to Florida."

Tawny huffed with exasperation. "Why can't you just be honest with me? I'd accept that better than you trying to bribe me with a phony vacation. I wish you wouldn't treat me like some juror you want to manipulate."

"You're right. I'm an asshole." His scary but sexy gaze melted her every time. "Why do you put up with me?"

She made a face. "Because nobody else will." She twined fingers through his springy black curls as he bent to kiss her. Soft, warm lips pressed against hers. Lord, the man was annoying but irresistible.

The kitchen door banged shut in the opposite end of the bungalow. Their host, Smoky Lido, clumped into the living room, lugging two cases of Corona. "Tillman, take your tongue out of that nice girl's throat and go unload the ice from my trunk."

Tillman released Tawny. "Smoke, you always did have lousy timing."

"Not fast enough. That's why I became a coach, not a player." He set the beer on the dining table. "I'll never forgive you, son, for not going pro. I'd've made millions as your manager. I should be living in a Boca Raton high-rise. Instead I'm stuck in a hovel in New Port Richey. Now, go get the goddamn ice before it melts."

Tillman winked at Tawny and headed outside.

Smoky adjusted the air conditioner thermostat and flapped the tail of his Hawaiian shirt, a garish pink with orange hibiscus, to unstick it from his damp back. "Gonna be a hot mess when the power gets knocked out."

"What's the latest prediction?" Tawny asked.

"Irma's supposed to hit late tonight. Then we rock and roll." A grin creased his cauliflower features. He reminded Tawny of a gangster from 1930s movies, thick in the torso, knuckles like walnuts, grizzled sandy-gray hair, deep-water tan. A large emerald stud sparkled in one earlobe. "As long as we don't run out of beer and propane for the barbecue, we're fine. We grill steaks as they thaw out in the freezer. We can last for days."

Tawny was skeptical about Smoky's optimism. No air conditioning or refrigeration at ninety-five degrees sounded like hell. Tillman's crack about the roof tearing off didn't ease her apprehension.

Back home in Montana, she'd endured long power outages during blizzards. She knew how to prepare for a winter emergency—extra firewood, canned food, blankets, and battery-powered lanterns.

A Stage Four hurricane was another story.

Smoky flipped on a ceiling light to brighten the now-gloomy room and studied her. "What's the matter, darlin'? Your first time, right? Don't you worry, this ole boy knows how to throw the best damn hurricane party you ever saw." He cracked open a beer.

Tawny sank onto the turquoise and lime-green cushions of the wicker couch. "Who are you going to invite? Looks like all your neighbors evacuated to shelters."

"Wimps." He lowered himself into the matching wicker chair, hitching khaki cargo shorts above his prosthetic leg. "Thanks for pitching in. You're a good sport. Tillman hit the all-time Powerball with you."

Tawny smiled at the gnarly older man, recalling stories Tillman had told her about how he'd been a caring substitute father, unlike Tillman's dad. "What else can we do to get ready?"

"Have a beer, darlin'."

Getting drunk didn't sound like the best storm preparation to Tawny. "I'm good, thanks."

Tillman elbowed through the kitchen door, a twenty-pound sack of ice in each hand. "Where do you want this, Smoke?"

"Chest freezer in the laundry room."

A second later, Tillman's deep baritone voice called, "Freezer's locked."

Tawny caught a frown skip over Smoky's features. He heaved himself to his feet. "Never mind, I'll get it. Come in here and keep your lovely lady company." He lumbered out of sight.

Tillman joined Tawny on the couch. "Got a line on a generator." He leaned close, flicking the screen of his phone, and showed her a photo. "Last one in three counties. Up in Hudson."

"How far is that?" she asked.

"About twenty miles north of here but, with evacuation traffic, it could take a while."

She frowned. "Is it worth the trip?"

"It will be if the power's out for long. Might be days or even weeks. At least food will stay cold and we'll have air conditioning." He gently touched her nose. "You're already burned."

As a lifelong Montanan, Tawny and heat didn't get along. The brief hour working in Florida humidity had sapped her energy. Even with sunscreen, her pale complexion burned, unlike Tillman's darker skin, a gift from his African grandmother.

His thumb and index finger expanded the photo. "See, it's dual fuel—runs on either gasoline or propane. If we run out of gas, we just rob barbecue tanks."

Smoky returned to the living room, his steps sounding odd because he wore a flip-flop on his foot and a sneaker on his prosthetic. "Went by Wally World this morning. Shelves stripped empty, every department. I get why flashlights and batteries are sold out but curtain rods? Why the hell does anyone need curtain rods right now?" He shook his head. "Only food I saw was a dented can of cat food—giblets and liver. Probably should have bought it."

Outside, the wind suddenly kicked up, banging tree branches against the house. A volley of sharp cracks rang out.

Tawny and Tillman jumped. "Are those gunshots?" she asked.

Smoky wagged his head. "Acorns. From that big, ancient oak outside. When they hit the metal roof, sounds just like a three-fifty-seven. Scared the living crap out of me until I got used to them. Don't worry, just an early band moving through. Roars like a dragon one second, then silence so thick your ears pop. The downpour will hit later."

He clicked on the TV. On the screen, wind and sideways rain whipped a weather reporter crouched against a building as waves crested over a sea wall. "...clocked gusts up to a hundred and forty miles an hour here on Marco Island and the storm surge could impact structures as far as five miles inland."

The TV went black for a moment, video and audio dead. When it resumed, the camera captured the collapse of a wooden dock at a marina. Massive waves smashed boards into kindling. Pleasure boats tossed and collided in jumbled wreckage.

Tawny sank her fingernails into the bright cushion. "How far away is that?"

Smoky said, "More than a hundred and fifty miles south."

Tillman rose. "Told the guy with the generator that I'd duke him an extra hundred if he held it for me. I better head for Hudson now."

Tawny stood, panic washing over her. "Tillman? Don't go. This is crazy."

He fingered her braid. "When we're sitting here in air-conditioned comfort with ice-cold beer, while the rest of Florida swelters without electricity, you'll thank me." He jerked his chin at Smoky. "Give me your keys."

The old coach dug in his pocket and tossed them across the coffee table to Tillman. "Tank's three-quarters full. Got the last drop of gas at the Wawa station before they ran out. Heard from a trucker that it's bone dry all the way to Ocala."

Tawny bit her lip as she and Smoky followed Tillman to the kitchen door.

"Got a spare pistol?" Tillman asked.

Smoky looked sheepish. "You know that would violate my parole."

Tillman gave him a hard stare. "This is a privileged, confidential communication with your attorney."

Smoky grinned, disappeared into his bedroom, and emerged a moment later with a .380 Beretta that he offered to Tillman.

The small pistol disappeared in Tillman's big palm. "You got anything else here for protection?" He gestured toward Tawny. "She's good with a gun, too. Better than I am."

Smoky winked at her. "Beauty and skill. What a combination." He tipped his head toward his bedroom. "Got an old twelve-gauge."

They went outside to the two-stall carport where, as Smoky had predicted, the wind had died down. Tillman awkwardly folded his long legs into Smoky's little aqua retro Thunderbird convertible. Earlier, they had to remove the hard top when they discovered Tillman was too tall to sit in the car with the roof on.

Tawny bent to kiss him, her heart clenched in a knot. "Come back to me safe."

"Yeah."

His offhand tone didn't reassure her. He started the engine and backed out onto the deserted street, dodging fallen palm fronds that littered the pavement.

As the T-bird disappeared around a corner, Smoky squeezed her arm. "He'll be fine. Nothing stops him."

Tawny sighed. "That's what I'm afraid of."

A red jasmine vine climbed up one of the carport's supports. Smoky broke off a twig full of flowers and handed it to her. "Take a sniff."

The gentle gesture from the rough-and-tumble old man surprised her. She lifted the fragrant flowers to her nose and inhaled. "Lovely."

He waved his arm toward the rear of the property. "While it's still calm, come on, I wanna show you the nature preserve." He limped across the grass through the back yard to a lake surrounded by cypress trees, lacy with Spanish moss.

Dank, swampy air hung heavy in the eerie quiet.

"Usually there's all kinds of herons and sand hill cranes and egrets hanging around." He pointed at the top of a dead tree where a three-foot-wide nest was built from branches and sticks. "Ospreys, too. Irma's scared 'em someplace safer."

"The birds are a lot smarter than we are, getting the hell out of here," Tawny said. "Any alligators?"

Smoky guffawed. "This is Florida. Every puddle bigger than a soup bowl has a gator in it. A seven, eight-footer cruises out there. They leave you alone. I don't recommend swimming in the lake, though."

"Never crossed my mind." She dodged rounded knobs of wood protruding from the ground. "What are these weird-looking things?"

"Cypress knees. They grow off the roots of cypress trees."

"What do they do?"

"Mostly they trip up tourists walking by the lake." His blue eyes crinkled with humor. "Actually, nobody really knows what they're for. Just a strange natural outgrowth, like an appendix."

Tawny gazed toward the sun dropping in the west. A growing breeze rippled the lake. "Will you get storm surge here?"

"Glad you reminded me," Smoky said. "Gotta sandbag around the doors. Want to help?"

"Is that part of the all-inclusive vacation package?"

A grin creased his rumpled features. "How'd Tillman get so lucky to find you?"

Tawny slowed her normal pace for the limping man as they walked back toward the carport. "He kept me out of prison." Despite her light tone, the past still weighed heavily on her.

Smoky's voice dropped low and somber. "Me, too, darlin'."
Their eyes met and a brief glimpse of unspoken understanding
passed between them. Neither had to explain the gratitude they felt
toward Tillman for saving them from dire trouble. An odd yet
powerful kinship linked two strangers, with Tillman as the glue
between them.

Although Tawny was curious about Smoky's past, she didn't
want to ask about his record because he might expect her to
reciprocate with her own. It was never easy to explain how she'd
killed a man in self-defense.

Fortunately, Smoky didn't seem eager to open up either. It was
enough for now that they both loved Tillman.

Smoky gestured at long tubular sacks full of sand, piled where
the driveway met the street. "Boy Scouts dropped these off a couple
days ago at the houses of old folks and disabled people. I may be on
Social Security but I'm not ready to be called 'old.' Still, I appreciate
the help."

Tawny lifted a bag, at least twenty-five pounds. Underneath, a
snake with red, black, and yellow stripes lay coiled. She gasped,
jumped backwards, and dropped the bag. It hit the ground with a
dull thump.

Smoky stamped his flip-flop near the snake and it slithered
away. "Not to worry, darlin'. Just a little corn snake."

Her breaths came in jerks. "Is it poisonous?"

"Nah. But coral snakes look similar and they *are* poisonous."
He pointed at the serpent as it wiggled across the pavement. "See,
on this guy, the red stripes are next to the black. There's a rhyme to
help you tell the difference: *Red touch black, you're all right, Jack.
Red touch yellow, you're a dead fellow.*"

Tawny shivered. "Not likely to check out stripes when I'm
running in the opposite direction."

He smiled. "Tell you what, you lug sandbags while I chase off
snakes." He picked up the dropped bag and handed it to her. "Stack
'em about three or four high around the front door. I'll do the kitchen
door. When we're done, I wanna hear more about you and my boy."

"Deal." She carried bags, two at a time, to the front of the house,
as memories flushed over her—how Montana's most famous and
expensive lawyer had represented her when she had no way to pay
him. How he'd seen past her dyslexia and lack of education and

offered her an investigator job she knew she couldn't live up to. How her first assignment almost got her killed.

That close call had torn down the barrier between boss and employee even though they both knew it was felony stupid to get involved.

Yet they did.

But the longer they were together, the more conflicts arose.

She wished their relationship was as simple as piling up sandbags.

When she finished, she helped Smoky stack the last layer across the kitchen door. He struggled to bend down.

"Do you mind talking about how you lost your leg?" she asked.

He straightened, placed hands on hips, and arched his back. "Actually, it's a pretty damn funny story."

Funny? "I'm all ears."

"Working on a commercial fishing boat out of Panama three years ago. Halfway to Hawaii, way the hell out, hundreds of miles from the nearest port. Swells got rocky. Bunch of us were on deck, trying to keep stuff from washing overboard. A winch cable wrapped around my leg and, right then, this big wave knocked us sideways. Cable tightened down, mangled the hell out of my leg."

"How awful," Tawny murmured.

"All things considered I was pretty damn lucky. Another guy on the crew was a butcher from Argentina. Knew more about anatomy than most doctors. Took me below and poured a quart of Cuban rum down my gullet. Then he went to work with a boning knife. Saved my life."

"Wow, that's amazing." Tawny hadn't known Smoky long enough to judge how much of his story might be B.S., trying to impress her.

He thumped another sandbag on the stack. "Funniest part though, my butcher buddy was damn near as drunk as I was. He had this notion that surgeons could reattach the leg when we got into port. So, he wrapped it up in plastic and tossed it down in the hold with the frozen fish."

"Ugh, I don't think I'll eat fish anytime soon."

Smoky chortled. "Not to worry. Never made it to market." He fiddled with the emerald stud in his earlobe. "Know what I miss most?"

"What?"

"Toes. Sports physiology taught me how the body depends on toes for balance and maneuverability. But just moving around, everyday stuff like bucking sandbags. I miss my damn toes." He inspected the barrier they had erected. "Looks pretty good. That better do it because we're out of bags."

Tawny was again drenched with perspiration and weary from lugging heavy sand. "I'm going inside to enjoy the air conditioner while the power's still on."

He waved. "I'll be there pretty quick."

She pushed the door inward and stepped over the makeshift wall into the kitchen. With the windows boarded up, the house was a claustrophobic little cocoon. In the bathroom, she wet a washcloth and wiped her flushed face and burning neck. As she peered in the mirror, she was glad her brown eyes were growing more far-sighted, blurring new wrinkles she'd earned since meeting Tillman.

What the hell mess have you dragged me into now?

That was life with a criminal attorney—everyone you met was in deep trouble.

Although she liked Smoky, she sensed the man, like most clients, would dump a bucket of crap in Tillman's lap then expect magic to fix his problems.

With a sigh, she pinned her braid up with a hair clip then returned to the living room to check for the latest weather update.

On the TV screen, a different newscaster in raingear staggered against the wind down a deserted street. Palm trees bent sideways and whipped the leaden sky. The scene switched to Interstate 75, a solid block of vehicles stopped dead on northbound lanes as people tried to evacuate. The camera caught an embarrassing shot of a guy taking a leak at the side of the road.

Dammit, why did Tillman insist on making a dangerous trip right now to buy a generator? Too many things could go wrong with the entire state in a panic.

And his one-legged pal Smoky was nearly as bad—staying put when sensible people had moved to public shelters.

She heard faint shouts from outside. Although the louvered kitchen windows were boarded over, the seal wasn't tight against the metal frame. She cracked open the back door.

9

A black Hummer had parked crookedly on the sidewalk, blocking the driveway to the carport. Two white men, burly and burlier, were advancing on Smoky. His lumpy face was pinched and he appeared to be pleading with them.

A third man with light-brown skin, slight and elegantly dressed, stood beside the open rear door of the Hummer. Tawny immediately pegged him as the boss because the other two looked to him for direction. She couldn't hear the leader's quiet words.

Smoky talked faster but apparently not convincingly. The leader gave a slight nod and the two thugs jumped Smoky. One held his arms behind his back while the other gut-punched him.

Holy crap!

Where the hell did Smoky keep his shotgun?

Tawny ran into his dim bedroom and flicked on the light switch. She rooted through Hawaiian shirts in the closet and searched duffel bags on the floor. No shotgun.

She dropped to her knees on the tile and ran her arm under the bed. There, she found a long, canvas case. She yanked it out and unzipped it. A pump shotgun rested on the padded lining with a box of twelve-gauge shells beside it. She thumbed shells into it then raced from the bedroom to the back door.

Smoky now lay on the sidewalk, curled into a ball, as the bigger of the two thugs kicked his back and side. His prosthesis had detached, lying a couple of feet away.

Tawny hopped over the sandbags, ran to the edge of the carport, and jacked the slide.

At the loud metallic *clack*, the three men whirled to face her.

"Get out now!" she yelled, swinging the barrel toward them. She aimed at the boss, figuring the underlings would follow his lead.

He stood still, handsome in designer casual clothes and a small, neat fedora. After a few seconds of staring, he smiled at her. Then he climbed into the back seat of the Hummer. The other two got in front. The SUV swerved in a U-turn, climbing up over fallen tree limbs then thudding down on the pavement. In seconds, it was out of sight.

Tawny ran to Smoky and squatted beside him, setting the shotgun on the ground. "Can you get up?"

With her help, he rolled to a seated position. "Motherfucker kicked Annalise off," he muttered, adjusting the sock around his stump. When he twisted to reach for the prosthesis, a deep groan of pain slipped out. He faced Tawny. "I think one of my ribs must have dented that guy's boot."

For a second, she thought his confused words meant a concussion. Then she recognized his dark humor, the same nonchalance toward violent injury she'd heard from her son, Neal, an Army sergeant. She grabbed the prosthetic and set it next to him. "Do you have crutches?"

Smoky pulled the liner into place and fitted the socket onto the stump. "Nah, that'd only make the ribs hurt worse. Crutches are a bitch. Threw 'em away the day I got Annalise here." He tapped the hard plastic affectionately.

"You named your leg?"

"Why not? She's stuck with me longer than my wives did." He tested the suction then rested a heavy hand on Tawny's shoulder. "OK, let's give this a try."

Amid grunts and dripping sweat, she steadied him as they struggled to stand.

Once he was on his feet, she noticed blood trickling from his bruised nose. He dug his tongue into his cheek. "Tooth's loose."

Tawny scanned the street, worried the thugs might return, and retrieved the shotgun. "Come on, let's get inside."

With his arm slung across her shoulder, they climbed awkwardly over the sandbag wall and entered the house. She locked the door and set the shotgun beside it.

"Help me to bed, darlin'," Smoky mumbled. His words came in painful, breathy gasps. She supported him down the short hallway into his room. He sank on the mattress.

Tawny pulled her phone from the pocket of her shorts. "I'm calling nine-one-one."

"No point. They're busy evacuating. They won't come for piss-ant stuff like this."

"Smoky, those men assaulted you."

"Darlin', you've lived in small-town Montana too long. This is nothin' for Florida." Blood flowed faster from his nose, dripping onto his shirt. He hugged a pillow against his injured side. "Just lemme rest. Get me a little anesthetic? Rum and coke."

Tawny went to the kitchen and poured the drink but didn't find any ice in the top refrigerator compartment. In the laundry room, the chest freezer was locked. She grabbed a box of tissues and returned to the bedroom. "Smoky, where's the freezer key? I'll get ice for your drink."

"Never mind that. It's OK warm." He accepted the tissue she offered and daubed his nose. Then he took the glass from her, swigged several large swallows, and belched. His brow eased a little. "Thanks."

She perched on the edge of a papasan chair. "Who are those guys, Smoky?"

He drank again, big hand spread flat in a *wait-a-sec* gesture. He tried to take a deep breath but it caught in a groan.

Tawny knew he should get his ribs X-rayed but how? Tillman had taken the only car. With the hurricane bearing down, 911 wouldn't send an ambulance for anything less than a gushing artery or a heart attack...and maybe not even then.

When she and Tillman had arrived at midday, Smoky's neighborhood had appeared nearly deserted, the last few residents fleeing in their vehicles stuffed with precious possessions. Why did the aging coach insist on staying? He'd mentioned the house was a rental that he didn't own, so he wasn't guarding personal turf.

Under his tan, the skin had turned grayish. She peered into his light blue eyes, checking pupil size. Equal and apparently normal. "Smoky?"

"What, darlin'?"

"Who were those guys?" she repeated.

"Not my biggest fans."

"I figured that out. What do they want?"

One shoulder twitched. "What does everyone want? Money."

"Gambling debt?"

He hugged the pillow tighter. "Tillman told you, huh?"

"Not much."

"Not much to tell. I bet. I lost. They wanna get paid. But I don't know how they found me."

"You've been hiding out?"

"Yeah. Been here over two years, under the radar. Pay rent in cash. That makes my landlady happy. She likes me because I don't trash her fancy decorating." He gestured at the drapes, bedspread, and upholstery on the papasan chair, all matching yellow linen printed with brightly colored parrots. "She keeps the utilities and cable on her account so my name doesn't turn up anywhere. The T-bird is registered to an LLC. I keep my cell in a Faraday bag."

"What's that?"

"Blocks radio frequency signals so location trackers can't find it."

Tawny remembered the vague, mysterious texts from Smoky to Tillman earlier in the day. "Is that why you refused to give us your address when we were coming from the airport?"

"Uber logs every trip. I don't want to show up in anyone's database."

Now she understood the bizarre rendezvous Smoky insisted on. They had met at a gas station at the intersection of Highways 19 and 54 because he claimed the Uber driver wouldn't be able to find his house. He'd lied. The place was an easy mile away, tucked on a quiet back street of lookalike cinderblock boxes built in the 1950s.

Getting both guests to his house had taken two trips. Smoky's T-bird was a squeeze for average-sized adults and had no back seat. Smoky had first driven Tawny home then returned to the gas station to pick up Tillman, leaving her time to ponder why the coach was so secretive.

The arrival of the three thugs, moments ago, had answered that question.

She leaned forward on the chair. "How much do you owe those guys, Smoky?"

"Let's just say, it's more than the change in the sofa cushions."

"That's why you called Tillman last week?"

"Nah." A mischievous grin split his face. "I called him because I had to meet the lady who made him give up his vow to never get married again."

Uh-oh, how did this conversation suddenly veer from Smoky's problems to hers? "That's not going to happen for a long time." No matter how much she loved Tillman, she'd resolved not to marry him until he stopped manipulating her with deception. Like a Florida vacation that turned into a rescue mission for a problem gambler.

Smoky winked. "Whenever wedding bells ring, I want an invitation." He gestured at her left hand, where she still wore her plain gold band. "Gotta say, with Tillman's dough, I'd expect him to spring for a nicer engagement ring."

She shifted on the chair, wanting to avoid long explanations. "This is from my husband. He died a few years ago." And she would never take off Dwight's ring.

Smoky's gaze lowered in shame. "Well, darlin', let me remove my fat foot from my big mouth and apologize. I didn't know."

"No reason you should." She had to get him back on track. "Let's talk about right now. How do you think Tillman can help you?"

He finished his drink and lay on his side. "Darlin', nobody can help me." He pulled the bedspread over his head, a clear enough signal for Tawny to back off.

Chapter 2 – Six Million and Two

In the living room, Tawny watched the telecast as giant waves crashed into a coastal town called Naples. At a high-rise hotel overlooking the Gulf of Mexico, a massive picture window shattered under the onslaught. Wind blew broken glass like sparkling shrapnel.

She clicked to a different channel that showed gridlock on the interstates and major highways. All traffic lanes had been redirected, going north only. Troopers guarded onramps and exits. Even if Tillman reached Hudson, he wouldn't be allowed to return.

She tapped his number. He needed to get back. Fast.

A recording announced all circuits were busy. Everybody and their dog must be calling family and friends. Twenty million people scrambled to get out of the way of angry Mother Nature. The news played continuous footage of uprooted trees, cars bogged in mud, and fallen power lines that sparked and danced on floodwaters.

An emergency manager came on the TV with an announcement: "Evacuate to a shelter *now*. First responders will *not* be able to rescue people who stay behind."

Without Smoky's car, they couldn't get to a shelter.

Tawny tapped a text, hoping it might go through even though calls didn't. *3 thugs beat up Smoky, gambling debts. Come back now!!!*

With the windows covered, she couldn't see outside to know if the men returned. She explored the rest of the bungalow, looking for the safest defensible position, both from gangsters and the hurricane.

The house had two small bedrooms, Smoky's and the guest room where she and Tillman were going to sleep…if he made it back. In between was the bathroom with a tub shower, a small window above it that she and Tillman had covered with plywood. Off the kitchen, only the laundry room had a solid block wall without windows. Probably the safest place to hunker down when the storm hit.

She studied the freezer. It was an old rounded chest style, about five feet long and three feet deep, speckled with rust. It looked similar to the Hotpoint model her grandparents had bought right after electricity finally made it out to their Montana farm in the early 1950s. She tried the chrome handle. It didn't budge.

Tillman always said Tawny's job was to dig out secrets his clients were too afraid to tell him. And Smoky looked less like an old friend and more like a client who desperately needed a lawyer.

The kitchen door to the carport only had a flimsy knob lock. She listened to the rising wind buffeting outside and opened it for a quick peek. The sky had turned black and angry with a thin band of eerie yellow light glowing low on the horizon. Almost sunset.

She fought to push the door closed. Next, she looked around for something heavy to barricade it. The furniture was all lightweight wicker, airy and charming for a Florida vacation getaway but lousy for protection against goons bent on collecting money. She tried to move the refrigerator but it refused to budge.

In a kitchen junk drawer, she found a hank of rope. A waist-high cinderblock wall separated the kitchen from the living room. She anchored one end of the rope through a decorative cutout in the concrete divider and tied the other end around the doorknob.

At least the front door had a deadbolt. Even so, it rattled against its frame as wind gusts roared and fell.

Sudden clattering sounded on the metal roof. Rain hammered loudly enough to overpower the TV's volume.

"Here she comes." Smoky appeared from his bedroom, swaying slightly. He limped to the kitchen, poured more rum and coke in his empty glass, then gestured toward her with it. "Want to join me?"

Tawny shook her head and tried Tillman again. *Your call cannot be completed.* Dammit.

"If you want to take a shower," Smoky said, "might as well do it now. Electricity could go down anytime."

Humidity and hard work had made her sticky but she wondered about being alone and naked around a man she barely knew. Yet, despite his gambling problems, Smoky seemed like a gentleman. And Tillman thought the world of him. She decided to take the chance. "OK, thanks, I will."

"When you're done, fill up the bathtub. We'll use it to wash and do dishes. After the floods, there'll be a boil order on tap water because of busted pipes and overflowing sewers. Hot and cold running e-coli."

She wrinkled her nose. "Gross. Remind me again why people live in Florida."

"You don't have to shovel rain."

***

After a refreshing shower, Tawny scrubbed the tub then left the water running to fill it. Wearing clean shorts and a tank top, she came out of the bathroom to the delicious aroma of steak frying. Smoky stood at the stove. "Medium rare OK?"

"Perfect."

"I was planning to barbecue for you guys but..." He flicked a spatula at the ceiling as rain thundered on the roof. "I'll hold off cooking Tillman's steak until he gets here. Any word from him?"

Tawny checked her phone for at least the fifth time since he'd left. "Nothing. Shouldn't he be back by now? It's only twenty miles."

"Traffic's a bitch." He jerked his head toward the refrigerator. "Chop up some lettuce for salad, will you? There's tomatoes, avocados, and red onions, too."

As Tawny removed vegetables from the crisper, she watched his movements for lingering signs of pain but he seemed better. Or maybe just more anesthetized. "How are your ribs?"

"Sore, but no worse than the day after some football games I played when I was a pup." He raised his full glass, now clinking with ice cubes. "*Cuba Libre* is a miracle cure."

The unfamiliar sounds of banging and cracking outside made Tawny uneasy. She forced herself to focus on making salad.

Smoky spread butter on both halves of a loaf of Cuban bread. He sprinkled garlic salt and parmesan on top then slid a pan into the broiler.

In the living room, the TV was drowned out by the rain racket. She asked, "What's the latest on Irma?"

"Downgraded to a Category Three. Eye's approaching Sarasota now."

"How far is that from here?"

"About seventy-five miles. Next, she'll hammer St. Pete then Tampa. Once she's over land, that should take more punch out of her. If we're lucky, she'll be down to a Two when she gets here. But

17

she's moving slow and dumping a helluva lot of rain. Flooding's gonna be our biggest problem."

Where was Tillman? She thought of Smoky's car without a roof and prayed he could find shelter. She tried calling him again. Now the screen read: *Emergency calls only.*

Smoky flipped steaks out of the frying pan and nodded toward Tawny's makeshift rope lock as he carried plates to the table. "I like your security system."

She stooped to pull the garlic bread out of the broiler. "Do you think those guys will come back?"

"Not tonight. They hightailed it for their hole." He held Tawny's chair for her then sat across the table. "Think I figured out how they tracked me down."

She served salad on their plates. "How?"

"That goddamn phone of Tillman's. He's been texting me and they can trace your keystrokes. I keep my phone dark unless I'm several miles from home. But, if they figured out that he was meeting me, they could just follow *his* phone to me."

Tawny knew too well how smartphones could become tracking devices, having herself been the victim of a stalker. "How did they connect Tillman with you?"

Smoky cut into his steak, blue eyes wistful. "He's the only one I stay in touch with from the old days in Montana."

"You miss Montana?"

He chewed for a thoughtful minute. "Life was simpler back then. Friendly wagers with buddies over brewskis. Then I got caught betting on college games. Drummed me out of the state. Tillman had just graduated law school around then. I was gonna be his first case. He wanted to help me but, hell, rather than going through hearings and appeals and shit, it just seemed easier to move on…and on…and on. So here I am."

She remembered the water running and rose. "I better check the bathtub."

"Good idea," Smoky answered. "We don't need a flood *inside,* too."

In the bathroom, the tub was nearly full. Tawny turned off the water and stood for a moment, grasping the shower curtain rod to stretch her back. "Dammit, Tillman," she whispered, a choke in her throat, "please don't get yourself killed out there."

Back at the table, Smoky washed down his steak with more rum and coke and continued reminiscing. "Coached in Michigan for a while. Indiana. Then Nevada. That's where I really got in deep. Only state where college betting is legal. I loved it. Every game, every day. Better than sex." He hunched shoulders up around his neck. "If you ever tell Tillman I said that, I'll hunt you down and kill you."

She laughed. "I won't." The weird secrets people confided in her never failed to amaze.

He went on: "Did some time in the state pen. Decided to start fresh, new career. Commercial fishing, all over the globe. I like the sea, out there in the sky and sun and that salty taste on your lips. Managed to stay clear of gambling for years. Well, mostly." He fingered the emerald stud in his earlobe. "Won this little sweetheart playing poker. My three sevens beat two pair, queens and aces. Loser was a guy from Cartagena who got this working in the emerald mines near Bogota. Almost a carat."

Tawny leaned closer to admire the sparkling green gem. "It's really beautiful."

He tore off a hunk of crusty bread. "Then that damn cable ruined my leg. Couldn't work on the boats anymore and fell back into my old ways. Wound up lying low in this hovel." He sopped bread in steak juice. "The only people that give a shit about me want to kick my ass."

The self-pity was an all-too-familiar refrain. Tawny took a bite of garlic bread and watched Smoky's rumpled face as he slowly chewed, distant memories flickering in his eyes. The dreams of what might have been. She'd seen the same expression in the eyes of her father at the rare times when he was sober. The regrets were the same, whether felt by an alcoholic or a gambler.

Smoky studied her for a long moment, as if contemplating a decision. At last, he murmured, "Tillman doesn't know but I got a little girl I've never seen. Tried to send money for her but her mom sends it back. Won't tell me her name or her birthday. Not that I blame her—*I* wouldn't want me around my daughter." He pushed his plate away. "I wish I'd been a better man." He leaned forearms on the table. "And that, darlin', is the sad, boring tale of my wasted life."

Tawny remembered the stories Tillman had told her about how Smoky had mentored him when he was a kid badly in need of a friend. No matter what mistakes the man had made, his kindness to Tillman counted for a lot. She reached across the table and squeezed the coach's arm. "Couldn't have all been wasted. You mean everything to Tillman."

He shrugged. "Yeah, well, when he comes to my funeral, at least his car won't get door-dinged." He leaned on the back legs of his chair. "Damn, that boy was one fine athlete. First time I saw him, I knew he was going places. He could pull miracles out of his baseball mitt. Most of the time, he pitched, a real cannon. But I remember one all-state game when he was playing left field. The hitter knocked a sure home run, looked for all the world like it would clear the fence.

"Tillman leapt up in the air and, I swear to God, he took flight. Flashed the leather and snagged that ball right out of the sky. The final out that won the game. The batter was so pissed, he flung his bat into the stands and hit the vice principal. Poor sonofabitch got suspended."

Tawny munched on salad, enjoying the vicarious glimpse of Tillman in his youth, long before she knew the hard-charging, aggressive lawyer. "He still pulls miracles out of the sky. I've watched him do it in the courtroom."

Smoky gave her a small, fond smile. "I bet he does. Still, damn shame to waste that talent. When he was in high school, he and I used to fly down to Tampa for Yankees' spring training. I hooked him up with some scouts. He could have been another Honus Wagner."

"Who?" Tawny asked.

"Greatest baseball player of all time. Played for the Pirates in the early nineteen-hundreds. Helluva hitter. He was smart, too, like Tillman. Once he psyched out a pitcher, that guy was doomed. Tillman coulda matched him. I knew it in my gut then. Used to call the boy *Honus Rosenbaum.*"

"Why didn't Tillman go pro?"

"He got offers but he was set on college and law school. He'd say, what if his arm went out, what would he do then? That's the difference between him and me. He played the long game, looking way into the future. I only cared about beating today's point spread."

Tawny wondered what miracle Smoky expected from Tillman to get him out of his current trouble.

He finished his drink, got up to pour another, thudding across the tile floor with his unique gait, sneaker-clump and flip-flop slap. Facing away, he mumbled something she couldn't hear above the hammering rain.

"Sorry?" she said.

He turned to her and repeated, loudly, "I love that boy." Tears glinted in his eyes.

Her heart wrenched for the sad old coach. "I do, too, Smoky."

After washing dishes, they settled in front of the TV and watched footage of a tin roof peeling off a warehouse. The roof cartwheeled down a street, crashing into abandoned cars and bouncing off bowed-over palm trees. Weathercasters tracked Irma's relentless march into St. Petersburg and Tampa.

A studio reporter said, "It's predicted that six million people will lose electricity by morning."

Then the house went black. Completely and totally black.

TV and air conditioner abruptly fell silent. Only the racket of the constant wind and rain swirled outside.

The darkness was all consuming, as if Irma had sucked every speck of light and air from the room, like a vacuum chamber. As if Jonah's whale had swallowed Tawny and she floundered deep in its belly, unable to breathe or escape. Strangling fear gripped her.

From out of the darkness, Smoky said, "Make that six million and two."

Chapter 3 – Into the Hurricane Eye

Tillman drummed both hands hard on the steering wheel of Smoky's little T-bird. The solid line of traffic snaked forward mere inches at a time. The trip to Hudson to buy a generator should have taken a half hour tops, a straight shot north on Highway 19. Instead, all vehicles had been diverted east to SR 52, pushed inland, away from the expected storm surge, toward the Suncoast Parkway. Angry gusts buffeted the T-bird sideways. Exhaust billowed from the tailpipe of the diesel truck ahead of him but the rising winds carried it away before he smelled the stink.

He'd now been gone for four hours, funneled into the evacuation route by cops, sheriff deputies, and state troopers who blocked off access to any side roads where he could turn around. Tumbling black clouds promised imminent rain and the damn car had no roof.

Tillman worried about Tawny and Smoky stuck without transportation. Storm surge might swamp Smoky's bungalow.

He remembered the stricken expression on Tawny's face when she all but begged him not to go, dread haunting her brown eyes. She wasn't used to Florida's heat. The searing sun had already burned her pale skin but she didn't complain. A generator to run the air conditioner would ease her discomfort. But he'd failed and was coming back empty-handed, a wasted trip. He pounded the steering wheel.

When he tried to access GPS on his phone for alternate routes, the screen read *Emergency calls only*. The slow-moving but relentless current of traffic forced him north and east, farther away from his destination. He kept constant watch for a place to slide past law enforcement roadblocks and return to Smoky's.

Although Tillman was glad to see his old coach, Smoky pissed him off. His long history of gambling problems always reached critical mass at the most inconvenient times, like when a hurricane was bearing down on Florida.

Still, Tillman reminded himself, Smoke was aging fast. There might not be many more chances to see the friend who had prevented him from killing his father.

Stuck in traffic, Tillman's mind reached back to when he was sixteen, burning with righteous indignation and testosterone. He remembered stroking the knife blade across the sharpening stone hundreds of times, honing the edge so fine that his old man would never feel the slicing open of his carotids. Tillman planned every detail, including where he'd dispose of the weapon, the rain slicker, gloves, and boots he'd wear to shield him from the blood.

But Smoky had recognized the reckless fire in Tillman's eyes and stepped in.

He listened for hours to Tillman's reasons why his old man deserved to die. How his mother's life would be better, rid of a philandering husband. How Tillman was smart enough to cover the angles and not get caught.

Smoky didn't threaten him or try to talk him out of it. Instead, he walked Tillman further into the future, beyond the old man's death, beyond the satisfaction of his immediate rage. "You're smart," he'd said. "But even the best plan can turn to shit. What kind of life will your mom have if she has to visit you in prison?"

And the question that finally pierced his resolve: "*We* know he's a prick but she can't help loving him. You gonna be able to look in her eyes after you kill him?"

That night, Tillman changed his course and decided to play the long game. Gather data, look ahead, measure the odds, anticipate repercussions. Not give into the lust for immediate gratification. He used his brains, went to law school, and built a successful career. No one except Smoky knew how close he'd come to killing the old man, not even Tawny.

His father didn't die. He continued to drag down the lives of others.

But not Tillman's.

The coach's wisdom had pulled an angry boy back from the brink yet he couldn't follow it in his own life. That irony frustrated Tillman. Why didn't Smoky walk the walk?

Over the years, the roles reversed as Tillman interceded in one gambling crisis after another. Each time, Smoky swore Tillman would never have to rescue him again. There was always a next time.

But he loved that goddamned degenerate gambler and he'd pull Smoky back from the brink once more.

A sudden downpour drenched Tillman's hair, ran down his neck, and soaked his shirt. Even on high speed, the windshield wipers didn't keep up. The headlights couldn't pierce the darkness but only reflected on sheets of rain. With no top on the car, he felt every lash of wind, every stinging drop.

It was going to be a long night.

***

Tawny remained fixed to her chair, gripping the arms. The sound of Smoky's clack-thump steps reassured her as he moved around the house, familiar to him even in darkness. He turned on battery-operated lanterns, casting small, hopeful pools of brightness in the dim rooms. He spent several minutes in the kitchen then returned to the living room and handed her an icy glass.

She sniffed rum and coke and decided *why not?* It tasted sweet and strong. Warmth spread through her chest, relaxing muscles that felt too tense to breathe. "Thanks."

Smoky settled back in his chair with his own refilled glass. "I'd be one lousy host if I didn't bring you a little nightcap. But, after this, we should probably go to bed to save battery power. Is your phone OK?"

She went to the side table and unplugged her cell from the now-useless charger. "Ninety-five percent."

"Good. Any word from Tillman?"

She'd checked for texts throughout the evening. "Still nothing."

"Don't worry about that boy. Smart, wily, resourceful as hell. He'll be fine. Probably found himself a nice cozy restaurant that still has electricity and is enjoying a big T-bone and some fine scotch."

Smoky meant well, trying to reassure her, but concern still gnawed in her gut. A car without a roof didn't provide any protection from the violent weather. She sat again and sipped the strong drink. A flush worked up her neck to her face. "What do we do now? Tell ghost stories?"

He chuckled. "Halloween's coming. Got me a dandy costume planned. Eyepatch, black tri-cornered hat. Pirate's dagger clenched in my teeth. Stuffed parrot perched on my shoulder. Slather red dye all over my stump and attach a plastic gator. What do you think?"

She had to laugh at the picture he'd conjured. "Sounds like a prize-winner."

"I'd like to head down to the Keys. They know how to throw a Halloween bash. But Irma's probably torn that place up pretty bad. Course, a little flooding and wind never stopped Key Westers from a good party."

She knew he was trying to take her mind off worrying about Tillman and liked him for the effort. But concerns beyond the hurricane still bothered her. "Tell me something, Smoky."

"What, darlin'?"

"How do you expect Tillman to help with your...problem?"

The shadows around his eyes deepened. "I don't think he can. I really dug myself a deep hole this time."

"Do you want to tell me about it?"

He shook his head. "Won't do either of us any good."

"Then why did you ask Tillman to come?"

He gulped his drink. "Wanted to see my boy again."

The sudden shift to sadness in his tone distressed her. Like he meant to say goodbye. A last goodbye.

Outside, an explosive crack sounded from the back yard, followed by a rending, tearing groan. A loud *thunk* shook the whole house.

They both jumped up. Smoky clumped to the kitchen. Tawny grabbed a lantern and followed him.

"Dammit, bet that old oak went down," he grumbled as he untied the rope around the knob.

Rain still hammered the roof. He opened the door a sliver, using his bulky body to block it from blowing wide, and peered out into utter blackness. Tawny squeezed beside him and shone the lantern through the narrow opening.

As he suspected, an oak tree had crashed onto the carport roof, buckling the metal. One side had been folded flat to the ground. The leafy crown intruded almost into the doorway.

Smoky pushed the door closed, locked it, and retied the rope. "Close one. A little more left, it woulda caved in the roof over the kitchen. Then we'd be in one soggy mess."

Tawny leaned against the counter, took deep breaths, and waited for her heart to return to normal. The lantern weighed heavy in her shaking hands.

He noticed her trembling. "That's the only big tree close to the house. Now that it's down, nothing else to worry about. Get some sleep." He took the lantern from her and set it on the counter, then handed her a two-cell plastic flashlight. "Take this to bed with you, darlin'."

He limped out of the kitchen toward his bedroom and started to shut his door.

She clutched the flashlight as her quaking subsided. "Smoky?"

He paused and looked at her. "What is it?"

"Thanks for calming me down. I don't know what—"

"You're gonna be OK, darlin'." The shadows of his smile deepened in the flashlight glow. He blew her a kiss then closed his door.

She turned off the lanterns in the living room and retrieved her phone. In the kitchen, she picked up the shotgun she'd left by the door earlier and found her way to the spare bedroom. She propped the shotgun beside the bed then lay on top of the comforter. Heat and humidity settled over her like hot, soggy blankets. She hated to turn off the flashlight because it would plunge her again into stifling blackness.

Even in the remotest Montana wilderness at night, stars and moonlight tempered the darkness. Here, inside the windowless cinderblock prison, there was no such relief.

She took a deep breath and forced herself to click the switch off, gripping the flashlight in her hand like a lifeline.

***

"Tawny! Are you all right?" Although far off, Tillman's deep baritone was unmistakable.

She sat up, struggling out of sleep, trying to remember where she was. Darkness and humidity smothered her. She patted the bed, trying to orient herself, and touched a plastic tube. The flashlight.

She clicked it on. The beam illuminated an unfamiliar bedroom. Then she remembered.

At Smoky's house. In Florida. During a hurricane.

Rain still rattled on the roof but the wailing wind had died down.

"Tawny! Where are you?"

She clambered off the bed and hurried toward his voice, coming from the kitchen. The back door was pushed slightly ajar but prevented from opening by the makeshift rope lock she'd rigged. "It's OK, I'm here," she called. "Give me a minute." She switched on the lantern Smoky had left on the kitchen counter.

Through the crack in the door, Tillman snarled, "What the hell is going on? I've been yelling for five minutes."

She fumbled with the knots, knowing his angry tone masked his fear for her safety.

"I drove in and saw that tree down," he said. "Then you didn't answer. I was about to tear off the plywood with my bare hands and bust a window."

She finished unwinding the loops around the knob. At last, she flung the door open.

A tangle of branches, twigs, and oak leaves from the fallen tree surrounded Tillman. He stepped over the sandbag wall and slammed the door behind him. Tawny threw her arms around his neck, relief coursing through her.

His clothes were sodden and chilly against her, his hair dripping in her face. He lifted her off her feet. "You OK?"

"I am now."

His mouth found hers for a hot, deep kiss that signaled he was all right, not hurt.

When he let her go, all her pent-up worry tumbled out. "Oh, Tillman, I was afraid you were dead. The phone didn't work. The power went off."

"Helluva welcome, locking me out."

Her fingertips traced the grin she couldn't see in the dark. She pulled him to the kitchen table and turned on another lantern.

In the light, he looked weary, black curls plastered to his skull. She unbuttoned his shirt and peeled the soaked fabric away from his skin then ran to the bathroom for towels. He dried his arms and back, unzipped his shorts, and kicked them aside then toed off his deck shoes. She gazed at him, standing in his briefs, toweling his hair, as relief washed over her again. God, he looked wonderful. "I was so scared."

He looped the towel around her and pulled her close. "Hate to disappoint you but I didn't get the generator."

"Like that's all I was worried about."

"Where's Smoky?"

She leaned away and looked up into his dark eyes. "Some thugs beat him up because of his gambling debts. I chased them off with his shotgun but he might have broken ribs. He's asleep." She gestured toward the closed door of his bedroom.

"Surprised my bellowing didn't wake him up." Tillman moved to the door and rapped with his knuckles. "Hey, Smoky, what the hell mess did Tawny have to rescue you from?"

No answer.

He thumped harder. "Smoke?" He frowned then turned the knob. Tawny handed him the flashlight. He pointed the beam at the bed.

Empty.

Swept it around the room.

Not there.

In less than three minutes, they'd searched the entire bungalow but Smoky had vanished.

"How far could he get," Tillman asked, "with one leg and no car?"

Tawny tried the front door. "He must have gone out this way and locked the deadbolt from the outside."

They each grabbed lanterns and put on already-wet shoes. Tillman pulled two rain ponchos from the coat rack, handing one to Tawny, and threw the other on over his briefs. Outside, they paused on the porch. He said, "I'll check around back. You look on the street." He disappeared into sheets of rain, calling Smoky's name.

Tawny swept her light along the sidewalk, darkness as far as she could see. The beam only shone a few yards in the downpour, making raindrops sparkle and reflect back at her. She sloshed through water, moving toward dark lumps in the shadows, worried they might be Smoky, lying on the ground. As she closed in, she recognized a child's big wheel tricycle on its side and a crumpled wad of heavy roofing paper.

Flotsam rushed down the street that had now become a river. Several thin, ghost-like arms waved from the swirling water—the broken ribs of a patio umbrella.

She yelled his name but her voice didn't project like Tillman's.

Smoky was nowhere to be seen. She waded back to the front steps and stood on top of the sandbag wall, sweeping the light back and forth, calling out. Not a soul, human or animal, moved in the desolation. The porch overhang offered no protection from the wind-driven rain.

After ten minutes of fruitless searching, Tillman slogged from behind the house and shook his head. "Nobody around here for miles."

They went inside and took off their ponchos, leaving puddles on the tile floor. Tawny felt sweaty yet chilled at the same time. Despite the rain, the temperature remained uncomfortably warm.

"Where the hell could he be?" Tillman hung his poncho on the coat rack.

She followed with her own. "He knocked down a fair amount of rum and coke but he didn't seem drunk when we went to bed around midnight." She sucked in a breath. "Do you think those thugs could have come back for him?"

"How did they get in? After they kicked the crap out of him, I can't see him welcoming them in for a drink."

"Tillman, it doesn't make any sense."

His arm circled her shoulders. "I know. But nothing to do until it gets light. Maybe the rain will let up by morning. We'll search then."

They moved into the bedroom and undressed. Together, they slipped under the sheet, lying on their sides, facing each other.

"He sounded kind of melancholy tonight," Tawny murmured as Tillman's hand slowly slid along her back, over her hip, coming to rest on her bottom in a sensual massage.

"Melancholy?"

She wrapped her leg around his. "Full of regrets for screwing up his life. Then he said how much he loved you and he was almost crying."

"Doesn't sound like the Smoky I know." His lips explored her neck, warm breath tickling her skin.

"I only just met him but it didn't sound right to me either. Almost like the reason he wanted you to come to Florida was so he could tell you goodbye."

When his tongue flicked her hardening nipple, her concern slipped into the background. She pulled him closer, full of gratitude that he was safe. Together in the dark, they shared the unspoken realization they could have lost each other in the hurricane.

Chapter 4 – Safe and Well

The morning dawned sticky and sultry. Occasional tailing bands blew through that dropped drenching rain for several moments, followed by blazing sun that made steam rise from puddles. As Smoky had predicted, Irma lost her punch over land.

But she had also blown down electricity and cell service. Neither Tawny's nor Tillman's phones could capture a signal. His laptop had a full battery but couldn't connect to the internet for news.

Outside the bungalow, Tillman used a claw hammer to wrench nails out of the plywood covering the windows. He propped up the damaged carport with a long plank. Removing the broken oak tree would require a chainsaw.

Tawny cooked breakfast outside on the propane barbecue grill—Tillman's leftover steak, scrambled eggs, and cowboy coffee, grounds boiled in a saucepan. They sat at the kitchen table, sunlight streaming through open windows. He dug into the food with enthusiasm. "Best breakfast ever."

Tawny smiled. "That's because you didn't get any dinner last night. What was the road trip like?"

He shoveled in more eggs. "Everything closed, boarded up tight. Cops were funneling traffic to evacuation routes only, not allowing anyone into neighborhoods. I told them I needed to get to this address to rescue my wheelchair-bound, ninety-eight-year-old granny."

Tawny shook her head. "Tillman, you're bad. Leaving poor old granny to fend for herself."

He shot her a sardonic smile then sawed into his steak. "State troopers weren't impressed with my story, wouldn't let me past. On top of that, it's raining like hell and the damn car has no roof. Interior's soaked. Smoky's going to have a major mold problem with it." He paused to chew the meat then continued: "I finally sneaked past the cops, turned around, and headed back here. That's why we don't have a generator."

Tawny ran her hand along his muscular thigh. "Doesn't matter. I'd rather have *you* back safe." Despite sweltering heat, she had clung to him all night, afraid to let him go.

Heavy silence invaded the kitchen and settled over them.

She finally asked, "Where could Smoky have gone?" She knew Tillman was already pondering the same question.

"Nearest shelter is about five miles from here. He couldn't make it that far on foot. He might have boosted a car but I doubt it. Any rig left behind probably doesn't run."

"Maybe he went to a neighbor's house."

"Most everyone around here evacuated." He reached for her hand. "Let's check the shelters in the area if you don't mind riding in a soggy car."

"OK."

Tillman pinned her with his intense stare. "I'm not giving up on Smoky."

"I know you aren't."

"I'll find him, dead or alive."

Tillman always anticipated the worst but Tawny realized the fatal possibility was all too real in the catastrophe of the hurricane.

After breakfast, they decided to first search the surrounding neighborhood on foot, moving in opposite directions from Smoky's house. Tawny wore an oversized pair of Smoky's heavy rain boots that flopped against her calves and clumped with each awkward step. But they offered better protection than her sneakers from hazards lurking the dirty river that flowed down the street.

She picked past uprooted vegetation, scattered furniture, shingles, broken glass, and garbage. A twenty-foot-long sailboat lay on its side, the mast dug into the mud, apparently blown in from the beach two miles away. A raggedy couch had run aground, caught by a clump of palm trees.

Floodwaters lapped the sides of low-lying homes. In the next block, another big oak tree had toppled onto a travel trailer, caving in the roof and tearing the walls into jagged aluminum tongues.

Humidity made each breath feel like drowning. Tawny slogged through stinking, brackish water and mud to knock at the doors of cinderblock boxes that looked just like Smoky's. No one responded. Residents had not yet ventured back after evacuation. In the distance, she heard Tillman's deep, resonant shouts for Smoky.

Otherwise, the area was eerily quiet. No bird sounds, no traffic, no human noise.

She'd checked a three-block radius before she finally found one person at home. A toothless, unshaven man in a wife-beater undershirt cracked open his door, swore at her, and slammed the door.

Tawny gave up then and headed back.

A flock of seagulls arrived from the Gulf and wheeled overhead. Their raucous screeches were a welcome distraction from the heavy, dead silence.

A basketball floated by in a drainage ditch. As she climbed over a submerged tree branch, a red, yellow, and black snake slithered in front of her. She jumped sideways, nearly losing her balance.

Smoky's rhyme echoed in her memory: *Red touch black, you're all right, Jack. Red touch yellow, you're a dead fellow.*

Red touched yellow on this snake.

She backed away as quickly as she could, struggling not to stumble in the sucking mud that pulled at her boots. The snake disappeared under a tangle of twigs. She hurried toward home.

More gulls gathered and circled, their cries insistent. They seemed focused on an area in the nature preserve behind Smoky's house.

Had the gulls found a dead creature to feed on?

Tawny picked up her pace, slipping on muddy sidewalks in her urgency.

Please, not Smoky.

She met Tillman at the driveway, her steps crunching on leaves from the fallen oak. He also watched the gulls and silently shared her worry. Together, they slopped through Smoky's back yard to the lake. A soggy trail led into the swamp. They tripped over cypress knees hidden in puddles and swatted vines out of their faces as they drew closer to the racket made by the gulls.

Perhaps a hundred yards into the jungle, the trail opened into a clearing. On the shoreline of the murky lake, gulls hopped around a swollen form, half-sunken and covered in mud.

Tawny and Tillman moved toward it. She held her breath, partly because of the smell but mostly from fear of what they'd find.

Tillman stomped ahead, shouting and waving his arms to chase the scavengers away.

It was a bloated deer, belly torn open, entrails pulled out. Flies buzzed thick around its open eyes and crawled over the exposed intestines.

"Thank God," she breathed, leaning into Tillman. "I was afraid it was Smoky."

His arm came around her for a quick hug. "Let's get out of here."

They retraced their path to Smoky's yard, not talking, relieved, yet knowing the carcass could just as easily have been Tillman's old coach. At the front door, they paused to pull off boots. Rainwater filled a bucket and they washed their muddy arms and legs before going inside.

In the kitchen, Tawny opened the refrigerator, grabbed a gallon jar of sun tea, and quickly closed the door to retain the dwindling cold. "Want iced tea?"

"Sure." Tillman checked his phone. "Damn, still no signal."

She went to the chest freezer, opened it, and scooped two glasses full of ice, then realized it was no longer locked. She poked inside, wondering if Smoky had taken a hidden treasure when he disappeared. There was an empty space among packages of frozen food where something might have been removed. She closed the lid and checked the tile floor for telltale signs of anything he had dropped. Except for her own grubby bare footprints, she saw nothing.

Back in the kitchen, she poured tea and handed Tillman his glass. "Did you notice Smoky acted kind of weird about his freezer?"

His brow furrowed. "Weird?"

"He kept it locked. Didn't want me getting ice last night. Make kind of big deal out of it. But now it's unlocked."

"You're thinking...?"

"He stashed something in there for safekeeping. When he left, he took it with him."

"Like what?"

"I don't know. What do you lock up? Drugs, money, weapons. There's an open space about this big." She held her hands eighteen inches apart.

He raised an eyebrow. "The size of a Mach Ten or an Uzi. He's already violating parole with that Beretta. Might as well go whole hog."

She thought back to the previous night. "Those guys who beat him. Do you suppose he had something that belonged to them? Maybe it wasn't a gambling debt they were after."

Tillman pulled on his chin. "That could induce him to get the hell out of Dodge, even in the middle of a hurricane."

She gulped tea, grateful for the coolness in her overheated body. "What has your old buddy gotten himself into?"

"Damned if I know."

***

After a lunch of peanut butter and jelly sandwiches and sliced oranges, Tawny and Tillman sopped up the worst of the water in the T-bird, parked in the driveway. The leather seats dried off easily but the carpets were soaked. As she wiped puddles from the dashboard, she said, "I'm surprised the electrical panel didn't short out."

"Still might," Tillman answered. "Things rust fast in this humidity." He folded into the driver's seat. "See if it starts." The engine coughed and sputtered. After a moment, it smoothed out. "Let's go check out the shelters. Bring the shotgun." He jerked his head at the road. "Out there, we might run into people who'd like to take this car off our hands."

Tawny retrieved the weapon from their bedroom, wrapping it in a black plastic garbage bag. She locked the house and climbed into the passenger side. The cushion squelched under her weight. She hid the shotgun behind the seat but still handy.

They backed into the street, tires flinging mud. Tawny turned on the radio and scanned channels until she found an operational news station. Millions of people were without electricity. Shelters were overcrowded. The Anclote River was rising and expected to flood soon.

Sun beat down on them as they moved through deserted streets. Tillman drove slowly, watching for submerged debris. Tawny turned on the air conditioner to blow across their faces even though, without a top, it couldn't cool the car.

She tried to latch onto wi-fi connections with Tillman's tablet. At last, she found one. He pulled over and parked under a shade tree, giving welcome relief from the searing sun. She handed him the tablet.

For several minutes, his long fingers flicked over the screen. A half-dozen red arrows dotted the map he'd pulled up. "In Pasco County," he said, "shelters are in elementary schools." He gave the tablet back to her. "That one's the closest. We head there first."

She directed him where to turn until they found the school. Parked cars jammed surrounding streets and packed the playground, except for a few open areas where children chased each other, laughing and tossing balls, resilient in the face of disaster. Tawny imagined their parents were inside the building, worrying if they had homes to go back to.

A truck moved out and Tillman pulled into the vacant space. "I'll go check for Smoky." He got out and walked around to her side. "Mind staying here? Shouldn't leave the shotgun in a car we can't lock."

"OK." She watched his long strides toward the entrance. Her fair skin was quickly burning under the bright sun. She got out and stood in the shade of the building, wishing they'd brought hats and go-cups of iced tea.

Fifteen minutes passed before Tillman came out, carrying two water bottles. He shook his head that he hadn't found Smoky and handed one to her. They stood in the shade, gratefully guzzling lukewarm water.

After emptying his bottle, he said, "Well, that was an eye opener. There's no roster of who goes into shelters. Some bullshit about confidentiality. Red Cross has a website where people can enter their phone number or address so family knows they're *safe and well*." He made finger quotes. "But unless you have internet, which isn't working in most places, you can't access the site. They suggested checking Facebook, too. Not damn likely with Smoky. He won't advertise for the guys chasing him."

Tawny ran her arm across her burning forehead. "Yeah, he told me he's pretty paranoid about staying off the grid. Keeps his cell in a Faraday cage. He thinks the texts from your phone are how those guys found him." She finished her water. "So, what do we do now?"

"Keep going from shelter to shelter in hopes of spotting him."

Three fruitless hours later, in the parking lot of the sixth school, Tillman started the engine and studied Tawny. "You've got to get out of the sun. You look like a lobster."

She felt like one, too, simmering in sweat. She pressed the bare skin on her thigh with a finger. Red skin turned white. She closed her eyes, trying to ignore dizziness from her pounding headache. Her pale complexion wasn't tough enough for tropical sun. Even Tillman's skin, already bronze from his Ethiopian grandmother, looked burnished. "OK. But what else can we do to find Smoky?"

He peered at the dashboard. "Only an eighth of a tank left. We can't waste more gas aimlessly wandering around. Let's head back to Smoky's."

As he drove, Tawny finished her sixth bottle of warm water, replenished at each shelter they had stopped at. Because she'd sweated so much, she hadn't gone to the bathroom since early morning. It was now nearly four in the afternoon.

Tillman steered past floating lumber in rising brown water. "Not sure we can get back the same way."

Ahead, a Honda sat abandoned on the side of the road, water edging up to its door handles. An orange bucket from a home improvement store floated past.

"Shit," he muttered, putting the T-bird in reverse. He backed all the way down the block to the next intersection and stopped. They peered at the cross streets but the floodwaters flowed deeper and deeper, overtaking the car from every direction. He made a U-turn, heading inland, searching for a road that wasn't completely submerged. Even at a cautious fifteen miles an hour, the wake behind the T-bird looked like a speedboat.

Tawny sniffed sewage that tainted the nasty-smelling garbage soup. The car's footwells filled. She lifted her feet but her socks and sneakers were long past soaked. "I wonder if typhoid or cholera seeps through skin," she said.

Tillman swore at water rising through openings around the gas and brake pedals.

Several blocks away, they spotted the flashing roof lights of a public works truck. The T-bird engine coughed and surged, barely running until they finally climbed a slight rise, out of deep water. Two workers in reflective vests were setting out *Road Closed* signs. One hailed them and Tillman stopped.

"Dude," the man said, "you're lucky you got out of that area when you did. Anclote River's flooding. Another few minutes and everybody's gonna be swimming."

"We're headed home." Tillman rattled off Smoky's address. "Any roads still open to get there?"

The man went to his truck and returned, swiping a tablet. He held the screen so Tillman and Tawny could see it. "These here are satellite photos. Last update was about fifteen minutes ago."

The screen showed vast areas of brown water as high as the windowsills of houses. Muddy sludge covered cars up to their roofs. Square residential blocks could be defined but long sections of road disappeared under water. The river no longer had any boundaries, spreading like dirty chocolate milk spilled across a flat table of land.

The man swiped through aerial views of roofs and bundles of treetops. "That road is still OK. You might get through if you go around this way." His fingertip traced a circuitous route. "Looks like your house might still be in a dry area."

Tillman asked, "Any reports of dead bodies?"

Tawny chewed her lip. Tillman was always quick to expect the worst and, unfortunately, often turned out to be right.

The man frowned. "Not that I've run across. Nothing's come over our radios."

"A friend of ours went missing during the storm. We've been checking shelters."

"You could try hospitals or the sheriff's office. But good luck getting through. Phone lines are jammed and a lotta cell towers are down."

"Thanks for your help."

The man flipped a salute. "Hope you locate your buddy."

They drove the zigzag route, frequently hitting dead-ends and backtracking, but finally turned onto Smoky's street. A few residents had returned to the neighborhood, slogging through mud to survey the damage around their homes.

Tillman pulled into the driveway, avoiding the fallen oak tree. Tawny got out and stepped into the shade of the house, relieved to be out of the blistering sun.

Water had crept from the lake across Smoky's back yard and lapped at the sandbag barrier he and Tawny had built the day before.

She stood atop it and unlocked the back door, swinging it inward. Tillman followed, sloshing through puddles behind her.

The kitchen floor was still dry so the sandbag barrier had done its job...so far. If no more rain fell, Smoky's home might not flood.

The inside of the house felt nearly as sweltering as the outdoors, even though they'd left the windows open, but at least the sun no longer beat down on them. Without ceiling fans, the air hung heavy and stagnant.

Tillman toed out of his mud-filled sneakers. "I'd sell my children for a shower right now."

She peeled off socks so rotten that no amount of bleach could clean them. "I'd buy your children for a shower right now." Wet shorts chafed the insides of her thighs. She took his hand and led him to the bathroom, their muddy footprints leaving a trail on the tile. They undressed and dipped towels in the water stored in the bathtub to wipe down their sweaty, naked bodies. She patted her sunburned skin, fearing layers might peel off if she scrubbed too hard. But the cool water felt good.

With two fingers, she picked up their smelly clothes from the floor. "I'd like to wash these but we should save the clean water."

"Hang 'em over the towel rack to dry. Best we can do for now." He studied her red skin then opened bathroom cupboards. "Smoky's got to have something to take the sting out of that burn." He grabbed a bottle of green jelly-looking stuff. "Aloe's supposed to be good." He squeezed some in his hand and gently coated her face, neck, arms, and legs, anywhere her t-shirt and shorts hadn't covered.

"How about you?" she asked, taking the bottle from him.

"Don't need it. Thanks to my grandmother." His brow crinkled as he stroked damp hair off her forehead. "This isn't quite the vacation I planned. I thought we'd get Smoky's problem settled right off then go to a nice hotel on Clearwater Beach. Drink those frozen Margaritas you like."

Slushy lime and tequila sounded good but the only thing she truly craved right now was air conditioning. The unit in the living room remained silent, useless without electricity. Despite her worry the night before, she now wished Tillman *had* brought back a generator.

In the bedroom, she threw on one of his big t-shirts, light on her tender skin. He stepped into clean shorts but didn't put on a shirt.

She rubbed his bare chest, dark hair tickling her palm. "Want some dinner?" she asked. "I'll see if more steaks thawed with the power off."

He kissed her, his lips salty from perspiration. "You're my beautiful calm harbor amid the storm."

"You weren't here when the lights first went off. I didn't feel very calm then."

"I'd bet big money you were a helluva lot better than Rochelle would've been. Can you imagine the screaming tantrum she'd throw without electricity?"

The mention of Tillman's ex made Tawny squirm because the subject usually led to a fight about his children.

She pulled from his embrace and went to the kitchen. "I had to throw out the salad greens because they got slimy but maybe there are canned veggies."

As she searched the cupboard, he checked his phone. "I texted the kids when we got into cell range. Judah texted back. He's pissed he didn't get to come with us. He thinks being in a hurricane would be 'bitchen.' His word."

Tawny smiled. "Big adventure for a thirteen-year-old."

"I almost brought them."

She watched him watching her, testing for a reaction, and hoped her expression stayed neutral. As much as she cherished Mimi, Arielle, and Judah, she desperately tried to avoid the ongoing custody fight.

He added, "We could have made the trip into a family vacation."

Tawny didn't answer. She'd been careful not to overstep boundaries. Tillman and Rochelle were the parents and had to work out their children's future between them. No amount of love could change the fact that Tawny was not the one who'd given birth to them. She would never have the rights Rochelle did.

His voice deepened, serious. "If I went to the mat, I could get sole custody."

"Tillman, no matter what, she *is* their mother." Tawny faced the cupboard again.

"They could use a better one." He came up behind her, encircling her waist. "Someone who's the way a mom *should* be."

She selected two cans from the shelf. "Do you want baked beans and corn? Smoky has plenty of those."

"You're avoiding the subject."

"Yes, I am." She slid sideways from him, set the cans on the counter, and moved to the freezer in the laundry room. She opened it. The interior was still cold but, when she pressed a finger on the top package of T-bones, they felt soft. She pulled them out and quickly closed the lid to keep the remaining cold in as long as possible.

When she turned around, Tillman filled the doorway, blocking her way, his gaze penetrating her soul, recognizing the apprehension that gripped her.

He knew, even better than she did, that if Tawny joined his fight for his children, Rochelle's jealousy would rocket off the scale. Her vengeance could destroy the entire family.

And poison Tawny's relationship with Tillman.

"Tawny."

"Just let me fix dinner, OK?"

"Let's get married."

Her head throbbed from too much sun. The sting of her sunburn worsened by the minute.

There was no escape from the cinderblock hot box or the disease-filled, snake-infested waters lapping outside the house.

Or Tillman.

"You know how I feel about that," she murmured. "We should wait until the kids are grown. Rochelle already thinks I'm trying to steal them from her."

"You didn't steal them. They gave you their love freely. That's what she can't stand." He leaned an arm on the door frame. "I planned to bring the kids along and have the wedding here. Smoky as my best man."

Damn. He was always springing surprises on her. "Crap, Tillman, you have the rest of our lives all worked out but you didn't think to let me in on it?"

He offered a lopsided smile. "No reason to mention it because it didn't fly. Rochelle threatened to go to the judge if I tried to take the kids out of state without her permission. I would have prevailed but there wasn't enough time."

Tawny remembered her conversation with Smoky the previous night and his odd comment that Tillman could have sprung for a better ring. "Did you talk about this to Smoky?"

Sheepishness flitted across Tillman's face. "Did he spill the beans?"

"Not exactly. But he apparently knew more about this wedding plan than *I* did." She pinned him with a hard look. "You're not supposed to leave the bride out of the loop." She pushed past him, pressing the steak package into his bare belly.

The cold shock made him jerk back. He grasped the package then grinned. "Thanks, that felt refreshing."

On the kitchen table, Tillman's phone tinged with a new text. He set the steak on the counter then studied the screen. "From the guy with the generator. He says somebody else wants it, too, bidding the price up another hundred."

Thank goodness for the distraction from wedding talk. "Sounds like a shakedown."

"Could be. But if he's legit, it'd be worth it to run the AC."

She had to admit air conditioning sounded awfully good in her dehydrated, sunburned condition. "Is there enough gas in the T-bird to get there and back?"

"Should be OK. Maybe I can scrounge some en route."

Her head pounded and a wave of dizziness swept over her. She braced herself against the counter. "I'll stay here. I can't take any more sun."

"Good idea." He kissed her as he headed toward the back door. "Shouldn't be too long if I can avoid flooded roads. Back in time for steak." The door banged shut.

Her aching head lolled back. Damn that man but, damn, she loved him.

A minute later, he opened the door again, stripping the plastic bag from the shotgun. "You better keep this here. Radio just announced there's been looting." He handed the weapon to her.

"What about you?"

"Smoky's pistol is still in the glove box. If it hasn't turned to rust."

"Be careful."

His chin thrust out. She studied the towering, lean, shirtless giant, able to bench press more than three-hundred pounds. Anyone who challenged him would be a fool who came out second best.

Even so, Tawny worried. Plenty of danger still lingered in Irma's wake.

Chapter 5 – Unwelcome Visitors

Smoky's electric can opener didn't work without power. Tawny rattled utensils in the kitchen drawers, searching for a manual crank style, but didn't find one. Unless Tillman punched a knife through the metal lids when he returned, they'd have to eat steak without corn and beans.

In one drawer, she found a raggedy-looking address book. She put on her readers and tried to focus but even her eyeballs felt sunburned. Squinting, she paged through, sipping sun tea, now tepid because the ice had melted. Maybe she could trace Smoky's whereabouts through his friends. He'd printed first names only, in pencil with a heavy hand, no notations of who *Raul* or *Lyman* or *Dennis* were.

Tillman's name, private cell, home and office numbers were noted, as well as his children's names and their birthdays. There was also a smeary erasure that looked as if it once read *Rochelle*, Tillman's ex.

If Smoky had family listed, Tawny couldn't tell without last names.

When she checked her cell, it still showed no service. To follow up on Smoky's contacts, they would have to drive someplace where their phones worked.

If enough gas remained in the T-bird to go anywhere.

Since Irma, simple everyday conveniences—like can openers, phone service, and gas pumps—had become precious luxuries, as out of reach as the stars.

Through open glass louvers, she heard a screech of metal in wood. At the bungalow next door, an unshaven Hispanic man used a claw hammer to yank nails from the sheets of plywood covering his windows. He was in his thirties, wearing a ball cap, t-shirt, and cut-off jeans.

A girl about thirteen with dark brown braids walked around the yard, picking up storm-tossed trash and stuffing it in a garbage bag. A gangly black Labrador scampered alongside her, eagerly sniffing the strange smells brought by Irma's debris.

Maybe the neighbors had a clue where Smoky had gone.

Tawny again put on the oversized rain boots and went out the front door. Afternoon sun beat down, still brutal at five o'clock. Her throbbing headache ratcheted up another notch. She walked around puddles toward the house next door. "Hi," she called.

The dog bounced to her, tail wagging, excited to meet a new friend. Muddy paws slapped Tawny's sunburned thighs. She yelped as claws raked her painful skin. "No!" She shoved the dog away.

"Churro!" the girl shouted. "Get down!" She ran toward Tawny and grabbed Churro's collar. "Bad boy, don't jump up!" Her braids flipped as the dog twisted, trying to break loose. "Sorry, ma'am, I'm still training him. He's only a year old."

Tawny swallowed fresh pain that contracted her throat. Scratches scored her already-red skin. "It's OK. I'm a dog lover." Although, at the moment, she didn't love *this* dog.

The girl yanked on the collar. "Sit, Churro, sit."

After a short struggle, the dog obeyed. Tawny petted his shiny black fur. "Good dog, Churro." To the girl, she said, "I'm a friend of Smoky's. Have you seen him?

The girl shook her head. "We evacuated. Been at our church. Shelters don't allow dogs but the padre does. We just got home a little while ago."

The father walked over to join them, nodding at Tawny. "*Señora*." He gestured toward the fallen oak tree that had smashed Smoky's carport. "I have a chainsaw. I come over later and cut up the tree."

"*Gracias, señor*," Tawny answered. "That's very nice of you."

"Smoky, without his leg, it's hard for him to do work like that."

"You're a good neighbor."

The girl piped up. "Smoky's awesome. He's coaching me in track."

Tawny smiled at her. "Smoky coached my fiancé, too, when he played baseball in high school. But we're worried now because we can't find him. He left in the middle of the storm last night and disappeared."

The man pulled his chin back. "Disappeared?"

"Do you know where he might have gone? A friend's house, maybe?"

Both father and daughter shook their heads.

"Do you know any of his other friends?"

"Only Nyala, the lady who owns his house." The man shot an embarrassed look at his daughter. "Sometimes she…"

The girl broke in: "Smoky's girlfriend spends the night, only Papi doesn't want to come out and say that. Like it's some big scandal." Her eye roll asked *do you believe how old-fashioned he is?*

"Jessica." The father spoke a few gruff warning words in Spanish. To Tawny, he said, "Excuse my daughter, *señora*."

"Jessica? My name is Tawny Lindholm." She turned to the father. "*Señor?*"

"Raul Zaragoza, *señora*."

"*Mucho gusto*. Nice to meet you." She'd seen the name *Raul* in Smoky's address book and made a mental note to look up a number for Nyala. "Where does Nyala live?"

Raul jerked his head to the east. "Land O'Lakes. About twenty miles away. I hear many roads over there flooded, too, even worse than here."

"Does your cell phone work?"

"No. It worked OK at the church but when we get home, *nada*." He raised one shoulder. "I need to call, check with my job, see if the store will open tomorrow. But I have to find a cell tower that works."

"Where's your job?"

"Big warehouse hardware store over on Highway Nineteen. They close for the last three days. Everyone wants tools and generators but we sold out. Store is empty, like a big cave. Have to wait for trucks to bring new shipments." He removed his cap to run a sinewy arm across his perspiring forehead. "At church, I hear that trucks are getting stopped at Georgia state line. Can't come in." He splayed his hands. "Maybe I have job, maybe no."

Tawny's ears had perked up when he mentioned *generators*. "My friend is trying to buy a generator in Hudson but the deal sounds a little funny. If that doesn't work out, can we buy one from your store when you receive your shipment?"

He grinned. "I save one for you. How big do you want?"

"Can you get one to run an air conditioner, refrigerator, and the TV?" Especially the air conditioner. A wave of wooziness swept over her and she planted her feet to keep from swaying.

"Should be next shipment. If I had extra money, I would buy one, too, but my wife is stuck in Puerto Rico. She go there to help *abuela*..." He looked at Jessica for help.

"Grandmother," his daughter filled in. "She has cancer and Mama's been there with her for the last month. Then Irma hit. We can't call her. She can't call us. We don't know if she's safe. Puerto Rico got socked real bad."

Tawny's heart choked for the family in spite of the increasing fog in her brain. "That's scary."

Raul said, "I need to send money to her but no banks, no phones, no electricity, no way to get it to her. So, we must wait."

Behind his frown, Tawny recognized the same terror she'd faced when separated from Tillman. "I'm so sorry."

Jessica spoke up: "My uncle has a ham radio with solar power. He can talk to amateur radio operators in Puerto Rico. He's trying to find out where Mama and *Abuelita* are."

"My grandpa was a ham," Tawny said. "They're the only communication left when cell phones and the net are down."

An annoying hum grew louder inside her ears. She squinted into the searing sun. The continued heat was making her sicker. But walking away from the concerned family would be rude.

Jessica said, "My uncle helped FEMA and emergency services during Katrina. He's helping now, too." Her mouth twitched a little, fighting back a sob. "I hope he can find Mama and *Abuelita*."

"So do I, sweetie." Tawny squeezed her shoulder, trying not to sway from dizziness.

Jessica brightened. "I'm training Churro to be a search dog. He's going to find lost people in disasters."

Tawny forced enthusiasm into her voice. "Wow, that's great."

"There's training courses." The girl made a face. "But you have to be over eighteen. I read a book about a lady in Colorado who taught her dog how to find people in snow, under water, all kinds of weird places. She had a black Lab, too, just like Churro. I'm learning how from her book. Churro is a really good swimmer."

Tawny wanted badly to get out of the sun and lie down. "It's nice your whole family wants to help people."

Jessica thought for a moment. "I guess so."

Churro had wandered off toward the overflowing lake. Raul again spoke in Spanish to his daughter. She ducked her head, then ran to the dog, grabbed his collar, and dragged the reluctant Churro back through puddles.

Raul shot Tawny an indulgent father look. "Big dreams, this little girl. But she better watch her dog or a water moccasin will bite him."

Tawny shuddered. "I saw a coral snake this morning when we were checking around the neighborhood for Smoky."

"*Cuidate mucho*. Be careful. Snakes want to find a dry home. They go through broken water and sewer pipes to get inside the house."

Tawny shot him a horrified look, hoping he was just trying to scare the dumb tourist, but his expression was dead serious. Along with the desire to get out of the sun, she suddenly felt overwhelming homesickness for Montana. Grizzlies and mountain lions seemed less threatening than poisonous vipers wiggling inside through busted plumbing.

"Jessica, put Churro in the house," Raul said. "We need to go call my work." To Tawny, he said, "Excuse me, *señora*. I come tomorrow with my chain saw."

They shook hands and he headed for a Ford truck in his carport, angling between several fifty-five-gallon metal drums. The barrels had been placed to catch runoff from the roof and were brimming with rainwater collected from the downpour. Tawny felt a brief stab of envy, remembering the limited supply of fresh water in Smoky's bathtub.

More cars turned into their driveways as residents trickled back. She should ask other neighbors if they'd seen Smoky but the buzzing in her ears grew deafening. Those questions had to wait until she felt better.

A staggering wave of dizziness engulfed her. Her vision went shiny white. She stood still for a minute, hoping her knees didn't buckle.

After a few deep breaths, her disturbed vision cleared enough that she dared to walk back to the house. Inside, she locked the door and collapsed on the nearest chair. Head spinning, her heart thudded heavy in her chest. She gulped tea, now tepid and weak from melted ice.

Bracing herself on furniture and walls, she stumbled into the bathroom, sat on the edge of the tub, and dipped washcloths in the

47

precious, stored water. She draped one around the back of her neck and wiped her forehead with another. Her skin felt hot and dry as if every drop of sweat had been wrung from her body. She dipped a plastic cup into the tub and forced herself to drink the lukewarm water.

After a second cupful, nausea lurched in her stomach. Drank too much too fast. But she had to rehydrate. She rested for several moments then went to the chest freezer. She filled a tall glass with cold water from the plastic bags of melting ice then folded a handful of remaining cubes into a towel.

In the bedroom, she sipped more water and lay down with the ice-filled towel across her forehead. Even with her eyes closed, splintered mirrors drifted through her vision. The headache pounded in her ears.

She'd done all she could to treat heat stroke and faded into fuzziness.

***

A hand grasped Tawny's bare foot and wiggled it. She couldn't open her eyes and her tongue stuck thick in her dry mouth. "Don't, Tillman. I'm sick."

The hand continued to shake her foot.

She pulled it away, pushed herself up on one elbow, and rubbed the now-warm washcloth over her eyelids. When she forced them open, they felt like sandpaper scraping across her eyeballs.

Shadows darkened the bedroom, the last shimmer of daylight coming through the window. She made out a silhouette of a small man wearing a fedora.

Not Tillman.

Her mind flip-flopped in frenzy. How did he get in? Who was he?

She'd left the shotgun in the kitchen—nothing to defend herself with.

He stood between her and the doorway—nowhere to run. Panic tightened her throat.

As her eyes adjusted, she recognized the same man who'd ordered his thugs to beat up Smoky.

He smiled, that same strangely elegant smile. "Lovely lady, where is my dear friend, Smoky?"

Her heart pounded in her ears. "He's gone."

"I understand that. My colleagues and I have searched the house. Where did he go?"

Slowly she sat up, fighting dizziness. She couldn't pass out, not now. "I don't know. He left during the storm. I have no idea where he is." Would the truth be enough to convince the dapper man?

"Where is your very tall gentleman friend?"

Where *was* Tillman? He should have been back by now. "He'll be here any moment. You better get out. He's armed."

The man lifted the tail of his pressed silk shirt, showing a pistol grip in his waistband. "So am I, lovely lady." He hitched one hip up on the edge of the low dresser. "Smoky and I have known each other for a long time. I really don't want to lose track of him."

She sucked in a strangled breath. "I don't know where Smoky went. I can't help you. Just leave. You don't want to get into a gunfight over a guy who isn't here."

He folded his arms across his chest and regarded her for a long moment.

Despite faintness, she forced herself to maintain eye contact— her only means to prove she was telling the truth.

At last, he slid off the dresser. "I believe you. But when you see Smoky, please tell him I do need to talk with him."

Two larger figures darkened the doorway, waiting for their boss. He touched his hat then all three men disappeared down the hall. Seconds later, she heard the back door open and close.

Tawny pushed herself up from the bed. On wobbly legs, she peered out the window as the same black Hummer drove away into the descending dusk.

Supporting herself against the walls, she moved into the hall. Linen cupboard doors were open, the contents scattered on the floor. She stepped over rumpled piles of towels, sheets, and extra rolls of toilet paper.

In Smoky's bedroom, the mattress had been yanked off the box spring and lay folded in half on the floor, bedding torn loose. Clothes and duffel bags had been removed from his closet and thrashed through, dresser drawers pulled out and dumped.

Wicker furniture in the dim living room had been overturned, cushions on the floor. Drawers from end tables had been opened. The TV hung askew on its wall mount.

In the kitchen, sacks of chips and cereal had been swept from cupboards and were strewn around. The table and the chairs were toppled. She staggered across the room to the gaping refrigerator door and found the steaks she'd seasoned earlier for dinner still sat on a plate but other food was scooped out and dumped on the floor. She closed the door, a useless gesture since the cold had already escaped.

Something sharp pierced her heel—shards of glass in a puddle of rum. She plucked out the slivers and tiptoed away, avoiding the jagged neck of the broken bottle.

In the laundry room, packages of meat had been removed from the freezer and lay jumbled on the floor, along with the remaining plastic bags of ice, now almost completely melted. When she bent over to pick up the food, she had to grab the wall to keep from passing out. After several deep breaths, she gathered up the meat, threw it back in the freezer with the ice bags on top of it, and shut the lid.

Her legs quivered. She righted a kitchen chair and collapsed into it. The brief adrenaline rush from the surprise visit by the gangsters gave way to overwhelming weakness.

Amazingly, the men hadn't taken the shotgun propped against the cinderblock room divider. She grasped it in trembling hands and jacked the slide. Empty. They had ejected the shells. She set it down, weak from the weight of the heavy gun. Maybe they hadn't found the remaining box of shells under Smoky's bed. But her body felt too leaden to move the mattress to look for them.

She sucked deep gulps of air and clicked on the lantern sitting on the concrete divider. Thank goodness, the thugs hadn't smashed the light.

With the sun gone, the thermometer hanging on the wall now read eighty-seven, down from ninety-five earlier. Barely tolerable.

Why wasn't Tillman back? A battery clock above the stove said more than two hours had passed since he left.

How had the intruders gotten in? Then she noticed a gap in the louvered windows by the back door. Didn't take a crack burglar to slide out a glass pane and reach inside to unlock the knob.

Her mouth felt dry and sticky. She took a sip of tea she'd left on the counter earlier, surprised the glass hadn't been broken in the trashing of the house. Surveying the mess, she wondered how the noise hadn't wakened her. She must have been completely knocked out by heat stroke.

Headlights appeared down the street. Were the intruders coming back?

She jumped up and found a butcher knife amid utensils and frying pans on the floor. She turned off the lantern to prevent them from seeing inside the house. Gripping the knife, she watched through a window as the car approached.

It turned into Smoky's driveway and stopped. Against the last faint glow of twilight, she recognized Tillman's tall form unfolding from the low-slung T-bird.

She dropped the knife, flung open the back door, and stumbled over the sandbag wall, through the oak branches, to reach him. "Those men came back. The ones who beat up Smoky."

He grasped her arms. "Are you OK?"

She sucked in a breath. "They broke in and trashed the house."

"Jesus," he growled. "They didn't hurt you?"

"No, I'm all right."

Together, they went inside. Tawny sank weakly on the chair while Tillman turned on more lanterns and inspected the damage. When he returned to the kitchen, he studied her face in the light. "You don't look good." He handed her the glass of tea.

She drank a few swallows. "Heat stroke. I was kind of passed out in bed and didn't even hear them knocking over furniture."

"What did they say?"

"Just the leader talked. He wanted to know where Smoky was. I told him I didn't know. I guess he believed me and they left."

He peered closer. "You sure they didn't hurt you?"

She shook her head then regretted the movement because the pounding worsened. "I've got to lie down. The steak is in the fridge but they left the door open. Everything's probably spoiled."

"Don't worry about that." He helped her up and steadied her, his arm around her waist, a lantern in his other hand.

In the bedroom, she sank on the mattress. Even the pressure of the pillow against her head made the ache worse.

51

He went into the bathroom and came back with fresh wet towels and a plastic cup of water. Gently, he wiped her face and neck then folded the cool cloth onto her forehead. "Dammit." The low rumble of his baritone reverberated through his touch. "I shouldn't have left."

She closed her eyes, grateful for his presence. "Did you get the generator?"

"Like you thought. A scam. Guy had a new, sealed Honda box. I made him cut it open and inside was this rusted hulk that hadn't run since last century. I think he planned to mug me for the cash and take off. But, once he saw me, he decided it wasn't worth the risk."

She smiled weakly. "Size does matter."

He stroked her cheek. "You're burning hot. Drink more water." He held the glass for her. "I did score a couple of gallons of gas, though, so the trip wasn't a total waste."

"Where?"

"The guy had a jerry can in the back of his truck. I confiscated it for my inconvenience. Smells stale but it's better than nothing. I tossed the junk generator in a dumpster along with his truck keys. Left him digging through garbage looking for them."

"Captain Karma."

One side of his mouth lifted despite the concern still clouding his eyes. "Want anything?"

"I'm too sick to eat. You go ahead if the meat's not spoiled. But I couldn't find a manual can opener so you're out of luck for anything else."

"Just rest. I'll take care of everything." He bent to kiss her lightly.

How soft his lips felt on her hot, parched mouth. Her breath had to smell terrible. Then she remembered. "They didn't take the shotgun but they unloaded it. Earlier, I saw a box of shells under Smoky's bed. I don't know if they're still there."

"I'll find them." He left with the lantern and darkness took over the bedroom.

A faint, comforting glow came from the living room as she listened to Tillman moving furniture to straighten the mess, while she wavered in and out of sleep. A short time later, the aroma of steak sizzling on the grill outside drifted through the window. Such small, insignificant things as a glimmer of light and the smell of cooking food gave her hope that maybe the chaotic, flooded moonscape of Florida might eventually return to normal.

Tillman carried two plates into the bedroom. She managed to sit up and sip more water. As sick as she felt, the meat smelled good. He'd added a handful of potato chips.

"Take a few bites," he said. "You should eat something salty when you're dehydrated." He sat on the edge of the bed, cut up the steak, then handed her the plate.

She nibbled while he wolfed down his steak and crunched chips. After a few bites, her stomach rebelled. She set the plate aside, hoping the food would stay down. "I met the neighbors next door. They have a Lab puppy that might like the rest of my steak."

He smirked. "Don't I get first right of refusal?"

She pushed the plate to him. "The guy, Raul, works at a tool store on Highway Nineteen. He said he'd save us a generator when the next shipment arrives."

"Hell, I've driven around half the state and you waltz next door and charm the neighbor out of one." He wagged his head. "Amazing." He picked up the plates and rose. "Drink as much as you can then get some sleep."

She sipped from the glass and lay down, curling on her side. He took the plates to the kitchen. A moment later, he was back, towering over the bed. She felt a fresh, cool washcloth on her forehead. She reached for his hand and drifted off, holding it.

Chapter 6 – One Bag of Ice, Ten Gallons of Gas

During the night, Tillman had gotten up several times to replace the cloths on Tawny's forehead with fresh, cool ones. By morning, a lingering headache nagged but otherwise she felt stronger. He slathered more aloe on her burned skin, which had already started to peel. He skipped shaving to conserve the water in the bathtub.

Another scorching, muggy day without air conditioning lay ahead. Before Tawny had awakened, Tillman had taken a walk around the neighborhood to reconnoiter. None of the other neighbors who'd returned from evacuation had seen Smoky.

The milk was sour so they drank black coffee that Tillman made in a pan on the grill. For breakfast, they munched dry Cheerios. Oranges in the crisper drawer of the now-warm refrigerator had grown fuzzy gray coats but, once he peeled off the moldy rind, the fruit tasted wonderfully juicy.

After breakfast, Tawny tossed the mayonnaise and other perishable food into a garbage bag and placed it outside in the carport. Smoky's trash can was gone, blown away in the storm. "This is going to turn nasty real fast in the heat. Wonder when trash collection will start again?"

Tillman used the tail of his yellow polo shirt to mop his face. "Couple blocks away, there's a front-end loader from the road department, clearing fallen trees. So much crap blocking the streets, cars can't get through. The operator said he'd keep working until he ran out of fuel. Then everything comes to a screeching halt until there's electricity to run gas pumps." He shook his head. "What a cluster."

Outside, they stood in the shade of the house and surveyed the lake. Overnight, the flood waters had receded, almost back to the normal shoreline. Flotsam remained behind on the muddy grass. Irma's gusts had flung the aqua hardtop for the T-bird across the yard.

"What are we going to do today?" Tawny asked.

Tillman peered down at her. "You're staying out of the sun. The way you looked last night, you can't take any more heat." He stroked the side of her face, concern still in his dark gaze.

She did feel wrung out and weak, like the aftermath of a bad case of the flu. "I won't argue. But we still have to look for Smoky. I found an address book. His landlady's name is Nyala. They evidently have a romance going. Several other women's names in the book, too."

Tillman lifted an eyebrow. "Sounds like Smoky, all right. Maybe he's holed up with one of them."

Around the corner of the house, a chainsaw roared to life.

Tawny said, "That's probably the neighbor. He offered to help with the oak tree."

They walked to the carport and found Raul adjusting the choke on the saw as it sputtered then died. He looked up at their approach.

Tawny introduced them. The men shook hands and immediately began speaking in rapid Spanish too fast for her to follow, except for a few words. She left them discussing the best way to cut up the fallen tree.

Inside the house, wearing her readers, she pored over Smoky's address book again. She found Nyala's number and the first names of three other women. Smoky didn't bother alphabetizing, apparently randomly adding contacts as he met them.

Outside, the chainsaw engine repeatedly revved up and idled back. After thirty minutes, she checked again. Both men were now shirtless, their muscular chests shiny with perspiration as they worked together, bucking chunks of wood and stacking smaller branches in a growing brush pile.

She poured two glasses of tea, added the few remaining slivers of ice, then took the drinks outside to Tillman and Raul. They shut down the chainsaw and gratefully accepted the barely cool tea, tipping their heads back, Adam's apples moving up and down as they gulped.

Raul said, "I hear some places are getting electricity back on. Mostly down in Tampa. Not this far north yet. My store is still closed but may open later today if there is power."

"I thought of something," Tawny said to Tillman. "If we can put the hardtop back on the T-bird, I could drive somewhere that has cell coverage and try calling the numbers in Smoky's phone book."

Tillman's cheeks hollowed as he sucked ice. "Not a bad idea. But you being out alone isn't smart."

"It's the only way. You can't fit in the car with the roof on and I can't take the sun with the roof off." She read Tillman's worry. "Besides, I'll be in air conditioning, doors locked and windows rolled up. If any stores are open, maybe I can pick up more ice."

Tillman continued to frown at her, his disapproval clear. "You're sure?"

"I'll be careful," she said.

To Raul, Tillman said, "Give me a hand putting the hardtop back on the car?"

The men walked through the muddy grass, lifted the top, and carried it to the T-bird. They set it in place and lined up the pins to reattach it.

While they worked, Tawny went inside to get the address book and her phone. Still ninety percent charged.

Catching a glance in the bathroom mirror, her appearance startled her. Too much sun was not kind to redheads—face puffy, cracked lips, nose painful and peeling. She applied more aloe, giving her skin a faintly green sheen. Brushing her teeth didn't get rid of the fuzzy feel inside her mouth.

Her braid had come undone, loose strands stuck to her damp skin. Too much trouble to re-braid. She twisted the hair into a knot, and fastened it high on her head with a clip.

Dear God, she needed a shower and shampoo. She would never again take for granted the blessed luxury of unlimited, clean, running water.

Outside, the men had secured the hardtop on the car. The engine was idling. Tillman peered down at her. "Lot of roads still flooded and tons of debris. Don't take chances."

She slid her palm over his damp, naked chest. "I won't."

"I turned the AC on high. Should start getting cool soon. I put a go-cup of water in the holder. Stay hydrated."

For a lawyer who was normally harsh and arrogant, he had a tender, considerate side that he kept hidden from everyone except her and his children. "Thank you," she said.

His mouth firmed into a hard line. "Pistol's in the glove box. Loaded. Twelve rounds. Watch out for looters."

"OK." Doubt coiled in her stomach as she climbed into the car, closed the door, and gripped the wheel tightly.

Even a simple errand meant another frightening separation in the disrupted world after Irma.

***

The air conditioning had a slightly moldy smell but Tawny still relished the coolness after being overheated for so long. She drove slowly through the neighborhood streets, steering around obstacles and giant puddles. On a still-flooded side road, she watched a couple of teenage boys racing an air boat, whooping as they threw up rooster tails while they swerved across the water.

She debated whether to head west to Highway 19 toward the Gulf, or to go inland, farther from storm surge damage. The radio gave updates, mentioning the names of towns and roads she didn't recognize. She wished she had a map to track where the newscasters were talking about.

Electricity had been restored along the main corridor of Dale Mabry Highway, wherever that was, but power had not yet fanned out to surrounding areas. Up to twenty-two inches of rain had drenched some areas of the state. Flooding was widespread.

Few vehicles ventured out. Traffic lights didn't work. Several times, *road closed* barriers forced her to retrace her route.

She turned onto SR 54, a major highway, and headed east, away from the Gulf. Only occasionally did she see other cars across the expanse of six lanes. She passed darkened fast-food joints and closed supermarkets with vacant parking lots. After eight desolate miles, she spotted an open gas station and convenience store. A long line of cars snaked from the gas islands into the street. Customers pushed into the store, others coming out with armloads of groceries and ice.

Tawny joined the queue for the pumps behind a pickup truck. The driver stood outside his rig, smoking and pacing as he waited for the line to move. He nodded at her. "Ten-gallon limit as long as the gas lasts. I turned my engine off. Otherwise, I'll run out."

The T-bird gauge hovered near empty. Tawny followed the man's example and shut off the ignition. Without air conditioning, the car quickly heated up even with the windows open.

While waiting, she checked her phone and was elated to see four bars. She thumbed through Smoky's address book and tapped in Nyala's number. It rang five times then went to voice mail.

"Nyala, my name is Tawny Lindholm. I'm trying to locate Smoky Lido. He went missing in the storm and we're concerned about him. Please call me."

She tried the numbers beside the names of three other women. Two calls said *all circuits are busy, please try again later*. The third didn't even ring.

In the baking car, sweat trickled down her back. The line moved at a snail's pace as a few vehicles left the islands. She counted twenty ahead of her.

A heavyset black woman in her fifties wearing thick glasses left the store, trailed by a little boy about seven. The woman carried two bags of groceries while the boy hugged a ten-pound sack of ice to his chest. Both looked weary. As they walked past, his admiring gaze swept over the T-bird and he shyly made eye contact with Tawny.

She smiled at him. "That ice must be heavy but I bet it feels pretty good in this heat."

He smiled back and nodded. The woman pushed the boy ahead of her. "Don't bother the lady, Caleb."

Tawny regretted initiating the conversation and hoped the kid wouldn't get in trouble for responding. She was accustomed to her small Montana hometown, where chatting with strangers was normal, even expected. But this was a major urban area under siege. People were understandably suspicious.

She watched the pair trudge down the street. Evidently, they didn't have a car. She felt sorry for them walking in the searing sun, burdened with packages.

An incoming text chimed from Arielle, Tillman's fifteen-year-old middle child. *R U guys OK? Can't reach Dad. Did FL sink into the ocean? Luv U.*

The message lightened Tawny's heart. She tapped a reply: *We're OK, no electric, iffy cell svc. Don't believe everything U see on TV. Luv U 2.*

In front of her, the truck started up and moved forward a few car lengths. She followed then turned off the engine again. Fifteen cars still ahead of her. Would the gas supply last until she reached the island?

Her phone rang. Caller ID said: *Nyala.* Smoky's landlady and girlfriend.

"Hello, Nyala."

"Who are *you*?" The voice sounded half-hostile, half-curious.

If Smoky's paranoia extended to his friends, Tawny had to be careful not to scare the woman off. "Smoky was my fiancé's high school coach. We were staying at his house when Irma hit. I found your number in his address book." She hesitated, wondering how much more to reveal. If the woman cared about Smoky, she'd want to know he was missing. Tawny plunged ahead: "Smoky went out during the storm. We can't find him. We've checked shelters and neighbors. We're really concerned about him."

A long hesitation. "Is the house OK? Any damage?"

Nyala sounded like a property owner first and girlfriend second. Tawny answered, "It's all right except an oak tree fell on the carport and crushed it."

"Damn. I'll have to put in an insurance claim."

Irritation chafed Tawny. Didn't this woman care at all about Smoky? "Have you heard from Smoky?"

Another pause. "We talked a week ago."

"Do you have any idea where he might have gone, staying at another friend's house maybe?"

The woman scoffed. "He's got lots of *friends*."

Tawny couldn't decipher the meaning under her sarcasm. *Friends* as in other women or *friends* as in the thugs who beat the crap out of him? "Nyala, is there any way we could meet?"

"What for?"

"We want to make sure Smoky is safe. Maybe we can kick around ideas of where he might be."

The woman sighed. "I suppose I could drive out to the house. I'll need to see the damage and take photos for the insurance adjustor. Although, God knows, it'll be months before all the claims from the hurricane get handled. I own several other rentals in New Port Richey that I ought to check on, also."

"That would be great." Tawny didn't care what Nyala's reason was, as long as she agreed to talk. "Where are you?"

"Land O'Lakes. The power just came on here about fifteen minutes ago. But lots of roads are still underwater. Depending on flooding, I could be there sometime this afternoon."

"We'll see you then." Tawny disconnected and moved the car ahead again. She wondered if the woman would show up. How close was her friendship with Smoky if she sounded more worried about damage to her property than the missing man?

Then Tawny realized she'd called Tillman her *fiancé*.

Since the beginning, she'd struggled how to categorize their relationship. Initially, he'd been her attorney, her savior. Then he'd offered her a job that she desperately needed because Dwight's medical bills left her broke.

As a boss, Tillman had been rude, demanding, and impatient, yet, at times, surprisingly kind. Gradually his harshness eroded and he'd revealed his soft underbelly to her. She'd managed to teach him *please* and *thank you*, words foreign to his vocabulary before they'd met.

And, as they'd fallen in love, his rough edges smoothed a bit.

His longtime office manager, Esther, had recently made the crack, "What have you done with my boss and who is this cream puff who replaced him?"

Now Tillman wanted to marry Tawny but she resisted because of concern for his children. They were already torn between warring parents and she didn't want to add more complications. Yet maybe that was a false reason, built up in her head because she feared the ultimate commitment to the man who would do anything for her, yet was at times frighteningly volatile.

She remembered his admonition to stay hydrated and sipped water from the go-cup. It tasted awful, warm and plastic.

Another twenty sweltering minutes passed before she finally pulled beside the pump. An attendant walked between islands, repeating a chant: "Ten-gallon limit. No exceptions."

Tawny inserted a credit card. As she pumped gas, she asked the attendant, "What food is in the store?"

"Truck brought milk but it sold out in minutes. Might be lunch meat and cheese left."

The pump shut off automatically at ten gallons. She replaced the nozzle and gas cap then parked near the store entrance. Inside, a welcome blast of air conditioning hit her. The temperature had to be well over eighty but, compared to the muggy outdoors, it felt wonderfully dry and cool.

A harried-looking clerk marched up and down aisles, repeating an ongoing refrain: "Limit, one bag of ice per customer. One case of bottled water per customer. Ten gallons of gas per customer."

In front of the register, a couple in grubby clothes, carrying four sacks of ice, argued with the checker. "One bag of ice for each of us and my two girlfriends are in the car."

"If they want ice," the clerk answered, "they gotta come in and get it themselves. Boss's orders. Nobody walks outta here with more than one bag of ice. Take it or leave it."

The couple grumbled but relinquished the extra ice, paid, and left.

The smell of unwashed bodies hung in the air, including her own. Tawny edged between people at the glass-front coolers. Most racks had already emptied out. She filled a handbasket with a pint of half-and-half, a dozen eggs, a loaf of bread, and the last packages of smoked turkey and Swiss cheese. She grabbed a lone jar of pickles from an otherwise empty shelf. A hand-crank can opener hung on a hook. She picked it up and balanced the basket of groceries on a case of bottled water.

Beside the front counter, a burly clerk now blocked access to the freezer box and handed out only one bag of ice to each person in line. While the checker rang up her purchases, Tawny clasped the ice to her chest like a newborn.

In the eyes of other waiting customers, she recognized the same feeling she had—at this moment, cubes of frozen water were more precious than a sack of gold.

Outside, she put the food in the trunk.

Shouting erupted over at the gas islands. The attendant yelled to customers still waiting in line, "No more gas. Tank's empty. Get out of here!"

Angry customers protested as voices rose and tempers flared out of control. A man threw a punch, knocking the attendant backward into the hood of a Mercedes. Several bystanders piled on. Shoving and tussling broke out, spreading through the crowd in waves.

Tawny quickly jockeyed out of the lot onto the highway, barely escaping the fast-brewing riot. Her breath came in anxious gulps, knowing she'd been damn lucky to score gas, ice, and a little food without getting trampled by a mob.

A mile farther down the road, she caught movement on a side street. Two skinny white teenagers in gray hoodies and sagging jeans circled the grandmother and little boy she'd seen earlier. The woman was in a tug-of-war with one kid over her bag of groceries. The other one lay on the sidewalk, contents scattered. The second punk snatched the sack of ice from the boy and swung it like a bludgeon toward the woman. It struck her in the back of the head. She staggered but refused to turn loose of her bag.

Tawny grabbed the pistol from the glove box and veered onto the side street, accelerating toward the struggle. She screeched to a halt beside them and leaned on the horn. "Hey, leave them alone!" she shouted through the car window.

"Fuck off!" The teen with the ice came toward her, swinging the sack in a figure-eight pattern like nunchucks. Tawny gripped the gun in both hands and pointed it in his direction.

He jerked back, stopped, and dropped the ice. "Gun!" he yelled to his friend. "Get out of here!"

The second guy let go of the groceries. Both ran, dodging between parked cars, and disappeared into an apartment complex.

Tawny jumped out of the car and hurried toward the woman and child.

The boy, Caleb was pulling on the woman's t-shirt. "Grammy, did he hurt you?"

"Help me pick up the stuff, Caleb." The woman was breathing hard, face perspiring, as Tawny drew near. Behind coke-bottle glasses, her eyes focused in recognition. "Thanks," she said.

"You OK?" Tawny asked.

The woman gingerly touched the back of her head. "Damn punks. We waited an hour in the sun for the store to open 'cause I heard the truck was bringing food. Got the last half gallon of milk." She jerked her chin in the direction the muggers had fled. "Then *they* try to steal it." She hugged the precious bag to her breast.

Tawny became aware of how hard her heart was thumping. She tucked the pistol in her waistband under her t-shirt, relieved that showing it had been enough to scare off the thieves. She stooped to pick up the dropped bag of ice and a can of Vienna sausages that had rolled away.

The other plastic bag had ripped in the fight. A can of Spaghetti-Os, a box of mac and cheese, dog treats, and a package of Oreos had fallen to the sidewalk. Caleb retrieved them and approached his grandmother, juggling to keep from dropping the food.

Both looked wrung out and exhausted from walking in the heat, not to mention fighting off the thugs. Tawny scanned the area to see if they still lurked between the apartments. If she drove away, they might come back and take another run at the vulnerable pair.

"Let me give you a ride home," she said.

The woman studied Tawny, squinted at the car, then looked down at her grandson. The boy's face lit with hope at Tawny's offer.

"Please, Grammy, I'm tired," he pleaded.

The woman stared at Tawny once more. "Yeah, OK. It's about two miles from here."

Tawny helped them carry the groceries to the T-bird and opened the trunk. "My name's Tawny."

The woman set the milk in the trunk and placed the ice beside it. "Melba. And this is my grandson, Caleb."

"Glad to meet you, Caleb." Tawny took the cans and boxes from the kid and put them with the rest of the groceries.

He ran a hand over the fender. "When I get older, I want a nice ride just like this."

"OK, Caleb, let's go for a test drive." Tawny checked once more but didn't see the thieves.

With only two seats, Caleb perched on Melba's lap. The woman groaned as she shifted her grandson's position. "Boy, you're gettin' too big to be sittin' on your grammy."

He leaned sideways to study the dashboard. "Does it have the three-point-nine liter V-eight? What's zero to sixty in this? I like those portholes."

"Hush, Caleb." Melba rolled her eyes at Tawny. "Can't wait 'til he gets his driver's license." She gestured. "Turn right at the next corner."

Tawny followed her directions, veering around tree branches, a sodden mattress, and broken hunks of plastic pipe. With the fan on high, the car cooled quickly.

Melba heaved a deep sigh. "Jesus is my lord and savior but right now this air conditioning comes a close second."

Tawny answered, "If we could get enough gas, I'd sleep in the car with the AC."

A small amused grunt came from the woman. "My son and his wife, Caleb's folks, work for the road department. They been swamped with hurricane preparations and now this mess afterward."

Caleb chimed in: "Mama and Daddy ain't been home since Friday."

Melba scolded, "Don't say 'ain't.'" To Tawny, she added, "Food all spoiled when the refrigerator quit. Caleb didn't have milk."

"My dog's hungry, too," the boy piped up. "And we have to go to the bathroom in a bucket because the toilet's broke."

"Caleb!" The grandmother gave a warning shake to her grandson. To Tawny, she said, "Flood tore the plumbing out from under the house." She pointed. "Turn left here."

Tawny drove into a long driveway where an aging mobile home sat high on concrete blocks. The door was a good four feet above the ground but no stairs led to it. Instead, a rickety aluminum stepladder stood beside the entrance. Blue plastic tarps covered parts of the roof, secured with crisscrossed ropes and bungee cords.

After Tawny parked, Caleb clambered off Melba's lap and ran across the muddy yard. A smiling tan pit bull trotted to him. The pair romped, happy to be reunited.

While they unloaded the trunk, Melba said, "My son doesn't know how bad the roof's leaking. My cousins covered the worst places with those tarps. But inside, everything's soaked, all my furniture, my cross-stitch, my grandma's photo albums." She jerked her head toward a wooded area behind the mobile home. "Creek over there flooded. For a spell, it looked like the Mississippi River was rushing under the trailer. Used to have concrete stairs up to the door. Flood carried them right off, like they were made of cardboard. Lord only knows where they wound up. But we couldn't go to a shelter because Caleb wouldn't leave his dog behind."

"He's a loyal friend."

Melba clucked her tongue. "Boys and their dogs. And their cars."

Tawny helped carry packages as they walked to the stepladder entrance. The ladder teetered under Melba's weight. Tawny steadied it as the woman climbed. At the top, she unlocked the door then leaned down to take the groceries Tawny handed up to her. She set them on the floor in the entry. When they finished, she called, "Caleb, come here and tell this nice lady thank you."

The kid skipped across the yard, fresh mud specks spattered on his legs, trailed by the smiling dog whose tail never stopped wagging. "Thank you, Miss Tawny, for letting me ride in your T-bird. If you wanna sell it, you call me." He started to scamper away but an afterthought made him turn back. "Thank you for saving us from those assholes."

A sharp intake of breath sounded from Melba. "Caleb, your mouth!"

Tawny swallowed a chuckle.

She traded glances with Melba, who also suppressed a smile and muttered, "Gets that from his daddy." To Caleb, she said, "Go play now."

The boy and dog galloped through the yard, kicking up mud.

Melba grasped the package of Oreos and thrust them toward Tawny. "Thanks for saving us from those assholes."

Now Tawny had to laugh but shook her head. "No, I couldn't. Caleb must love Oreos."

"His teeth don't need that sugar." Melba patted her round rump. "And my booty sure don't need it either. Here." She pushed the cookies into Tawny's hands.

Tawny couldn't rebuff the woman's generous gesture and reluctantly accepted them. "Good luck."

She returned to the car, touched that, in time of crisis, Melba wanted to share the little she had.

Chapter 7 – Oreos

When Tawny pulled into Smoky's driveway, the fallen oak was gone, the trunk cut up, branches limbed and stacked in the back yard. The brush pile reached as high as the roof of the house. Only a stump remained.

With the crown of the tree gone, she could now see the damage to the broken supports of the carport, the metal roof folded like a sheet of paper, part still upright but much of it bent to the ground. She drove under the intact part, dodging the barbecue.

Tillman came out the back door as she popped the trunk.

A surge of gratitude lifted her spirits that they were safely together again. "I scavenged some ice, a little food, and ten gallons of gas."

Tillman evidently felt the same relief as he hugged her tight to his naked chest. He grabbed the bag of ice and the case of water. "You earned your pay today."

She gestured at the cut-up oak. "So did you." She pushed the door open for him. "Also, the landlady is coming later to look at the carport damage. She said she doesn't know where Smoky is but, maybe, when we're face to face, you can dig out more information than she would give me on the phone."

Tillman stowed the perishable food and ice in the chest freezer. Without electricity, the appliance served only as an oversized picnic cooler but its thick insulation retained cold better than the non-operating refrigerator.

He pulled the package of Oreos out of the grocery sack and gave her a down-the-nose look, as if he'd caught an alcoholic hiding a bottle. The month before, he'd given up all sugar and she'd been missing sweet treats.

"It was a gift," she said.

"A gift?"

She explained about meeting Melba and Caleb and their fight with the muggers. His expression hardened when she described the confrontation. "Damn glad you had the pistol. They're lucky you helped them. But this." Mischief crinkled the corners of his eyes as he held up the cookies. "This is not a healthy reward."

"Who appointed you the sugar police?" She reached for the Oreos but he lifted them high over his head, out of her reach. She tickled his exposed armpit. He laughed. She loved that deep, throaty sound because it happened so rarely.

He twisted away and they jostled back and forth, grabbing and tickling. At last, she slid her hand down the front of his shorts and grasped him where he was guaranteed to forget about sugar and most everything else.

He hooked his arm around her, low voice husky. "You must be feeling better."

"Mm-hmm." She kissed him. Then again, deeper, not caring that his whiskers scratched her face.

Then they both forgot about Oreos.

***

Sharp knocks on the front door startled them out of drowsy afterglow. Tillman rose from the bed, pulled his shorts on, and strode to the living room, bare feet slapping the tile. Tawny slipped on his t-shirt and followed.

He opened the door to a tall, stately, black woman about fifty, standing on the porch. She looked cool and immaculate in a form-fitting pink sheath and matching strappy sandals, better dressed and groomed than any other person Tawny had seen since the hurricane. The contrast made her realize how grubby and bedraggled she and Tillman looked, how badly they needed a shower and clean clothes.

The woman stared past Tillman toward her. "Are you Tawny?"

Tawny stepped forward. "You must be Nyala."

She scrutinized Tillman up and down. "You're Tillman Rosenbaum. Smoky said you were a giant. For once, he wasn't exaggerating. He also said you were part Ethiopian."

Tillman slipped into his formal courtroom manners that made his unshaven, shirtless appearance fade into the background. "Ms. Nyala, thank you for coming. My paternal grandmother was an Ethiopian Jew. Please come in and have a seat. We need to talk about Smoky."

Tawny recognized a model's or dancer's training in Nyala's walk, posture, and the way she crossed her legs when she sat in

Smoky's chair. "My great-great-grandparents were coffee growers from Ethiopia."

Tillman said, "One day, I plan to take my children there to research our family history. My younger daughter is especially interested." He sat beside Tawny on the couch and leaned forward, elbows on his knees. "Ms. Nyala, how did you and Smoky meet?"

She smiled, lovely and professional, as if she did it for a living. "He said you were all business. An attorney, and quite a famous one, correct?"

"I practice in Montana. You met Smoky when?"

"Oh, dear, I didn't prepare for cross-examination, counselor."

"Ms. Nyala, Smoky was my coach in high school. We've remained friends all these years since then. I'm concerned about him and I will do anything—anything—to find him. You understand, of course."

Green eyes appraised him, measuring. "Good friends are rare, Mr. Rosenbaum."

"They are, Ms. Nyala." His dark stare bored through her.

She uncrossed and re-crossed her legs. "I'm a flight attendant. Smoky and I met when he was on his way back from Panama shortly after his accident. He was in a wheelchair and his leg needed to be elevated. I'm also an RN so the responsibility for his wellbeing fell to me. It was a long trip, seven hours, if I recall, because of a layover in Atlanta. I accompanied him on both legs of the flight."

She laid one manicured hand atop the other on her knee. "I'm used to being hit on—goes with the job—but Smoky was a complete gentleman. He didn't use his injury to gain sympathy, he didn't demand extra attention even though I could tell he was in terrible pain. If I brought him an ice pack or a drink, he thanked me. Little things like that you notice when you deal with the public every day."

Tawny sneaked a glance at Tillman, remembering his abrasive rudeness when they'd first met. He also would have impressed Nyala—not in a good way.

The woman pressed her palms together, like a prayer. Her fingernails matched her dress. "He said he'd been a coach. I used to work in a sports medicine practice and we got talking physiology, slow-twitch and fast-twitch muscles, the use of ultrasound on soft tissue injuries. You know, esoteric shop talk that bores the average person to tears. But we enjoyed chatting. It made the time pass quickly.

"He needed a place to live. I own a number of vacation rental properties in this area. I was tired of weekenders trashing the place. He seemed like he'd be a good, responsible tenant who'd take care of the house. We came to an agreement and he's been here ever since."

That echoed the explanation Smoky had given to Tawny about the rental, except Nyala didn't mention he paid cash and hid under the radar by keeping the utilities in her name.

Nyala went on: "We became friends with benefits. Neither of us was looking for a long-term domestic arrangement. We see other people. And that, counselor, is the summation of our relationship."

Tillman inclined his head. "Very nicely done, concise, without extraneous details. Thank you."

Tawny had the strange sense, watching them stare at each other, that a different, unspoken conversation went on beneath the surface. A negotiation, a test.

Like two tigers circling each other, deciding if the fight was worth the risk.

Nyala broke eye contact first, her delicate nostrils flaring as she surveyed the room. "My, Smoky has been lax with his housekeeping since the last time I was here."

Although Tillman had up-righted the toppled furniture and cleaned up the kitchen, disarray from the three thugs still remained, along with their own dirty footprints on the tile.

"Some unwelcome visitors broke in." Tillman waited for her reaction but Nyala gave none.

Instead, she continued, "I told Tawny on the phone that I haven't seen Smoky since before Irma hit."

"Do you know his business associates?"

A little smile. "You mean, his bookies? No, I stay out of that. I'm a business woman. I prefer to invest my money in more tangible assets than Sunday's point spread."

"Do you know who he owes money to?"

"As long as it's not me, I don't concern myself. He's always paid his rent on time."

Tillman switched gears. "Where does Smoky hang out? A particular watering hole?"

"There's a bar down in Tarpon Springs on the Anclote River. Exiles. A real Florida bubba dive, not for tourists. Sometimes we'd take a boat out for the day then come back and have drinks and listen to the band."

"Whose boat?"

"When I worked at the orthopedic clinic, I met football and baseball players from the Tampa Bay Buccaneers and the Rays. Several have boats in Tarpon or Palm Harbor. They let me use them." A dainty shrug.

In exchange for *benefits*? Tawny wondered.

Tillman kept pressing. "Names?"

"They are *my* friends, not Smoky's. I'm hesitant to mention them over something that's really not their concern."

"A missing man wouldn't concern them?"

"I'm merely saying, they barely know Smoky so there'd be no way they could help you."

"How about the other ladies Smoky was seeing? Do you know any of them?"

"Really?" She arched her brows with an *are-you-kidding* grimace. "No strings but we're not so coarse as to flaunt friends in each other's faces." She rose and smoothed her tight pink dress. "Now, I'd like to see the carport damage." She moved gracefully on her high-heeled sandals through the living room, kitchen, and out the back door.

Tawny and Tillman exchanged glances. His raised eyebrow told her she'd been right about the strange undercurrent. They followed Nyala outside.

She walked around the carport, snapping photos from different angles with her phone. She noticed the cut-up wood. "You did that?"

Tillman strode closer. "Raul, the neighbor, and I did."

Her smile was gracious, practiced. "Thank you."

"Ms. Nyala." He loomed tall above her. "I *am* going to find Smoky."

Her neck craned up and she met his eyes, steady, unblinking. "I have no doubt, Mr. Rosenbaum." She took a business card from her pink clutch and handed it to him. "Well, I'm off to inspect my other properties. Do call if you have any problems with the house. How long are you staying?"

Tillman took the card and folded long arms across his bare chest. "Until we find Smoky."

She dipped her head slightly with another professional smile. She neatly avoided puddles and debris as she walked around to the front of the house then slid into a pearl-colored Lexus and drove away.

Tawny slouched back on one hip. "What was *that* all about?"

He held the business card at arm's length to read it without his glasses. "She's lying. What I can't figure out is if she wants to convince me she *doesn't* know anything or convince me she *does*."

Chapter 8 – High Water Mark

The internet and phones started working at four-thirty that afternoon but still no electricity.

While Tawny made turkey, cheese, and pickle sandwiches for dinner, Tillman called the other women listed in Smoky's address book. After careful questioning, he decided they were telling the truth when they claimed they hadn't heard from the missing man in months.

"Look at this." With readers perched on his nose, he carried his laptop to the counter where Tawny was cutting sandwiches in half. "This is video taken at that bar Nyala mentioned where Smoky hangs out." He tapped the screen.

Tawny put on her glasses and watched as the camera scanned the exterior of a rickety clapboard building sitting atop a wooden dock that leaned like a parallelogram. It appeared close to collapsing in the river. Above the entrance, spray-painted letters read *X-Isles*.

Tillman grunted. "Wonder if they didn't know how to spell *exiles* or it's intentional."

Nearby on the shoreline, a rowboat hung suspended several feet above the ground in the spreading branches of a tree. On its side, spray-painted words read: *HIgH WaTeR marK, 1993*.

"What's that mean?" Tawny asked.

"Evidently a flood raised the river enough that it left that boat hanging in the tree."

She shook her head in amazement. "Looks like a deep breath could blow the whole dump over."

He indicated a date on the screen. "This You Tube's from a couple years ago. Since Irma hit, that dump might not be standing anymore."

The video continued to play, showing a four-piece band—fiddle, guitar, bass, mandolin—and a raucous-voiced blond singing "Proud Mary" while people danced.

Another clip showed a fisherman outside on the dock. His bare leg bore a tattoo of a yardstick and he held his catch against his calf to measure it. Next, a biker in a do-rag grabbed the ample breast of his girlfriend who mugged for the camera.

When the video ended, Tawny looked at Tillman. "So that's Smoky's favorite hangout?"

"Been to some backwoods Montana bars like that, tracking down witnesses."

"Want to check out the place?"

He frowned at her. "You're kidding, right?"

"If that's where Smoky's friends are, they might know something Nyala wouldn't tell us."

"If it didn't wash down the river." He tapped the bar's number and put the phone on speaker.

After five rings, a gruff voice answered, "X-Isles."

Surprise widened Tillman's eyes. "You're open?"

"Hell yeah. It takes worse than a little blowjob from Irma to shut us down." Laughter sounded in the background.

"Do you have electricity?"

"Shit, who needs electricity when you got rum and weed."

"OK, thanks." Tillman disconnected and faced Tawny. "Sounds lively."

"Sounds like a lead to follow."

He cupped the side of her face. "Sure you're up to it? Heat stroke laid you pretty low."

Her headache still nagged but time in the air-conditioned car had helped. Ice in drinking water improved the taste and she felt rehydrated. She gestured out the window. "Sun's going down. Pretty soon, it won't be as hot. Besides we can stay here and sweat or go there and sweat."

He pretended to appear annoyed but his eyes glowed. "You're a trooper."

She smiled and pushed the paper plate at him. "Eat your dinner. I've been slaving all day in a hot kitchen."

He grabbed up the sandwich, took a big bite, and chewed. "Best turkey, cheese, and pickle sandwich I ever ate. Of course, it's the only one I ever ate."

***

Tawny drove while Tillman leaned through the open passenger window to keep from being crushed by the low roof of the T-bird. "I feel like a damn dog," he grumbled.

"Let your tongue hang out and wag your tail."

He shot her a sour look.

The sun was setting over Tarpon Springs, reflecting bright orange on the inlet where the Anclote River emptied into the Gulf. The village's Greek bakeries, restaurants, and souvenir shops were shuttered. The scenic sponge docks were empty of tourists.

In a vacant dirt lot, a scattering of pickup trucks and motorcycles sat parked, the only indication they'd found their destination.

"Are you sure this is it?" Tawny asked. "I don't see any bar."

Tillman pointed to a rough wood plank nailed to a tree, an arrow pointing toward a jungle-shrouded trail. Burned into the sign were the letters *X-Isles*. He got out of the car, stretching from the cramped position. "Guess we hike in."

Tawny curled her fingers into a fist to keep from nervously scratching her sunburn. Growing up with her dad's alcoholism, she'd been in and out of too many dive bars, trying to coax him home. She followed Tillman on the darkening trail as he held vines out of the way.

Through the dank, still air, a saxophone whined a soulful, bluesy tune.

"Think we're getting close." Tillman turned to her then stopped. "Sure you're OK?"

Her discomfort must have shown. She set her jaw. "I'm fine."

He saw through her lie. "Stay in the car if you want."

She shook her head. "No way, I'm coming with you."

He took her hand with a reassuring squeeze then continued, ducking under low branches.

Fifty yards down the trail, a clearing opened on the shore of a river channel. It looked like an outdoor living room with old bench-style car seats, beer barrels for tables, and rusty boat anchors as decorations. Several bikers lounged outside, wearing jeans, chains, and leather vests over naked chests. They passed around a joint, the pungent odor drifting in the air.

They stared at Tillman and her, mostly Tillman. All were burly and heavyset but nowhere near Tillman's six-seven.

"Good evening, gentlemen." He flicked a casual salute and continued walking toward the sagging, dilapidated building, holding Tawny's hand, neither challenging them nor giving anyone a chance to challenge him. The bikers watched them pass. One dipped his head in a slight bow to Tawny. Being with Tillman insulated her from unwanted advances. Even bad-asses, if they were smart, steered clear of the formidable giant.

The rickety wood dock creaked under their weight. The bar entrance looked as if the builder had forgotten to finish the job—no door or frame, just an open gap between rotting studs. A crooked sign was nailed over it: *Guys—no shirt, NO service. Gals—no shirt, FREE DRINKS!*

Inside, the plank floor was uneven and sloping, making Tawny feel off-balance, as if she'd already had too much to drink. Bras hung from exposed rafters. Posters for beer, motorcycles, and condoms covered rough-hewn walls. Old-fashioned lanterns gave off a warm, kerosene smell with their soft, flickering light. Tawny wondered if they'd been salvaged from pirate vessels.

Tillman made his way to the bar, his size easily parting the crowd. Tawny stayed close in his wake. The counter was chipped orange Formica, as if recycled from a kitchen remodel project. He cleared enough space for her to stand beside him as he leaned across to talk to the bartender.

The man had a bristly red beard, wore a mustard-yellow do-rag and wife-beater undershirt. "We're on ice rations because of Irma," he said. "One cube to a customer. Or English beer is free."

"Scotch neat," Tillman said, "and give my ice cube to the lady in her *Cuba Libre*."

The bearded man set up a shot glass of scotch. He reached into a picnic cooler under the bar and plucked out two ice cubes, which he dropped in a plastic cup, then added rum and coke.

"What's English beer?" Tawny muttered in Tillman's ear.

"Warm."

"Ugh." She took a sip from the plastic cup. Strong, sweet, and barely cool. The ice cubes were already melting.

Tillman slapped a hundred on the counter. "We're Smoky Lido's friends. We came all the way from Montana to visit him." He stuck his hand out. "I'm Tillman and this is Tawny."

The bartender assessed the big hand thrust toward him and, after a second, shook it. "Parrot."

"Good to meet you, Parrot. Run a tab, if that's OK. I'd like to buy drinks for Smoky's friends who are here tonight. Appreciate if you'd point them out so I can say hello." He surveyed the room and found a vacant space to sit. "We'll be over there," he said to Parrot then took Tawny's arm.

They moved to an old bus stop bench against a wall with a spindly table in front of it. The wood surface was inlaid with a checkerboard, marred with whitish rings where years of drinks had sweated condensation.

They sat side by side, Tillman's arm around her, and listened to the sharp crack of pool balls from a game in an adjacent alcove.

"Quite a place," she murmured.

"The real, unvarnished Florida," he answered.

"You think Parrot's going to help us?"

"Have to wait and see. He wants to check us out for a little while. So, we sit tight, enjoy our drinks, and smile at everybody."

The saxophonist was a bulky woman with bare, tattooed arms. She started to play "Old Time Rock and Roll." The song brought people to their feet, dancing, bobbing, and singing along.

By the time Tawny and Tillman had finished their first drinks, the music switched tempo to the mournful wailing of "Baker Street."

He asked, "Want to dance?"

She realized they had never danced together before. "Sure." They rose, staying close to the bench to hold their seats.

He folded his arms around her and they swayed to the plaintive melody. It felt nice, even in this crazy environment.

She had just started to relax when she caught a glimpse of three men entering the bar. "Tillman, it's the guys who beat up Smoky."

He continued to sway but asked, "Where?"

"Just coming in."

He deftly spun her around so he faced the entrance. "In the hat?"

"Yes. The guy carries a gun. I'm sure the others do, too."

"OK, sit down. If the mood turns nasty, get the hell out. I'll meet you back at the car."

Great.

He released her and crossed to the bar. He leaned over and spoke to Parrot who shot a quick glance at the newcomers.

Then Tillman moved to block the way of the man in the fedora. He loomed a foot taller. Tawny couldn't make out his words but heard the rumbling baritone reverberation.

The two strong-arms pushed forward. Tillman stepped closer to their leader and grasped the man's hand as if to shake it, or, more likely, flip him over his shoulder.

Tawny held her breath, expecting a fight to break out, worried the thugs would go for their weapons.

Tillman and Fedora exchanged more words. The thugs backed away slightly.

To her surprise, Tillman gestured toward where she sat on the bus bench. Fedora met her gaze and smiled that same elegant smile.

At last, Tillman released the man's hand which, Tawny suspected, was throbbing from pain even though he didn't show it. Tillman returned to their bench while Fedora went to the bar and ordered.

Tillman leaned down to her ear. "He'll be over to join us after he gets his drink."

Tawny's jaw ached from clenching her teeth. "What's going on?"

"He wants to apologize. You don't have to talk. Just listen."

"OK." What was Tillman up to?

Fedora waited at the bar. Meanwhile, four bikers approached Fedora's companions, one at each arm, friendly as circling sharks. The bikers walked the thugs outside as if they were all going for a smoke. The whole encounter was over in seconds, without ruffling the drinking crowd.

Fedora wove through the dancers, carrying two full shot glasses in one hand and a tall plastic cup in the other. He stopped a few feet from where Tawny and Tillman sat on the bus bench and smiled down at her with a slight bow.

Even with Tillman beside her, the seat turned to concrete under her butt.

The man spoke: "Lovely lady, my behavior the last time we met was unforgivable. I sincerely hope you weren't traumatized. I meant you no harm."

She glanced sideways at Tillman for a cue.

"The lady accepts your apology," he said.

Fedora smiled and offered the plastic cup and one of the shot glasses to Tillman. "The bartender said the lady is drinking *Cuba Libre* and you have scotch. I hope that's correct."

Tillman accepted their drinks. "Join us?" He handed the cup to Tawny. Three ice cubes floated in the rum and coke. Evidently Fedora had donated his ice to her.

The man dragged over a wooden Shaker-style chair with slats missing from its back. He sat and raised his glass in a silent toast.

Tawny watched to see if Tillman drank. When he did, she also took a sip, hoping the man hadn't slipped in a drug.

He set down his glass and folded his hands neatly on the inlaid checkerboard. "My name is Gabriel Marquez Garcia, not to be confused with Gabriel Garcia Marquez, the brilliant author of *One Hundred Years of Solitude*." He smiled again.

Tillman remained silent, impassive, his courtroom expression firmly in place, waiting. Tawny willed herself to fade into the woodwork but the man kept focusing on her, pulling her into the one-sided conversation.

Gabriel continued: "I've known Smoky for some years now. Initially, our relationship was mutually profitable. I run an internet sports book along with an ancillary memorabilia business. Smoky had a keen eye, both for talent and for collectibles whose value would increase with time." He shifted his focus to Tillman. "I understand you once considered pro ball. Smoky pinned great hopes on you. He has never gotten over his disappointment that you didn't follow through with that career."

Tillman's voice deepened even lower than normal. "I can be of more use to Smoky as legal counsel than I ever could have been as a pitcher."

Gabriel lifted one shoulder. "If you'd had a few winning seasons, as Smoky fully expected you would, you could now have an ongoing profitable career with endorsements, merchandising, memorabilia, and commentator positions that far exceed that of an attorney."

Now Tillman smiled, a harsh, humorless expression. "My loss." He finished his scotch. "The problem we need to solve today is how to get you off Smoky's back."

Gabriel sipped his drink, green eyes watching Tillman over the rim. He lowered the glass and turned it around between his hands. They were meticulously manicured, nails buffed. "I don't believe there's a practical solution that you could proffer."

"How much does he owe you?"

"If only it were as simple as dollars. Some things have value beyond monetary worth. Like friendship and loyalty." Gabriel inclined his head toward Tawny. "Unfortunately, Smoky disappointed me in those areas. I believed we were friends and that he would not betray me. Sadly, he did. Trust is priceless and not recoverable."

"Agreed." Tillman leaned forward. "But you must have some figure in mind as compensation for that loss."

"That compensation can only be worked out between Smoky and myself."

Tillman straightened. "Then it appears we're at a stalemate. None of us knows where Smoky is, therefore, nothing can be accomplished."

"That is true." Gabriel rose. "So that means we'll continue to work on parallel tracks to find our missing friend." He bowed to Tawny. "Good evening." He threaded his way through the patrons to the exit.

Tawny gripped Tillman's thigh. "He wants to kill Smoky."

He heaved a sigh. "That means we have to find him before Gabriel does."

The saxophone player started up again as Parrot lumbered through the crowd, carrying two more drinks. He handed them to Tawny and Tillman. He flipped around the chair Gabriel had vacated and straddled it. "This round's on the house for keeping the lid on. No big deal when regulars mix it up but I don't like strangers coming in and causing problems."

Tillman raised his glass in thanks. "What happened to the other two guys?"

"The boys took 'em outside to feed the gators."

Tawny jerked then realized it had to be a joke…didn't it?

The fresh drink chilled her hand since it was full of ice cubes. Apparently, Parrot had called off rationing for friends of Smoky.

Parrot leaned forearms across the chair back. "Smoky's here most nights. Week or so back, he told me he had friends coming from Montana and said he'd bring you guys around. I asked but nobody's seen him since before the hurricane. Something stinks."

Tillman turned to Tawny. "Tell him what happened."

She took a deep breath. "The afternoon before Irma hit, those two thugs beat the crap out of Smoky in his driveway under

Gabriel's orders. I think they broke some ribs. A few hours later, the power went off. I went to bed and I thought Smoky had, too."

Tillman picked up the narrative: "I didn't get to his house until almost three in the morning. That's when we looked in his bedroom and discovered he was gone. We've searched the area, checked shelters, asked neighbors and friends but he's vanished. We figure he's on the run because of those guys."

Parrot scratched his beard. A notion flitted through Tawny's mind that something might live in the thicket of red hair. He thought for a moment then said, "Sounds likely. What are you going to do?"

"Keep looking," Tillman answered. "We're not leaving until we find out what happened to him."

Parrot stood. "To my mind, if a man wants to disappear, it's his own business. But I'll keep an ear open." He returned to the bar.

Tawny studied Tillman, deep in thought. She grasped his hand. "We'll find him. Somehow."

He listened for a moment to the sax's wail. "Recognize that song?"

She shook her head.

"Springsteen's 'Born to Run.' Fitting, isn't it?" He rose. "Let's get some air."

To avoid insulting Parrot, Tawny carried her ice-filled drink outside, even though she had no intention of finishing it. She staggered on the uneven planks of the dock.

Tillman steadied her. "You're a cheap date."

"Yeah, I'm a lightweight," she answered, "especially compared to you." They stood at the rail.

He took the *Cuba Libre* from her and downed it then handed the cup back. "Left you the ice cubes to suck on."

"Thanks a lot." Despite her sarcasm, she appreciated his solution because she was thirsty but didn't want more alcohol. In the muggy night, ice tasted better than anything she could imagine.

Across the channel, splashing drew their attention. A bright flashlight beam shot from the roof of X-Isles to the shore, about a hundred feet away. It lit up two figures clambering out of the water. They briefly turned to face the brightness but held their arms over their eyes.

Tawny squinted. "Isn't that...?"

"Yeah," Tillman said.

Gabriel's two henchmen, soaking and muddy, slogged along the riverbank and disappeared into the trees.

The bright beam from the roof turned off. A few seconds later, a biker appeared from around the corner of the building. He flipped his flashlight in a wave at Tawny and Tillman. "Guess the gators weren't hungry," he said then went inside the bar.

She slid her hand into Tillman's. "Parrot meant business when he said he didn't like strangers causing a ruckus."

"Good thing he likes *you*. Even gave you extra ice."

Insects chirped in the dark marsh. Humidity still hung heavy in the air but the temperature had dropped into the eighties. Below the dock, waves lapped against several motorboats tied to pilings. A glowing ember passed between a couple sitting in one boat, the smell of weed rising in the air.

Tawny leaned against the railing. "I've been thinking about something Nyala said."

"What's that?"

"Could he have fled by boat?"

"Into the middle of a hurricane? Doesn't sound very smart and Smoky isn't stupid."

"But he's desperate."

He rocked slightly. "It's possible."

"He told me how much he liked being at sea, the salt air, the freedom, the peace."

Tillman pulled on his chin. "If so, we'll never find him. Unless his body washes ashore."

The grim vision pinched Tawny's gut. Finding the dead deer at the lake had been unpleasant. She didn't want to imagine Tillman's old friend like that.

Despite Tillman's matter-of-fact tone, she knew if Smoky died, it would hit him hard. But to be left wondering forever if he was dead or alive would haunt Tillman without mercy.

Unfinished, unknown, unsettled.

She clasped his hand between both of hers and brought it to her lips for a long moment while she wracked her brain. "Should we start checking marinas?"

He snorted. "Yeah, we'll go door to door. Hi, are you missing a boat that disappeared during the hurricane? That's like asking a

Montana rancher with a half-million acres, say, are you missing a cow?"

She sighed. He was right, of course. "Maybe we're going at it from the wrong direction. How did he leave the house? You had his T-bird. Unless he had another car stashed somewhere, he'd be on foot. And he couldn't have walked very far, right?"

"Hell, even in the car, I was fighting to make headway in ninety-mile-an-hour wind and rain."

"So," Tawny mused, "he had to call somebody to pick him up."

"I found his phone under the mattress after Gabriel's buddies tossed the place. The only recent calls in the log were to my cell when we were coming from the airport."

"Just his phone? Not the pouch he kept it in? That Faraday bag to block tracking?"

"Phone only." Tillman pondered a few seconds. "He probably had a second burner phone. Left the first behind, used the second to call someone then put it in the Faraday bag, and took it with him. No way to trace it."

"Which brings us back to his address book," Tawny said. "Who did he trust enough to call?"

"The three women I talked to didn't sound like they knew anything. One said she'd told Smoky never to call her again because she was patching things up with her husband, didn't want him suspicious. Sounded like she'd washed her hands of Ol' Smoke."

"So, we start calling the rest of his friends."

"Until our phones run out of charge."

Tawny heaved a sigh. "Living in the dark ages sucks.

Chapter 9 – Scent Object

Day three without electricity dawned hot and humid again. Tawny's peeling sunburn was shedding like lizard skin. Growing stubble darkened Tillman's face. Their clothes felt stiff, crusty, and smelled like a boys' middle school gym.

While Tawny cooked eggs on the barbecue, Tillman sat on the back steps and used a putty knife to scrape God-knows-what from his sneakers.

"We're going to contract jungle rot," he muttered, "wearing shoes that never dry out."

"Typhoid will kill us first." She plucked toasted bread slices from the grill and turned off the fire. "Hope the propane holds out until the power comes back on."

The jingle of dog tags caused them to look out in the back yard. Jessica's black Lab galloped around the brush pile, spotted Tawny, and beelined for her, pink tongue lolling out the side of his mouth.

This time, she was prepared, lifting her knee to block the dog from jumping on her. "Down, Churro." He wagged his tail and bounced on his toes. She pinched a scrap of scrambled egg and showed it to him. "Sit." His butt hit the ground instantly. "Be gentle." She offered him the egg, which he nibbled with a soft mouth. "Good boy." She ruffled his velvety ears.

"Who's this?" Tillman asked, rising.

Churro lumbered over and plunged his nose hard into Tillman's crotch.

He jumped back. "Whoa, easy on the family jewels."

"Churro!" Jessica's voice rang out from a distance. Seconds later, she came running from next door. "Churro, bad dog! Don't run away!"

The dog smiled, wagged his tail, then faced Tawny and plopped his butt on the ground again, staring hopefully at the eggs.

She held the pan out of reach. "Jessica, this is Tillman. Remember I told you the other day that Smoky used to be his coach?"

The girl looked nervous, craning her neck up at the towering man, but Tillman squatted low and offered his hand. "Hi, Jessica. I have a son about your age."

She tentatively took his hand. "Is he as big as you?"

"Not yet, but he's growing."

Tawny's heart warmed at the uncharacteristic softness in his deep voice. She said, "Jessica is training her dog to search for lost people."

The girl brightened. "Did you find Smoky yet?"

Tillman shook his head.

"Well, me and Churro will help you. It'll be good practice for him."

"That's a great idea," Tawny said.

Tillman straightened and rolled his eyes at Tawny, out of Jessica's sight. The rambunctious pup had made a lousy first impression.

Jessica's tone turned earnest. "First thing, you have to give him a scent object."

"What's that?" Tawny asked.

"Something that smells like Smoky. Y'know, like dirty socks or underwear."

Tawny and Tillman exchanged a look. "There's plenty of dirty socks around here," he said wryly, "but they don't belong to Smoky."

"Well, see if you can find something. Then seal it in a baggie and give it to me. Churro sticks his nose in the bag, gets a big sniff, and I tell him to go find Smoky."

"OK, we'll look." Tillman winked at Tawny. "Now, it's time for our breakfast. See you later."

The girl and dog skipped off.

Tillman held the door as Tawny carried the eggs and toast into the kitchen. "Her heart's in the right place," she said.

He rolled his eyes again. "Shee-it. And you gave that damn dog some of my eggs."

After breakfast, Tillman called his office in Billings while Tawny worked through the names in Smoky's address book. An hour later, she'd reached almost every listing, her cell battery had dropped to twenty percent, but no one knew anything about Smoky.

Discouraged, she went into the bathroom to slather more aloe on her face. The sunburn pain had decreased but peeling skin itched down her arms and legs. She sighed at the pile of dirty clothes on the floor. This morning, she'd put on her last clean panties. Because they conserved water only for necessities, the bathtub remained half full. Maybe she'd splurge on a bucketful to do laundry.

She heard a knock at the door and came out of the bathroom to find Tillman talking with Raul. Tillman looked elated as he clapped the neighbor on the shoulder. "That's great. I'll follow you." He lifted his chin toward Tawny. "Shipment of generators just arrived at Raul's store. We're heading out to get one."

"Wonderful! *Muchas gracias*, Raul." Gratitude overwhelmed her.

Raul shrugged apologetically. "They only send us small generators, like suitcases. Not much capacity. They run a refrigerator and TV but not big enough for the air conditioner or water heater."

"A refrigerator is a huge luxury." A luxury that almost dissolved Tawny to tears. The strain of the past several days caught up with her. She sank into a chair and bit her quivering lip.

Raul said, "Maybe I ask you to keep some food for Jessica and me until the power comes back on. It's hard to get enough ice for the cooler."

"Of course." Her voice choked. "Whatever you want."

"I leave soon." Raul flicked his hand goodbye and headed outside.

Tillman gazed down as tears welled in Tawny's eyes. She buried her face in his belly and hugged him tight. He laid a light hand on her shoulder. "If I'd known you'd get this excited about a refrigerator, I'd have bought you one a long time ago."

She laughed through sniffles then turned her face up to him. "Raul said he wanted a generator but he's saving his money to send to his wife who's stuck in Puerto Rico."

He stroked her hair. "In that case, I'll pick up two, one for us and one for him."

She rose and hugged his neck. "You're sweet."

"No, I'm not. I'm an asshole." He held her, rocking gently. "When I called the office, I told Esther to pay you a hazardous duty bonus."

"If you keep doing nice things, you'll never convince me you're an asshole."

He leaned away. "Raul's probably waiting for me to follow him. Want to go?"

She shook her head. "No, generators are guy things. I'll stay here and do girl things like wash clothes."

"No starch in my underwear."

She mock-punched his hard belly.

***

Tawny scrubbed mud-caked socks, filthy shorts, and t-shirts in a bucket of soapy water that quickly turned brown. She squeezed them out and rinsed them in a second bucket. When delivery trucks could run again and stores were restocked, she resolved to buy new clothes and throw away these dingy, stained ones. She hung them over the shower rod to dry.

In Smoky's room, she tackled the mess Gabriel's men had left. In a tipped-over wicker laundry hamper, she ran across socks and remembered Jessica's request. Doing a quick sniff test, she found the grimiest sock. Holding it between two fingers, she went to the kitchen and sealed it in a baggie then washed her hands.

Back in Smoky's bedroom, she hung up Hawaiian shirts that had been ripped out of the closet and searched through duffels and boxes. What were Gabriel's men looking for? She gathered scattered magazines that had been yanked from a bookcase. She flipped through pages of baseball history books and sports physiology texts, searching for hints. Finding nothing, she replaced them on the shelves.

What did the old coach have that Gabriel wanted so badly?

Smoky admitted to a gambling addiction and implied he owed money to Gabriel. Yet the strange, smiling man in the fedora had rebuffed Tillman's offer of cash to settle the debt.

As her fingers fluttered through a magazine, a full-page ad made her pause. It featured sports memorabilia and collectibles, like trading cards, autographed game balls, and World Series rings. The company also offered full-service auctions, appraisals, and authentication.

She thumbed through, finding more ads for similar businesses. Gabriel had mentioned he operated a sport memorabilia business. Was his shop featured in one of these ads?

She carried the magazine to the coffee table in the living room where she opened Tillman's laptop. Wearing her readers, she typed on the search bar: "Sports memorabilia business in Florida, Gabriel Marquez Garcia." Pages of listings appeared. Slowly, she pored through but his name didn't appear in any of them. Odd. It was almost impossible to fly below the radar without popping up somewhere in Google.

She continued to search for a business name, a location, any thread that might lead to the mysterious, well-dressed man in the fedora. Nothing obvious jumped out.

She scanned Smoky's address book again, looking for Gabriel's name. Nothing. But she did find a pencil notation for *Sports of Yesteryear*. She entered the name and phone number on the search bar and tapped *enter.*

Images of old team photos and hundreds of historical news articles about sports were listed from the early 1900s to the 1990s. She scrolled through. On the seventh page, she found a business named Sports of Yesteryear in St. Petersburg. The address yielded a street-view photo of a small storefront secured behind folding burglar bars. She clicked on it.

Interior pictures of the store showed glass display cabinets of collector cards and autographs in plastic sleeves. Players' jerseys hung on the walls. Off to one side, the camera had inadvertently caught a man crouched over a box, apparently unpacking it.

His build looked familiar. Tawny zoomed in for a close-up. Although his face was fuzzy, she made out his features.

One of Gabriel's bodyguards. The big guy who'd kicked Smoky's ribs.

This had to be Gabriel's business.

She went to the Florida Secretary of State website and searched business registrations for Sports of Yesteryear. The corporation showed as inactive, with a different address. Its last annual report had been filed four years earlier.

When she scrolled down to the registered agent's name, her breath caught.

Nyala Obregon.

Smoky's landlady and sometimes girlfriend. How did she connect to Gabriel?

She googled "Nyala Obregon." Few women had similar names. She found an address in Land O'Lakes, Florida. Following that trail led to a real estate broker's license, tax statements for several properties in New Port Richey, and a Facebook page with photos of the cool, attractive woman.

When Tillman returned, he'd have hard questions for Ms. Nyala.

In the kitchen, Tawny dropped a few precious ice cubes into sun tea and drank a tall glass. Through the window, she spotted Jessica next door in the yard, throwing a stick with Churro eagerly retrieving it.

Tawny grabbed Smoky's sock and carried it outside. "Jessica," she called and held up the baggie.

The girl ran to her, long legs graceful, the dog bounding beside her. "Is that the scent article?"

"Yes." Tawny handed the baggie over. "No school?"

Jessica shook her head. "Still closed. Churro and me will work on finding Smoky today because, if the electricity comes back on, I have to go to school tomorrow."

She ordered the dog to sit, opened the baggie, and held it to his nose. "That's Smoky's sock. Smell it." Churro snuffled, tail wagging. She resealed the bag and stared into his eyes. "Go find Smoky."

The dog zigzagged around the yard, nose to the ground. He paused and looked back at Jessica then galloped toward the lake, tail high. He stopped abruptly, sniffed, and pawed the dirt. Soon he was digging, throwing up muddy clods. Then he flopped down and rolled on his back, twisting this way and that.

Jessica heaved a big sigh. "He's probably rubbing in poop. Disgusting habit he has."

Tawny pressed her lips together and kept silent. She didn't want to discourage the girl's aspirations but Churro didn't show much promise as a tracker.

"Smoky keeps a little fishing boat at the other end of the lake," Jessica said. "He likes to go out to the Gulf and catch flounder. I'm gonna take Churro and see if the boat's still there. Maybe Churro can pick up Smoky's scent."

"How does he get from the lake to the Gulf?" Tawny asked.

"The channels around here all connect up to the river. You can get lost easy but if you know the right canal, it takes you out to the Gulf." She skipped toward the swamp. The dog trotted ahead to the trail that bordered the water's edge.

As Tawny watched them move into the cypress trees, she remembered the snake she'd nearly stumbled over. She worried about the girl going into the jungle alone. "Jessica, wait!" She hurried to catch up. "Is that a good idea?"

The girl made a face. "Me and Churro explore all the time."

One missing person was enough for Tawny. "Listen, how about if I go with you?"

"Sure, if you want to." A shy smile signaled she was happy for Tawny's interest.

Back home in Montana, Tawny would take her revolver and bear spray on a hike. But she didn't have either with her to venture into a Florida bog full of unknown dangers. "Might be a good idea to have a weapon."

"Papi has a machete."

"Let's bring that."

While Jessica ran to her house, Tawny checked her cell. Only fifteen percent charge left. She texted Tillman: *Looking for Smoky at lake with Jessica.*

The girl came back moments later, swinging a machete like a pirate, the curved blade whooshing through the air.

The reckless slashing made Tawny nervous. "Let me carry that."

"If you want. It's kinda heavy."

"I don't mind." Besides, it was much safer in Tawny's hands than Jessica's. She grasped the wood handle.

Jessica and Churro scurried ahead, Tawny walking behind. The trail wound around the irregular lake, some areas swampy mud, others spongy duff. After a half mile, they reached a little inlet. Scraps of a collapsed wooden pier floated near the water line, planks bumping the shore.

"This is the dock where Smoky used to tie his boat up, at least what's left of it," Jessica said. "Boat's gone. Maybe Churro can find it." She opened the baggie and gave the dog another sniff of Smoky's sock.

Tawny wondered if Smoky had taken the small craft or Irma had blown it away. Seemed crazy to venture out in a hurricane in a boat but walking out of his house during the storm was crazy, too.

Churro lifted his nose high while he paced back and forth along the shoreline. He waded into the lake and began to dog-paddle toward a little island. A tree had fallen on the mud hump, roots splayed in the air.

"Churro, come back here, you bad dog." Jessica faced Tawny. "He loves to swim but he gets all mucky and nasty. Churro, get over here!" The girl waded out to thigh-level. "Churro, come!"

Tawny didn't like either Jessica or the dog in the murky swamp with alligators and snakes. "Please come back on land, Jessica."

As disobedient as her dog, the girl continued out, water lapping the bottoms of her short-shorts.

In an area dappled with shadows, Churro headed toward a dark object about five feet long barely breaking the water.

Could it be a gator?

Or a body?

Tawny ran around the edge of the shore, trying to get a better view, heart quickening with each step. A sideways glance showed Jessica up to her waist in the lake. "Get out of the water, now!" Tawny shouted.

The dog reached the dark object and pawed at it, pushing it into sunlight. To Tawny's great relief, it wasn't a body, only a submerged log.

But relief vanished when the triangular head of a gray-brown snake reared up from the log, white-rimmed mouth open wide.

Jessica shrieked, "Churro!"

The cottonmouth struck at the dog. He yelped, splashed wildly, and reversed direction, swimming hard back toward his owner. His pitiful cries echoed in the silent jungle.

The snake slid into the water. In an S-pattern, it skimmed after the dog, head raised, white mouth wide open.

Jessica's arms windmilled in a desperate crawl stroke toward her pet, yelling his name.

Tawny plunged into the lake, holding the machete over her head, moving as fast as she could. Her sneakers sunk deep into the sucking mud but she pushed forward until the water reached her armpits. She angled to place herself between Jessica and the snake.

She might not be able to prevent the snake from attacking Churro but she had to cut it off before it reached the girl.

She made a desperate lunge toward the cottonmouth, swiping the machete through the murky water. It slid under the snake and she yanked it up quickly, catching the reptile on the edge of the blade. She flung it as hard as she could away from the girl and the dog. It hurtled through the air and landed with a splash, twenty feet away.

Churro was still yelping, trying to swim but panicked. His front paws landed on Tawny's shoulders, rear paws raking her belly as he tried to climb on top of her. She shoved him away to keep him from being cut with the machete in his mad scrambling. Then she hurled the weapon toward the shore. She grabbed his collar and the loose scruff of his back and dragged him through the water.

Meanwhile, Jessica clambered out of the lake and ran around the shoreline, trying to get closer to her dog. "Churro! Churro!"

Tawny hauled the dog up on dry ground. He stood, trembling, the dark centers of his eyes surrounded by white, a front paw lifted off the ground. Blood dripped from the leg and it was already swelling. The cottonmouth had scored a solid hit.

Jessica grabbed him around the neck. "Churro, don't die." She stared up at Tawny, tears glistening. "Don't let him die."

Tawny pulled her cell from the pocket of her dripping shorts, hoping it had survived the drenching. When it lit up, elation rushed through her. She punched 911. It rang eight times. A recording announced all circuits were busy. Dammit. She tried Tillman's number and heard the same message. With shaking fingers, she tapped a text to him: *Snake bit Jessica's dog. Help! Hurry!*

Cursing Irma for destroying communication, Tawny squatted and gathered the dog in her arms. Churro had to weigh more than fifty pounds. She struggled to rise. He craned his neck around to stare at her with terror in his dark molasses eyes. "It's OK, Churro, I'm going to help you. Jessica, you lead."

The girl grabbed the machete and hurried ahead, holding vines out of the way as Tawny plodded through muck and tree roots. The dog whimpered.

"You're going to be fine," Tawny murmured, wondering whom she was trying to convince, the dog or herself.

In her pocket, her phone chimed an incoming text but she couldn't stop to check. *Please let it be Tillman saying he's back.* She forged ahead, panting as hard as the dog from the effort of lugging him over the rough trail. Soon, his breathing fell to shallow and rapid. His head dropped low while shudders spasmed through his body. The leg quickly swelled into a painful-looking balloon covered with black fur.

Fifteen long minutes later, they emerged from the jungle to Smoky's back yard.

Tillman loped from the carport toward them as Tawny staggered from exhaustion, knees like jelly. He grabbed the dog out of her arms and carried him to the carport.

Tawny paused to catch her breath and noticed the open trunk of the T-bird. A red and black generator box was inside, rope tying down the trunk lid.

The dog's eyes were almost closed, jowls slack, drooling.

"Where's your vet?" Tillman asked the girl.

"She's over on Fifty-four."

Tawny watched Tillman's eyes as he pondered the same questions she had—how to stuff himself, Tawny, a thirteen-year-old girl, and a fifty-pound dog in a two-seater. "I'll stay here," she offered.

New panic crossed Jessica's face. "No, you have to come. You saved Churro."

"Honey," Tillman spoke softly, "there isn't enough space in the car for everyone."

"We can take my mom's van. It's got lots of room. Papi filled it with gas before Irma. C'mon!" She ran across the adjoining yard to Raul's carport where an older Dodge minivan was parked. Tawny and Tillman followed, the dog quivering in his arms.

Jessica raced into the house and returned a moment later with keys. She unlocked the van and slid the side door open. Tawny climbed in the back seat and Tillman placed the trembling dog on her lap. Tillman got in the driver's side with Jessica riding shotgun to direct him.

While Tillman sped, Tawny's jaw clenched as they passed closed stores, unlighted signs, and traffic signals that still didn't work. Without electricity, nearby vets wouldn't be open. How far would they have to drive to find a clinic with power? How long could the dog survive without treatment?

Jessica pointed to a strip mall. "That's where Churro's vet is." Her voice caught. "Oh, no, they're closed."

"Here." Tillman handed Jessica his phone. "Find vets closer to Dale Mabry Highway. Power's on in that area." He shot Tawny a black look over his shoulder. Expecting the worst, as he usually did.

Jessica thumbed the screen. "There's one on Gunn Highway. That's eight miles away."

Tillman took the phone back and tapped to call. Long seconds passed. "Are you open?" he barked then paused. "OK, listen, I'm bringing in a fifty-pound young Lab bitten by a cottonmouth about a half hour ago. Bad swelling of the front leg. We'll be there in ten."

He floored the van while Tawny struggled to hold Churro steady. The dog moaned. His drool ran down her leg. A weak heartbeat fluttered against her thigh. She stroked his mud-caked fur and cooed to him.

Tillman kept Jessica busy, telling him what had happened so she didn't have a chance to turn around in the seat and watch her suffering dog.

Few cars were on the roads since gas remained in short supply. They passed a newly reopened Publix market, jam-packed with people desperate for food.

Jessica told Tillman to turn south on Gunn Highway. Moments later, he parked in front of the clinic, jumped out, yanked the slider open, and took Churro from Tawny. Jessica ran ahead and held the entrance door.

Tawny rose on wobbly legs, her feet numb from the dead weight of the dog. She stepped down from the van and tried to brush off the mud and dog hair stuck to her skin. She closed the slider and followed them into the building. *Oh please, don't let us be too late.*

Tillman and the dog had disappeared, apparently taken to the back of the clinic by waiting vet techs. Jessica sat in a plastic chair in the reception area, feet up on the seat, hugging her legs, sniffling. Tawny took the chair beside her and wrapped her arm around the girl. In the air conditioning, their sodden clothes turned clammy.

"Papi's going to kill me," Jessica whimpered. "He told me not to let Churro go in the lake. But Churro loves water. He's a Lab. He can't help it." She leaned harder against Tawny. "Besides, I think he was after something, like he was tracking." When she dragged her arm across her runny nose, dried mud flaked off. "Did you see what happened? I gave him another smell of Smoky's sock. That's when, all of a sudden, he took off. I think he caught a scent and that's why he went in the water. Something on that little island interested him."

For a heart-stopping instant back at the lake, Tawny had believed the dark, partly-submerged log was Smoky's body. Now, though, she doubted the dog had been on the scent. He was just a goofy puppy that didn't know enough to avoid a snake.

She grabbed a box of tissues from the counter and handed several to Jessica. When she put the box back, the clerk behind the desk asked, "Are you the owner?"

Tawny shook her head. "We're neighbors. Jessica here owns Churro. Her dad's at work."

The clerk asked more questions, obviously concerned about who would pay the bill. Tawny spoke up, "We'll guarantee whatever Churro needs." Tillman might grumble but she knew he would never let Jessica's pet die for lack of money.

A few minutes later, Tillman came through the door from the treatment area and sat beside Tawny and Jessica. "They're giving him IV fluids and antivenin. Lucky the bite was pretty shallow, didn't hit a vein, which is good. The vet says he should make it." He pulled his cell from his pocket and handed it to Jessica. "Call your dad. Let him know where we are and that we're here with you."

She took the phone and moved across the waiting room. Soon, she was quietly speaking Spanish.

Tillman leaned down to Tawny's ear. "Antivenin is fifteen hundred bucks a vial. Just lucky they had some in stock."

Tawny whispered back, "I told the clerk we'd guarantee payment."

He rolled his eyes. "Figures." But, despite his grousing, he squeezed her leg. "Vet also said snake venom is most potent in the spring and toxicity tapers off later in the year. Churro's damn lucky it's autumn."

A solemn Jessica approached, holding the phone out to Tillman. "Papi wants to talk to you."

He took the device and lapsed into rapid Spanish that Tawny couldn't follow.

The girl's face was pinched. She murmured to Tawny, "Papi is really mad at me. He said if he has to pay vet bills, he doesn't have money to send to Mama in Puerto Rico. He says I should have thought of my Mama instead of letting Churro run loose and get in trouble. I have to find a job to pay the vet bill." Her lip trembled.

Tawny wrapped her arm around the girl and rocked her. "That's a hard lesson, sweetie." She felt sorry for Jessica but couldn't interfere with Raul's parenting.

Cuddled into Tawny, the girl listened intently to Tillman's side of the conversation. Tawny only caught a few words here and there.

When he disconnected, Jessica looked up at him with a shy smile. "Thank you for paying for Churro. I have thirty-five dollars saved. I'll give it to you when we get home. I promise I'll get a job and pay the rest. How much...?"

Tawny recognized the questions swirling in her brown eyes. She clearly had no clue how expensive the bill would be.

Tillman glanced at Tawny then frowned sternly at the girl. "I don't know yet. Probably about a hundred and fifty. It's OK, you can make payments."

Tawny jerked but caught herself. His slight headshake warned her to stay silent.

Twenty minutes later, the vet reported the dog was improving and beckoned to Jessica. She paused at the doorway to the treatment area and said, "I want to stay with Churro. Papi will pick me up here after work. You guys can leave if you want."

As the inner door closed, Tawny caught Tillman's eye. "You big softy. The bill's going to be more than two grand by the time everything's done."

His mouth pulled to one side. "I'm an asshole and don't you forget it."

She rubbed her cheek against his shoulder. "You know, for an asshole, you can be a pretty sweet guy."

"Raul said he wanted to teach Jessica responsibility. I'm charging her enough that she gets the message but it won't break her."

"Why do you hide your kind heart?"

He frowned. "Don't want to ruin my reputation."

She rose on tiptoes and kissed him. "It's our secret."

He left a deposit on his credit card. Then they drove home, eager to hook up the new generator.

At long last, electricity.

***

That night, Tawny and Tillman lay naked, side by side, on their backs in bed, a portable fan softly blowing air over them while the lamp on the bedside table glowed. Outside in the carport, the generator rumbled, its reassuring purr coming through the open window. Earlier, they had watched news on TV and their phones were charging, along with Tillman's laptop. In the kitchen, the refrigerator hummed once more, chilling the perishable groceries they'd splurged on after they left the vet's office.

Best of all, Tawny had enjoyed the most luxurious shower of her life, thanks to Raul's ingenuity.

When he had gotten home with Jessica and Churro, Raul had loaded one of his 55-gallon tanks full of rainwater on a dolly. Heated by the searing Florida sun, the water was perfect shower temperature. He set up the barrel outside Smoky's bathroom, connected the new generator to a pump, and ran a garden hose through the window. After days of washing in a bucket, Tawny had savored the makeshift shower.

She fluffed her freshly-shampooed hair across the pillow and sighed with pleasure.

Tillman rolled to face her. "So was the generator worth three hundred bucks?"

"Lord, yes! And Raul is an angel from heaven for jury-rigging that shower."

"The greedy princess used up all the warm water. Left me with a pail of cold water."

"You didn't go swimming in a filthy swamp and lug a smelly, wet dog all over. It took a long time to scrub off all that muck."

He suppressed a smile. "You deserved it."

"It'll be nice to have milk for our coffee in the morning. The little things you take for granted until you can't have them." She rubbed the stubble on his cheek. "Tomorrow, you'll have hot water to shave. You're giving me whisker burn."

"Might let the beard grow out. Think it would make me look wise?"

She giggled. "Wise ass, yes."

He rose on one elbow and pretended to glare at her. "If you insult me, I'll take the generator back."

She put her arms around his neck and pulled his face down to hers. "In that case, I love your whiskers."

He kissed her briefly but then surprised her when he didn't continue. Instead he rolled onto his back, away from her caresses. She watched him stare at the ceiling, brows furrowed.

After several quiet moments, she asked, "Thinking about Smoky?"

"Yeah."

She waited, knowing the turmoil inside his brilliant mind and aching heart. When he didn't say anything more, she curled closer to him. "Not knowing is the worst."

"If he's dead, he's dead. But, goddammit, I've *got* to know. People yammer about needing closure. I always thought that was bullshit. But, now, I see."

She wanted to reassure him. "Maybe he's alive and just underground on the run from Gabriel." She jerked with sudden recollection. "Oh, I forgot to tell you in all the excitement over the dog. I did some research online. Gabriel has a sports memorabilia business in St. Petersburg and the registered agent is Nyala Obregon."

Tillman sat up abruptly. "Smoky's girlfriend?"

"Yes. Maybe that's why she acted so odd when you were questioning her."

"If she thinks that interrogation was uncomfortable, wait until next time. I'll back her so far into the corner, she'll break her fingernails trying to climb up the wall." He swung long legs over the side of the bed. "Show me what you found."

"Tillman, it's almost midnight."

"Never mind. I'll look myself." He strode out of the bedroom. A lamp flashed on in the living room.

Tawny sighed and got up. Tillman wouldn't sleep until he found answers. And he needed to know for his friend's sake. She padded out to sit beside him on the couch, put on her readers, and called up the sites she'd found earlier.

97

He studied the photo she'd recognized and agreed it was one of Gabriel's thugs. He skimmed quickly through the business registry and Nyala's Facebook page. Then he dug deeper into more legal, tax, and business sites. After fifteen minutes, he came to the same conclusion she had. "Gabriel's purposely keeping his business unlisted."

"Why?" she asked. "Is he doing something illegal with it?"

"That's opposite of how it usually works. Criminals put up a legit business front to hide the illegitimate one. He's probably catering to restricted clientele and doesn't want the unwashed public bothering him."

"You mean, like us?" She stroked his inner thigh, hoping to coax him away from research and back into bed.

"We're not unwashed anymore." He cracked a small smile. "Good work, finding the connection."

She rested her head on his shoulder. "Thank you."

"Tomorrow, we'll have another chat with Ms. Nyala." He set the laptop on the table, rose, and pulled her up from the couch. "We better get some sleep."

She murmured, "It's nice to have light again. I never realized how much it means. Here we are, in the middle of millions of people, but we're all in the dark, like cavemen before fire."

In the bedroom, she stroked his unshaven face. "You feel like a wire brush."

He pushed her to sit on the edge of the mattress. "Just think of it as an exfoliate for your peeling sunburn." He turned off the light and knelt on the floor between her knees, pushing them apart. His hands slid lazily up the insides of her thighs.

She buried her fingers in his curls. A quiver of pleasurable anticipation ran through her. "I don't think I got burned down there."

His warm breath tickled her skin. "I better check anyway."

Chapter 10 – Wiener Special

On day four without electricity, in the early dawn, only Smoky's and Raul's houses glimmered with lights, powered by their new generators. Neighbors watched from their porches as Tillman and Raul refueled the gas tank.

After breakfast, the three of them sat in the shade at Raul's inlaid-tile concrete picnic table, the only patio furniture too heavy to be blown away. They drank coffee with milk, a welcome change now that their refrigerator ran. Tawny ran her fingertips along Tillman's smooth jaw, freshly shaven using water heated on the barbecue grill. "Hot water is a wonderful invention," she said.

Raul smiled at Tawny, embarrassment mingled with gratitude. "Thank you for helping my daughter's bad dog. His paw is not so big this morning." He turned to Tillman. "And I pay you back for the generator."

Tillman shook his head. "The price of the generator is a lot cheaper than hiring someone to cut up that oak tree. *Gracias*."

Raul gestured toward several people across the street. "My friends are very happy for the generator, too. Now their food won't spoil because they can borrow my refrigerator." He looked at a bedroom window in his bungalow. "Jessica is happy that school's still closed. She likes to sleep late." He sighed. "But I'm not happy until the electricity comes on."

Tawny asked, "Have you been able to reach your wife?"

He shook his head, brown eyes troubled. "My brother is leaving messages with other ham operators in Puerto Rico but so much confusion there." He rose and touched the brim of his cap. "I go to work now. Anything you need, anything I can do for you, you just say." He climbed in his truck and drove away.

"Poor guy," Tawny mused. "The news last night said hundreds of people are still missing in Puerto Rico. I hope his wife is OK."

Tillman grimaced. "We have our own missing person to look for."

They carried their mugs across the yard to Smoky's house. On the kitchen table, Tillman opened his laptop, peered through his readers, and tapped the keyboard. "Today's mission: Ms. Nyala Obregon."

"Want me to call her?"

"No. Based on what you found yesterday, I'm the last person she wants to talk to. No warning. We just show up." He pointed at the screen. "Look."

Tawny put on her glasses and leaned over his shoulder. A map showed streets twisting around numerous blue blobs that indicated bodies of water. "No wonder it's called Land O'Lakes. Is that red arrow where she lives?"

"Tax records show she owns six properties but I'm betting this one is her residence. A condo inside a gated community."

"How do we get in without tipping her off?"

He smirked. "I'm good."

She nudged his shoulder. "Yeah, and modest, too." As much as his arrogance sometimes annoyed her, she also recognized that was why, in nearly twenty years of practice, he'd won almost every case he'd tried. He *was* incredibly good.

He closed the laptop. "Want to come along?"

"Wouldn't miss it for the world."

"Sure you feel all right?" He lightly brushed the peeling skin on her arm. "It's going to be hot again today. Damn that crunched-up car of Smoky's. The air won't work with my head stuck out the open window."

She smiled at the image. "I'll be OK."

"I checked online for rental cars but there's nothing available for four hundred miles."

"Hey, what about Raul's van? He said if we needed anything…"

"Good idea. I'll call him." A slow smile spread across his face. "Even better, Nyala won't recognize it."

***

"Nyala lives in a nudist place?" Tawny stared at the sign on a solid concrete wall that blocked the gated community from view. She turned to Tillman in the driver's seat of Raul's borrowed van. "Did you know about this?"

One side of his mouth lifted. "Smoke mentioned once on the phone that he and a girlfriend liked to party at some resort where they'd get naked and skinny-dip."

Tawny shook her head. "Unbelievable."

"Makes it a snap to get in."

"Excuse me?"

"We buzz at the gate and say we want to visit for the day."

She grinned. "Are you going to take your clothes off?"

"Maybe. What about you?"

"Right. Like I'm not already peeling. No, thank you. Besides, the sign says *Clothing optional*. That means you can stay dressed, right?"

"Party pooper."

She wrinkled her nose at him. "Remember, we're here to work."

Tillman pulled into the entrance and pressed an intercom button. "Hi, we'd like a tour."

The disembodied voice answered, "Come on in. Turn right at the T in the road, then turn left and the office will be in front of you." The power gate slowly swung open.

"Nice they have electricity here," Tawny said. "Wonder if ours will ever come back on."

Once inside, Tillman turned left at the T.

"Didn't she say *right*?" Tawny asked.

"Yeah, but Google maps shows Nyala's address is to the left." He continued a short distance to another turn. Palm trees and oaks shaded the street. Ahead stood clusters of buildings, each painted a different bright color—orange, pink, turquoise, purple, green.

Tawny craned her neck, studying the surroundings. "All these colors. Looks like a tropical sunset."

A naked blond woman pedaled by on a bike and waved at them.

"Nice scenery," Tillman said, straight-faced.

Tawny poked his arm.

He stared down his nose at her. "I was referring to the sandhill cranes over there. What were *you* looking at?"

Sure enough, a pair of long-legged cranes minced on the shoreline of a pond with water lilies floating on it.

"What are you jealous of?" He kept his gaze lasered straight ahead. "You're much better looking than she was." He checked his laptop propped on the dashboard. "We should be getting close."

She knew he'd caught her grin in his peripheral vision.

"Here we are." He pulled next to a two-story green building that appeared to have ten units. The rear of the condos faced the parking lot.

They walked around to the front of the building to find the entrances overlooked a fifty-acre lake. Tawny paused to gaze at a wooden pier jutting into water that was the color of tea. Nude sunbathers lounged on chaises scattered along its length. A thick cypress forest, hung with Spanish moss, formed a border around the lake.

A squirrel jumped on the pier railing and chattered at Tawny. Snowy egrets poked in the mud at the edge of the lake. A brown rabbit emerged from ferns, nose twitching. Except for a few split trees and broken branches floating in the lake, Tawny didn't see much damage from the hurricane.

"It's like the Garden of Eden," she whispered to Tillman.

"Better watch out for the snake." He pointed at a unit. "Here's her place." He opened the door of a screened porch and they stepped inside.

Four white wicker chairs and a matching table furnished the porch. The blades of a ceiling fan slowly turned. Tillman had to duck sideways to avoid them. He rang the bell.

After a few seconds, the door opened only wide enough for Nyala Obregon to peek through. Her expression was impassive, no show of surprise at unexpected visitors. She wore a lime-colored sarong knotted above her breasts. Otherwise, nothing inside the condo was visible through the barely-cracked door.

Tillman bowed slightly. "Good morning, Ms. Nyala."

She waited, silent.

Tillman pulled a chair away from the patio table, as if inviting her. "May we sit down?" Without waiting for her answer, he lowered himself into the chair. Tawny took his cue and sat beside him.

Nyala slipped through the narrow opening and closed the door firmly behind her. She sat opposite them and laid a graceful forearm on the table. She propped her other elbow in her palm and rested her cheek against long, splayed fingers. "Is anything wrong with the house?"

"The house is fine," he answered. "We have a generator now. That makes life a little easier."

It occurred to Tawny that she viewed them as her employees, delivering a status report on her property.

Tillman sat easy in the chair, appearing relaxed but Tawny sensed the tight coils of his muscles. He said, "You are the registered agent for Sports of Yesteryear."

"I was. Not anymore."

"Tawny and I had a drink with Gabriel Marquez Garcia the other night."

"Really." She almost sounded bored.

"Did you know Gabriel had ordered his two employees to kick the shit out of Smoky? Likely broke some ribs."

She leaned back and folded her slim arms. "That was unnecessary."

Tillman answered, "Agreed. I attempted to come to an understanding with Gabriel that would satisfy Smoky's debt. He was not amenable to my offer."

"Gabriel can be stubborn."

"So can I."

Finally, a slight smile crossed her beautiful face. "I gathered that, Mr. Rosenbaum."

"Ms. Nyala, you have not been forthcoming."

"I didn't realize I was under an obligation to do so."

Now Tillman smiled. "You certainly are not. But, as Smoky's friend and attorney, I would be most appreciative if you were."

She leaned forward, back ramrod straight, both elbows on the table, chin resting in her palms. "Gabriel is my younger brother."

Tawny gasped then clamped her lips tight. Dammit, why couldn't she hide her emotions?

Nyala briefly noted Tawny's reaction then directed her attention back to Tillman. "My half-sibling, actually. Same mother, different fathers. I was eight when he was born. I bathed and diapered him from the day of his birth."

Tawny noticed the woman's delicate, narrow nose and realized Gabriel had the same nose. And the same green eyes. Only the windows into both of their souls were opaque.

"Even today," she continued, "when I look at him, I still see that smiling baby, kicking his chubby little legs as I tickled him." A faint sigh escaped through slightly flared nostrils. "As a man, though, I understand he has an unforgiving attitude in business."

Tillman watched Nyala. Tawny couldn't guess the strategy going on behind his courtroom expression.

After long seconds of silence, he spoke: "Given your relationship, are you willing to intercede with Gabriel? Convince him to accept a reasonable settlement and end the dispute between him and Smoky. That enmity can only cause both of them unnecessary grief."

She leaned back and inspected her manicured nails. Her hands stayed rock steady, no quiver or tremble. "I have no influence over Gabriel," she said. "He is his own man. I'm only a sentimental, foolish big sister."

"Foolish, you are not, Ms. Nyala," Tillman answered.

She rose. "I cannot help you, Mr. Rosenbaum." She went inside the condo and closed the door.

Tawny faced Tillman, eyebrows raised. His chin lifted slightly. They left the screened porch and walked back to the parking lot. Inside the van, she said, "That's weird. Brother and sister."

"Blood's thicker than water. Can't count on her to help Smoky...if he's still alive, that is." His jutting jaw firmed into granite as he started the engine. Nothing bothered Tillman as much as the inability to solve a problem. Impossible tasks never worried him but being helpless did.

They drove through the meandering lanes of the sprawling community, past blocks of condos and single-family residences. "There must be five hundred homes here," Tawny said. "Who knew so many people want to live naked?"

A chain link fence enclosed a central club complex with several swimming pools and dozens of nude people sunbathing on chaise lounges. Motel rooms and an octagonal open-air building were painted sky-blue with white trim and dark blue awnings, giving the resort a tropical feel. A spirited volleyball game was going on at an adjacent sand court.

Tawny gawked for a few seconds then nudged Tillman. "Is that uncomfortable for a guy, flopping around like that?"

He grinned and shook his head. "Want to check the place out?"

She raised a shoulder. "Why not? I'm getting hungry. You can buy me lunch."

They parked near the club entrance and went inside the lobby. A clerk wearing a tight t-shirt and a short black skirt greeted them and handed over an application form. While Tawny filled it out, Tillman pulled open a swinging door into a darkened bar. A central dancefloor was ringed with cocktail tables and chairs.

"The nightclub opens at eight," the clerk said. "It's lingerie night. Prizes for the sexiest costumes. If you pay the day fee, that covers entrance to the club tonight, also."

Tawny exchanged a look with Tillman then answered, "We'll think about it."

His wordless smirk called her a coward.

The clerk directed them to a rear door of the lobby and said a tour guide would join them in a few minutes.

Outside, umbrella tables and chaises ringed a hot tub and a curving conversation pool full of chatting skinny-dippers. The octagonal building turned out to be a tiki bar. At the entrance, a reader board advertised *$1 Wiener Special*. The tangy aroma of sauerkraut and mustard drifted in the air.

"Smells good," Tawny said, pulling Tillman toward the door.

Right at that moment, a man exited the bar, stark naked and swinging in the breeze. He carried a plastic cup of beer and a chili dog with onions in a paper boat. He smiled at them then headed to an outdoor table.

Tawny started through the door but Tillman caught her arm. He bent to her ear. "After seeing that, I'm not eating any goddamn wiener."

She giggled. "Chicken."

Chapter 11 – Orange Hibiscus

After lunch, Tawny and Tillman headed back to New Port Richey and found an open gas station on the way. They waited in line for a half-hour to fill Raul's van plus two gas cans for the generator. More traffic lights were now working and some businesses had reopened. Utility crews apparently restored power in commercial strips first then fanned out into residential areas. Smoky's neighborhood must have been way down their list.

When they parked the van in Raul's carport, Jessica ran out of the house, followed by her dog. Even with his paw bandaged, he trotted easily, as if yesterday's snake bite was a distant memory.

The girl was breathless with excitement. "I gotta show you what Churro found." She waved a scrap of cloth in front of Tawny's face as she climbed out of the van.

The fabric looked familiar—pink with orange hibiscus.

Tawny's heart sank. She shot a look at Tillman, striding around from the driver's side. His narrowed eyes said he also recognized the torn material.

He took it from Jessica, his voice a low rumble like an earthquake building underground. "That's the shirt Smoky was wearing."

"I *told* you Churro caught his scent," the girl insisted. "I *knew* it the way he jumped into the water to swim over to it."

Tillman moved to the concrete picnic table and spread the ragged cloth out. Reddish-brown stains marred the shredded edges. Tawny swallowed, knowing it was blood. Mostly likely, Smoky's.

Tillman's voice stayed low, tightly controlled. "Where'd you find this, Jessica?"

The girl gestured toward the lake. "Same place where me and Tawny went yesterday. Where the cottonmouth bit Churro." She looked up at Tawny. "Remember that little island?"

Tawny bit her lip, hard.

"The water's gone down since yesterday," Jessica said. "Today, we could walk across a little strip of mud and get to the island. This was all tangled in the roots of a tree that fell over."

"Show us," Tillman ordered.

The girl and dog practically bounced in anticipation of plunging back into the jungle.

Venturing into the swamp again filled Tawny with dread. "Wait, we should have a weapon."

Tillman retrieved the pistol from the T-bird's glove box.

Tawny bent low to Jessica's eager face. "Be very careful. If Churro gets bitten by another snake, he could die."

Tillman added, "And if *you* get bitten by a snake, your dad will kill *me*."

Guilt tinged the girl's smile, an acknowledgment of her mistakes the day before.

She led them on a different route, even more overgrown with vines that tangled around their shins. They twisted and turned through tree roots and cypress knees. Strings of Spanish moss brushed Tawny's face, making her skin itch. She stepped over a fallen log and, without warning, sank knee-deep in stinking slime. "Dammit."

Tillman offered a hand and pulled her out of the bog.

Churro darted ahead and Jessica sprinted after him, both disappearing into the thicket.

"Jessica!" Tawny called. "Slow down. Wait for us."

The girl ignored her.

"She's OK," Tillman said. "Raul told me she's been running around the swamp since she was a toddler. Says she knows the jungle better than the gators."

Tawny shot him what her son used to call the *worried-mom* look. "That went real well yesterday."

They slogged forward, trying to keep Jessica in sight as the path meandered along the ragged shoreline. After a half-mile, Tawny recognized the clearing and the little island. As Jessica had described, the water level had lowered enough to expose a narrow mud spit that connected the shore to the island.

Girl and dog were already out there, hunkered next to a toppled tree, its roots poking up in the air like gnarled fingers. Churro whined and pawed at the mud. The now-filthy bandages wrapping his foot were coming undone.

Tawny and Tillman picked their way carefully across the spit and joined Jessica.

She looked up at them. "He smells something."

The tree had split, part lying in the mud, but part still standing, a wide splinter of green wood sticking up. The fallen trunk sheltered a hollow underneath. Tillman pushed the dog aside and knelt down. He bent low with his face close to the ground and peered into the hollow.

When he reached deep inside, Tawny gasped. "Watch out for snakes."

He pulled out a flat object about six inches square, covered with mud. He swished it in a shallow puddle to clean it.

It was a wallet, brown, tooled leather. Still on his knees, Tillman carefully opened it, holding it far enough away that he could read without his glasses. His Adam's apple moved in his throat as he swallowed.

His hard, dark, impenetrable gaze met Tawny's. "It's Smoky's."

Please no. The unspoken fear that had haunted them since his disappearance couldn't be repressed any longer. Tears burned her eyes as he handed the wallet to her. Inside the water-soaked leather, a driver's license photo of Smoky's rumpled face smiled grimly through the plastic sleeve.

Tillman rose and stood close beside her as she flipped through several compartments. Smoky's saltwater fishing license was a plastic card with a blue marlin emblazoned across it. Other pockets held soggy, folded papers, business cards, and Nyala's photo with a seductive smile curving her lips. No credit cards. A twenty, three fives, and two ones made up the cash.

Tawny handed the wallet back to Tillman, squeezing his hand as it closed around the leather. "I'm sorry," she whispered.

Churro nudged her leg, smiling, tail sweeping back and forth, proud of himself.

She stroked his black velvet head. "Good boy." Her voice choked.

Jessica huddled on the ground, eyes round and stricken. Her teeth chattered.

Tawny wondered how she could be cold at ninety degrees then realized fear and shame were the true reasons for her distress. "Are you OK, sweetie?" She extended her hand to the girl.

Jessica grasped it and pulled herself to her feet then hunched her thin shoulders.

Tawny hugged her. "Honey, it's not your fault. You did great."

Jessica's tears dampened Tawny's tank top. "It's not like I thought it would be. I thought me and Churro would be heroes for finding lost people. And everyone would be happy." She sniffled. "I didn't know he'd find dead people."

***

The sheriff's substation smelled dank and a little moldy. Recent-looking water stains crept several inches up the walls. A fan oscillated back and forth, blowing on the damp plaster. A uniformed reservist stood behind a counter, talking on the phone, while other lines rang incessantly, unanswered. No one else appeared to be on duty. Earlier, Tawny had tried calling the station several times but couldn't get through. Now, she understood why.

While still on the phone, the reservist watched Tillman spread the contents of Smoky's wallet and the blood-stained scrap of pink fabric on the counter. After several minutes, he hung up and asked, "What's this?"

"We're reporting a missing person," Tillman said. "Smoky Lido. Age seventy-two. He disappeared during the height of the storm four days ago. We've searched shelters, talked with his neighbors and friends. No one has seen him. We just found his wallet in the swamp behind his house." He held up the fabric. "This is a piece of the shirt he was wearing when we last saw him." Tillman pointed at the stains. "Appears to be blood."

"That's all?"

Tillman's jaw tightened. "That's enough to start a search."

"Does he have dementia or any mental impairment?"

"No."

"Too bad," the reservist answered. "If mental impairment was a problem, given his age, we could issue a Silver Alert. But if he's an adult of sound mind and just decided to take off, there's not much we can do." The man answered the constantly ringing phone. "Can you hold, please?" He punched a button and again faced them. "Besides, we're understaffed. Fifty Pasco County deputies are on their way to relieve deputies in Collier County who've been up five days straight. They're falling over from exhaustion. There's a bunch of old people dying in a nursing home in Hollywood because they have no air conditioning. Irma left the whole state in chaos. I'll take the report but emergencies have priority. I can't promise anything. Could be weeks before personnel get freed up to look for him."

Fifteen minutes later, after filling out the paperwork, Tawny and Tillman left the substation. "Well, that was wasted," he muttered.

Tawny slipped her hand into his. "At least he gave you back the wallet and cloth. I have a feeling any evidence we left there would get lost in the shuffle."

As Tillman drove in silence, Tawny studied his profile. He was always hard to read. He was also no stranger to traumatic loss. Still, she worried and finally asked, "What are you thinking?"

"There's got to be more."

"More?"

"More than a wallet and a scrap of his shirt. He could have planted those himself."

"What about the blood?"

"Hell, I bleed worse when I cut myself shaving. He probably snagged a fish hook in his finger, tore a strip off his shirt, and wrapped it around the cut."

Tawny remembered details from that night. "After Gabriel's guys beat him up, his nose was bleeding. It was dripping on his shirt."

She felt torn. Should she try to reassure Tillman? Or point out that he was stretching too far for explanations to avoid the likely truth—that his friend was dead.

After a moment, she asked, "You think he's trying to fake his own death?"

"With Gabriel pissed off and after him, yeah. One way out of paying debts."

Tawny gazed through the side window, watching traffic grow heavier as the gradual return of electricity brought more normalcy to the storm-ravaged area. "If their dispute was just over money, why didn't Gabriel take you up on your offer?"

Tillman frowned. "I know. That bothered me, too. He's a businessman. As long as he gets paid, he wouldn't care where the money came from."

"Except he feels betrayed. He wants revenge."

Instead of turning on the street toward Smoky's house, Tillman veered onto Highway 19, heading south.

"Where are we going?"

"St. Pete. Look up the address to Sports of Yesteryear." He handed over his phone.

Tawny put on her readers and scrolled through their recent searches. "OK, what now?"

"Get directions from here."

She entered a starting point and the destination. "Got it. Stay on Nineteen. It goes through a bunch of little beach towns, Palm Harbor, Dunedin, and Clearwater. It's almost forty miles. We'll need to fill up Raul's van again."

Tawny waited, wondering if Tillman would explain the trip to Gabriel's business. When five minutes had passed without a word, she asked, "Why are we going there?"

Tillman turned right. "If Smoky wants the world to think he's dead, I'm going to back his play. I'm going to convince Gabriel that there's no use pursuing his revenge. Maybe I can buy Smoke more running time to get away."

She settled deeper into the seat. Tillman was nothing if not realistic, too realistic at times. Did he really think Smoky was alive? Or was he hoping against hope?

They passed through scenic beach towns, the aquamarine water of the Gulf stretching to the horizon. She rolled down the window to inhale the sea breeze. "Smells so fresh."

"Too bad you've gotten a lousy impression of Florida, so far," Tillman said. "When hurricanes aren't tearing up the landscape, it's a pretty place."

He was right. Even with bulldozers piling storm debris high along the road, the sun, sand, and water were beautiful, palm trees swaying. She'd never lived near the sea with its fresh, salty tang. "How long since you were here last?"

"Years." He shook his head. "First trip was after my bar mitzvah. I cashed the checks my parents' friends gave me and bought a ticket down here. Stayed with my uncle and went to some Yankee games during spring training. Then, in high school, Smoky brought me every year." He leaned back in the seat, stretching his long arms. "Know how he got the name *Smoky*?"

"How?"

"Radio announcer broadcasting the games. Used to say, 'Coach Lido smoked the other team again.' Name stuck." A faraway memory settled over him. "He was one helluva coach. Said I'd have a better chance to catch the eye of a scout down here than back in Montana. He was right. I got a couple of offers during my senior year trip."

"If you had it to do all over again, do you ever wish you'd gone pro?"

"You're waxing philosophical."

"Just curious."

He lifted one shoulder. "I was damn good. I could have gone as far as Smoky thought I could."

Tawny pursed her lips. "Know what I like best about you?"

He quirked an eyebrow.

"Your modesty and humility," she said.

He smirked then went on: "Too much in the game depends on luck and chance. Get traded to a loser club and you go down the drain with them. A ninety-mile-an-hour fast ball beans you and your career's over in a second. A law degree guaranteed a decent income and sometimes I can even do a little good."

She reached across the console and caressed the back of his neck, remembering how he'd saved her from prison. "Like getting me out of trouble."

"*That's* the best thing I ever did." For an instant, his hard, dark eyes softened as he gazed at her. Then he veered onto a causeway to the right. "See that big pink high-rise with two towers? Planned to stay there for a few days after we settled Smoky's problem. Didn't expect it to drag on this long."

"It's beautiful."

"Cross the street and you're on the white sand beach. There's an outdoor terrace overlooking the Gulf where they hold weddings." His sideways glance weighed heavy with significance.

She drew her hand back and hugged herself. "Please don't keep pushing me, Tillman."

"Why are you putting this off? We're together. We're going to be together unless you want out."

She stared at the ceiling of the van. The cloth headliner had a tear in it and sagged open. With one finger, she tried to tuck it back into place but it fell loose again. "I don't want out," she murmured.

A sudden turbulence of emotions churned in her stomach. She tried to pin them down, to separate the tangled feelings snarled like fishing lines. Was it that she'd already raised her children and didn't want the responsibility and heartaches of his?

His toxic ex-wife had wreaked irreparable damage and showed no signs of slowing down her efforts to alienate the three teenagers from their father. No matter how much Tawny loved them, she knew she couldn't undo the imprint of destruction on Mimi, Arielle, and Judah.

But other feelings intruded. Was it that she didn't want to tarnish her thirty-two years with Dwight? They'd struggled through problems and suffered their share of difficulties. Yet the bedrock underlying their marriage had always been solid. Nothing could ever come between them…except the cancer that had killed him.

She didn't feel that way with the volatile, impatient Tillman. A few months earlier, his temper had almost destroyed their relationship. The memory of his rage still stung.

Another factor was distance—four-hundred-fifty miles between Billings where his practice was and Kalispell where she'd always lived, where her roots were. He'd tried to convince her to move into his estate but she felt out of place and uncomfortable there. Recognizing her reluctance, he'd offered to buy a different home for them.

But she loved her creaky old house full of memories and the tree-shaded small town where she'd been born. If Tillman moved in there with her, where would those memories go? Would they be overwhelmed by his larger-than-life presence and shrink into the background like neglected, wilting flowers?

It all came down to fear. She was afraid.

With Dwight, she'd never experienced doubt, not even pre-wedding jitters. Being with him was right and she'd always known it.

But that feeling of certainty and security was missing with Tillman.

She took a deep breath. "I don't want out," she repeated. "But I'm scared."

His short laugh surprised her. "Well, hell, that's perfectly understandable with an asshole like me." He slid fingertips down the side of her face. "If you ever decide you're not scared anymore, let me know."

She grasped his hand and held it to her lips. "I will," she murmured against his long fingers.

"Anytime before tomorrow will be fine." Deadpan.

She grinned, relieved that he'd eased the tension. For now. "You know what else I like about you? Never any pressure."

Tillman's phone rang. The screen said *Raul*. He put the call on speaker.

"*Señor*, Jessica's dog found something else in the swamp."

Tillman frowned at Tawny. "What?"

"Bones. Not much left but they smell very bad."

"What kind of bones?"

"At first, I think maybe a deer leg. But they look different. I think you need to see this."

Chapter 12 – Bones

Tawny and Tillman abandoned the trip to Gabriel's store in St. Petersburg and instead sped back to New Port Richey.

There, they found Raul and Jessica at their picnic table, which was covered with newspapers. The girl leaned against her father, his arm around her shoulder. Churro sat beside them, pink tongue hanging out of his smiling mouth. When he spotted Tawny, his tail wagged.

On the newspaper lay two bones, about eighteen inches long, one thin, the other thicker, barely held together with strings of ligament, muscle, and discolored flesh.

Tawny breathed through her mouth, trying to avoid the stench of decay. The broken, ragged ends looked as if alligator jaws had shattered them. She asked Jessica, "Where did Churro find this?"

The girl shrugged. "I'm not sure. We went back to the island where we found the wallet. I gave him another sniff of Smoky's sock. He ran off along this inlet that leads to the river. I chased him but couldn't keep up. Then, all of a sudden, he's running back to me with these stinky bones in his mouth, jumping and wagging his tail, all excited." She swallowed hard. "The way Churro acted, they gotta be Smoky's." Her lip quivered.

Tillman stepped away from the stench and pulled out his phone. "Maybe *now* the sheriff will launch a search."

***

Three hours after Tillman's 911 call, a Pasco County detective named Boyd showed up. He was in his mid-thirties, with a shaved head and deep tan. His horn-rimmed glasses didn't hide the dark circles under his eyes. He mentioned he hadn't slept for the last seventy-two hours, trying to identify bodies and tracking down people who'd gone missing in Irma. He examined the bones on Raul's picnic table.

Tawny leaned against the side of Raul's house in the shade, feeling queasy. While waiting for the deputy to arrive, she'd brushed her teeth but the rotting smell still permeated her nostrils and mouth.

Jessica sat quiet and still on the ground beside Tawny, back propped against the cinderblock wall, hugging her knees. Churro lay with his head on her feet. His worried brown eyes flicked back and forth between the girl and the detective.

Boyd turned the bones around in his rubber-gloved hands. "Human, all right. A tibia and fibula. Little bit of the ankle structure is still attached." He ran his finger along a vertical crack in the thicker bone. "Gator probably munched on it. See the jagged way it's split here at the upper end. Fish and turtles ate most of the flesh. Doesn't take 'em long to clean all the soft tissue off. So, I'm guessing this hasn't been in the water more than a few days."

He dropped the bones into an evidence bag. "I'll call the dive team out to search the lake for more remains. But it may be a while. We're all spread pretty thin with Irma's mess—I haven't seen my wife and kids for four days. The divers are regular deputies with usual duties so, unless there's a known location where the victim likely is, they only do water searches when they have time."

"We just filed a missing person report on Smoky," Tillman said.

"You never know." One side of Boyd's mouth quirked. "These may not belong to him. He could still be alive. Meanwhile, can you give me something that has Mr. Lido's DNA on it for comparison? Something with blood or saliva."

Tawny straightened. "The night he got beat up, he complained about loose teeth. Maybe there's blood on his toothbrush."

Boyd's brow furrowed. "Beat up?"

Tillman folded his arms. "Yeah. The evening before Irma hit, three guys showed up and kicked the crap out of him. Tawny chased them off with a shotgun. We think it might have been over gambling debts but Smoky refused to say."

"Did you file a report?"

Tawny shook her head. "He didn't want to. Then the power went out and he disappeared. Since then, we've been more concerned about finding him."

Boyd asked, "You figured he'd gone on the run from the guys that beat him up?"

"That seemed likely," Tillman said. "But now, these bones make it look like he got lost and drowned. Goddammit." He kicked at an empty beer can left behind by the flood. It flew across the yard and clunked hard against the stump of the fallen oak tree.

Jessica rose and grasped Tawny's hand. The dog stood and leaned against her other side. Flanked by support, she spoke up. "Smoky's got a little fishing boat with a trolling motor. It isn't where he usually docked it. Maybe he took that out in the river and got swamped in the storm."

The detective studied Jessica. "It's your dog that found these bones?"

The girl laid a hand on Churro's back. "Yes. I want to train him as a search dog. I don't know exactly where he found them. He screwed up big time. He should have stayed with them and alerted me. But we haven't got that far in his training."

Boyd lifted an eyebrow. "Well, it's not exactly proper protocol for a search K-9 to chew on evidence but, hey, he did find them." His shrug said *don't beat yourself up.*

Relief washed over Jessica's face and she stood straighter. "I was afraid he'd get in big trouble."

The detective smiled. "Nah, he's just doing what dogs do."

Tawny liked him for reassuring the worried girl.

Churro wagged his tail, somehow understanding Jessica's tension had eased.

Boyd faced Tawny. "Mr. Lido's toothbrush might yield both blood and saliva. I'll need to get that from you."

She led him inside Smoky's house to the bathroom. In the medicine cabinet, he found the toothbrush and sealed it in a baggie.

Tillman had followed them and stood in the doorway. "How long for DNA testing?"

Boyd spread his hands. "There's quite a backlog. May be a month or more before we find out if there's a match."

He gave them his business card, said goodbye, and went out the back door. Through the kitchen window, Tawny watched him pause to speak to Jessica and to pet Churro, who wagged his tail. Then he headed for his cruiser and drove away.

Tawny faced Tillman. "Seems like a nice guy."

He huffed. "Nice and useless."

She waved her hand in front of her nose. "God, I can't get rid of the smell. It's seeped into my pores."

"Pretty rank," Tillman agreed.

"A month for DNA results. That's a long time to wait."

"Maybe we can fast-track that." He pulled a baggie from his pocket. Inside were a few small tan splinters. "Before the detective got here, I broke a couple of chips off the ragged end of the bone. Should be enough for a private lab to test. Too bad you had to give up the toothbrush but there's got to be something else around here with his DNA."

Tawny cocked her head at him. He always found a way to expedite what he needed. She returned to the bathroom. In a drawer, she found Smoky's brush, thick with grizzled salt and pepper hair. In the wastebasket, she picked out tissues spotted with blood that Smoky had used to stanch his battered nose after the beating. She carried the items to the kitchen table. "Think these will work?"

"Yeah," he answered but his mind was already elsewhere.

She put the brush and tissues in baggies and washed her hands. "What about the shirt with the blood?"

"We'll take that, too, even though that blood might not be Smoky's. Hell, if this was a criminal case, the whole chain of evidence would be an impossible cluster, between the dog and the swamp."

Tawny peered up at him. "What if it *is* a criminal case?"

"You mean, what if Gabriel and his guys are responsible? Yeah, I thought of that. But if they killed him and dumped his body in the lake, they'd know he was dead. They wouldn't have come back here to question you or go to that bar searching for him."

"Unless they weren't looking for *him*. What if they were looking for what he took from them?"

Tillman considered. "Makes sense. Fits the betrayal of trust Gabriel mentioned." His dark gaze hardened. He abruptly went outside, letting the door slam behind him.

A moment later, Tawny heard a *thunk*, then another. Through the kitchen window, she saw him raise an axe over his head then slam it down into the remaining stump of the oak tree. Over and over, chips flew into the air as his furious chopping continued.

She bit her lip, watching him pound his grief into the stump.

Chapter 13 – Honus Rosenbaum

Five long days after Irma knocked out the power, electricity finally came back on at Smoky's house. The air conditioner hummed to life, waking Tawny. Beside her, Tillman snored on his side after a restless night. She slipped out of bed and quietly closed the door, letting him sleep.

Rather than boiling grounds in a pan on the barbecue, she was able to brew coffee in the drip machine. She sliced a bagel and put it in the toaster, smiling as the coils grew red with heat. In the laundry room, she filled the washer with their filthy clothes and started the cycle. Simple electric luxuries swelled her heart with gratitude.

But she worried about Tillman. He'd been silent and turned inside himself since he had demolished the remains of the oak stump with powerful blows from the axe. Only chips remained, scattered across the grass like confetti.

She knew his brilliant brain couldn't stop analyzing Smoky's death, the many unknown ways it could have occurred, calculating the odds and probabilities, running each theory to ground, then moving on to the next. Despite his cold logic, each possibility ended in unspeakable grief for him.

God, she hoped the old coach was already dead by drowning before the alligator had torn his body apart. Would they find enough remains to bury?

She heard water running in the bathroom. After a few minutes, she carried a mug of coffee in there and peeked through the shower curtain. "Nice change to have hot water again?"

He said nothing, expression blank.

With her fingertips, she traced weary lines scoring his long face. "I wish you'd been able to sleep a little longer."

"Not much chance of that." He rinsed soap off and stepped out of the tub.

She perched on the toilet lid, watching him run a towel over his lean, muscular frame. God, he was sexy. Yet, last night, he'd turned away from her caresses. That had never happened before. The depth of his sorrow was palpable.

"What do you want to do today?" she asked.

He scrubbed the towel over his face. "Take those samples to a private lab to test for DNA. I don't care what it costs. If those bones are Smoky's, I want the answer *now*."

"Is there a lab around here?"

"Three choices in Tampa." He gulped coffee then shook a can of shaving cream and spread foam over his stubble.

Watching him shave was a silly little pleasure Tawny always enjoyed. "Do you think the sheriff's office will send divers?"

He scraped the razor up his neck and over his jutting jaw. "By the time they get around to a search, any remains will be long gone."

"What about Churro? He's done a pretty good job of finding evidence so far."

He scowled. "That damn dog probably destroyed more evidence than he brought back. I bet he buried Smoky's bones to snack on later."

Her gut clenched at the image. She should have been used to Tillman's harshness but, at times, he still shocked her. She forced her concentration back to the problem at hand. "I don't know, Tillman. If he hadn't found the shirt, wallet, and leg bones, we'd have nothing."

He exhaled heavily. "I suppose." He wiped the last traces of foam from his face and threw the towel over the shower rod.

She rose and slipped her arms around him from behind, her cheek pressing against the tense, knotted muscles of his back. "I'm sorry about Smoky."

He didn't respond. His body felt only slightly warmer than hugging a marble statue.

***

The DNA lab was a suite in a one-story strip mall on a busy Tampa boulevard. Tillman pulled Raul's van under a magnolia tree in the parking area. Inside, the receptionist listened to his request then led Tawny and Tillman to a small conference room.

Moments later, a lean, brown-skinned man about sixty entered the room. His gray hair was short and he sported a neat goatee. "I'm Dr. Rupert Thomas Jefferson. I'm the owner of this lab." He shook their hands then said with a wry smile, "To answer the first question many people ask me, yes, I am a descendant of Sally Hemings and our third president. That's what prompted my initial interest in DNA when I was a medical student. The field has opened up immensely in the past few decades."

As Tillman often did when meeting a person for the first time, he threw out a test. "My daughter would like to talk to you. She's working on a school project about our Ethiopian and Orthodox Jewish ancestors."

Jefferson took a business card from a holder on the table and wrote on the back. "This is my private number. Have her call me. I'd be glad to talk to her. It's important for young people to understand their origins."

Tillman put the doctor's card in his wallet and slid one of his own across the table. Tawny knew Dr. Jefferson had passed the test with his willingness to help Arielle. Tillman couldn't be bothered with anything beyond the here-and-now but he would encourage his daughter's interest in history.

Jefferson scanned the card. "Montana? You're a long way from home, Mr. Rosenbaum."

Tillman ignored the attempt at polite, small talk and pushed ahead: "Here is the reason for our visit today." On the conference table, he set out the baggies containing Smoky's hairbrush, tissues, the scrap of Smoky's shirt, and the bone chips. "My good friend, Smoky Lido, disappeared during the hurricane. This is his hairbrush and bloody tissues he used—known samples. He was wearing this shirt the last time we saw him. The stains on it appear to be blood. These are bits of bone. I want all these items tested to determine if the blood on the shirt and the bones belong to Smoky."

The doctor pulled on his goatee. "Interesting. Have you gone to the police?"

Tillman said, "To no avail. The sheriff's office is too overloaded to conduct even a cursory search. They have the rest of the bones but their DNA testing is backlogged." On his phone, he pulled up a photo he'd taken of the tibia and fibula and showed the doctor. "I broke chips off this splintered end."

Jefferson studied the photo then picked up the baggies and examined the contents. He regarded Tillman for a long moment, assessing. "Do I need to be concerned with chain of custody?"

Tawny knew problems might arise because Tillman had tampered with evidence. But he obviously didn't care.

His expression remained impassive. "Right now, doctor, I don't give a shit. I will pay for expedited processing. I want results ASAP. I need to know."

Jefferson fingered his goatee again.

Tillman read his hesitation. "There won't be any blowback on you. I'll pay cash and no one needs to find out about our visit today."

Jefferson rocked back in his chair. "I'll run the testing myself. You'll have answers tomorrow."

Tawny caught a fleeting quiver along Tillman's hard, jutting jaw. He rose. "Thank you, sir." He hurried from the room down the hall.

Tawny was used to his impatient rushing but knew this reaction meant more than that. She extended her hand to Jefferson. "We appreciate your help. Smoky was like a father to Tillman."

The doctor's grasp was warm and firm. "I understand." His eyes showed he really did. "This may sound strange but one of the most rewarding parts of my profession is identifying the remains of loved ones who've been missing. It's not a pleasant job. Still, I've found humans are equipped to deal with death but they don't deal well with uncertainty. When you can't find out if someone you love is alive or dead—that limbo is the worst torture of all."

Tawny recognized the truth in the doctor's words. "I'm glad we came to *your* lab."

He smiled. "Mr. Rosenbaum's daughter who's interested in family history. Is that your daughter also?"

"Yes," Tawny answered then realized what she'd said. "I mean, not by blood. I guess you'd call Arielle the daughter of my heart."

The doctor said, "Sometimes that's a more powerful connection than DNA. Like between Mr. Rosenbaum and his friend, Smoky."

At first, the parallel surprised her but then it made perfect sense. "You're very right, doctor. Thank you for taking the time with us."

Outside in the parking lot, Tillman was already sitting in the van. After Tawny climbed in, he said, "We're going to see Gabriel." His mouth was tight and grim.

"Are you OK?"

"No."

"Do you want to talk about it?

"No." He started the engine and pulled out onto the boulevard.

She faced him. "Dr. Jefferson is a good man."

He scanned the traffic. "He's not an asshole."

From the eternally cynical attorney, that was high praise.

She gave up trying to chip away at his armor and sat back for the ride.

As they drove over the Howard Frankland bridge to St. Petersburg, she admired the sparkling water of Tampa Bay. She rolled down the window to inhale the sea air.

And waited.

It was useless to push Tillman to open up before he wanted to. He would, eventually.

When she'd started working for him, long before she ever imagined they'd become lovers, he'd surprised her by confiding details of his mother's suicide years earlier. He'd recited the events with the same cold, clinical precision he did when he laid out a case in court. But red rimmed his eyes. When he'd reached for her hand, he gripped it so tightly that she had to hide her flinch.

That was the first time she'd realized her arrogant, demanding boss had a human side even though he kept his good heart hidden.

As they drove through the streets of St. Petersburg, Tillman remained silent. Some areas had been hit hard by Irma, where others appeared miraculously untouched. They passed apartments with boarded-up windows and balconies hanging by a thread, yet the next building in line was intact. She noticed an attractive two-story house that looked normal until they turned the corner to find an entire wall missing. Blue plastic tarps billowed in the wind. Splintered lumber poked through ragged clumps of fiberglass insulation.

In the downtown area, historic Spanish buildings with pink stucco walls and red tile roofs appeared undamaged. The solid, old buildings had endured storms before Irma and would, no doubt, survive future hurricanes, too.

On Pinellas Trail, they drove through an industrial area until they finally reached the address Tawny had found online.

The building was a small storefront, sandwiched between a wholesale warehouse and an auto repair shop. Iron bars covered the mirror-tinted window. No way to see inside.

Tillman drove around the block, looking for Gabriel's black Hummer but it wasn't on the street. They parked and approached.

The only signage was a metal plate that read *Sports of Yesteryear*, screwed into the block wall beside the wire mesh security door.

Tillman pressed a bell on an intercom box.

A gruff voice crackled through the speaker: "We're closed. By appointment only."

Tillman leaned down and rumbled, "We're here to see Gabriel." The window glass vibrated. Even when he didn't raise his voice, his tone still felt like a powerful bass woofer.

No answer.

Tillman glowered at a surveillance camera above the doorway.

A moment later, a buzzer released the lock and they pushed open the door.

Inside, a noisy air conditioner rattled one wall. The showroom was about twenty feet wide and ten feet deep. A glass display case held baseball cards, autographed balls, and old sports programs. A few jerseys and bats hung on the walls. Tawny doubted there was enough inventory to support a business. Something else was going on behind the scenes.

Gabriel emerged through a door from a back room. "Good afternoon." He smiled at Tawny. "It's nice to see you again." Then he faced Tillman with a pleasant, neutral expression.

Tillman removed Smoky's wallet from his pocket and opened it on the glass counter, showing the driver's license.

Gabriel stepped closer, studied the wallet without touching it, then looked up again at Tillman. "And this means…?"

"The shirt Smoky was wearing the night he disappeared has been recovered from the swamp behind his house. His blood is on the shirt. Bones with his DNA have also been recovered." He flipped through the wallet's inner compartments to display Nyala's photo.

The brother's eyes widened the slightest bit. "My sister is not involved in any business between Smoky and me." He leaned an elbow on the glass counter. "Why are you telling me this?"

Tillman loomed. God, his height still startled Tawny at times and he used the intimidation to his advantage. "I drew up Smoky's will and I am the executor. I will be filing a petition to have him declared deceased and to open probate. I'm informing you as a courtesy in the event you want to file a creditor's claim against the estate."

Gabriel gave a refined chuckle. "There aren't enough assets in his estate to settle my claim."

"Then you are out of luck. A dead man can't pay debts."

"I don't want money. I want my property back."

"What property?"

Gabriel bent low behind the showcase and brought up a leather-bound photo album. He carefully placed it on the counter and paged through it. When he found what he was looking for, he held the album open with both hands. "This."

Tawny and Tillman reached for their readers.

An eight-by-ten photo showed a closeup of a hand-painted baseball card with an orange background. The face on it was a homely man with a large beak nose and brown hair parted in the middle. He wore a gray shirt with a navy-blue collar, buttoned up to his neck. Lettering across his chest read *Pittsburg*. Small print below the picture said *Wagner, Pittsburg*.

Tawny looked to Tillman for a hint.

He studied the photo for several seconds longer. "Honus Wagner. Is this the cigarette card?"

Gabriel nodded solemnly. "Wagner was a prude who didn't want his name connected with smoking because it set a bad example for young boys. In 1909, Sweet Caporal Cigarettes used his image without permission. He sued, which cut short the run of these cards. The few that survive are very valuable."

"I heard about a sale for three million," Tillman said.

"That is correct. Which, you can understand, is why I want my property back."

Tillman folded his arms. "And you think Smoky had it?"

"I know he did." Gabriel closed the photo album and folded his hands atop the leather cover. "Smoky used to work for me. He had an eye for choosing memorabilia that would increase in value. He did very well for me for the past decade. I trusted him. I gave him large sums of cash to purchase assets on my behalf."

"As a straw man," Tillman interjected.

Gabriel pursed his lips. "I prefer to keep my ownership silent in most investments." He went on: "I knew his history and about the gambling problem. Still, he had a rare talent. In the beginning, I tested him with only small amounts of cash. He didn't disappoint me. Gradually, I allowed him to handle more money and high-value assets. We enjoyed some great successes and became close friends, almost like brothers. I foolishly believed he would never betray me. I gave him the combination to my safe where I kept the Honus Wagner card. Even my wife doesn't have the combination. That tells you the degree of trust I had in Smoky."

"What happened?" Tillman asked.

Gabriel smoothed the leather cover of the album. "I've asked myself that question many times. The only explanation I can pin to it is that when he lost his leg, he changed. At first, I thought it was a medical problem. Perhaps when he healed and got used to the prosthesis, he would go back to normal. In many ways, he did. But there was a subtle shift in attitude. I only realized the difference when I reviewed his behavior after the Wagner disappeared out of my safe."

"When was that?"

"A little over a month ago. He's been dodging me ever since. I tried to speak reasonably with him but he denied taking the card. He attempted to put me on the defensive—turn the accusation back on me, display outrage that I would question his integrity, feign hurt that I didn't trust him. In other words, make the whole thing my fault. I've been in business too long to fall for those tactics."

Tawny remembered Smoky's rationalizations during their conversation before he disappeared. His excuses had reminded her vividly of her father's arguments. Although she liked Smoky, she could almost understand Gabriel's anger—she'd felt similar frustration, rage, and betrayal when her dad caused the drunken wreck that killed her mom.

Yet a disabled old man didn't deserve the beating Gabriel's strong-arms had inflicted. She wondered how much further they would have gone if she hadn't stepped in with the shotgun. Would they have killed him? As she studied Gabriel's mild, smiling face, she glimpsed bitterness in the depths of his green eyes.

Yes, Smoky could have died at his hands.

She knew Tillman suspected Gabriel, also. What did he make of the accusation that Smoky was a thief? He showed no reaction, no hesitancy in facing down the man who was probably armed and whose two bodyguards were likely listening from the back room.

Gabriel replaced the photo album under the showcase. "Thank you for extending this courtesy to me. If the Wagner card is recovered in the course of settling the estate, I hope you will remember who it rightfully belongs to."

"The probate court will determine disposition. Good afternoon." Tillman grasped the door knob and stared at Gabriel until he released the lock. When it clicked, he held the door for Tawny as they left.

Back in the van, she asked, "Do you think he killed Smoky?"

Tillman's jaw was granite. "Not unless he got the card back first. But if his thugs chased Smoky into the storm, Gabriel could be the indirect cause of death."

"Is that enough to charge him with homicide?"

He pulled away from the curb. "No. Prosecution would have to prove he intentionally forced Smoky into a situation that caused his death. Gabriel wants the Honus Wagner back. He wouldn't kill Smoke until he recovered the card. Even then, doubtful. He might teach Smoky a lesson but why risk a murder charge if he got what he wanted?"

Tawny reviewed the conversation and had to agree with Tillman's conclusion. She also recalled what he'd told Gabriel about DNA. "You kind of exaggerated how much evidence we have."

He gave her the side eye. "I'm not testifying to the whole truth and nothing but the truth. My purpose was to get him off Smoky's butt in case he's still alive."

In case he's still alive?

Clinging to false hope didn't sound like Tillman at all. As an attorney, he lived in a world of evidence, hard facts, and harsh reality. Was the stress of losing his friend sending him over the edge?

She sat quiet for several minutes, worrying, but finally asked, "Do you believe Smoky stole the card?"

"Yeah." He spat the word out like a curse.

"Smoky told me he used to call you Honus Rosenbaum."

He didn't answer for a long time. When he spoke at last, the first softness she'd seen in two days crossed his face. "Yeah, he did."

She caressed his taut thigh. "I'd never heard of the guy until Smoky started talking about how good he was and that you could have matched him. He's not famous like Babe Ruth or Mantle or DiMaggio. Crazy that his card is worth so much money." An unexpected, new idea made her jerk up in the seat. "Do you think that's what Smoky had locked in the freezer?"

"You may be right." He rubbed his jaw. "Whatever. It's gone now."

At a stoplight, she watched bulldozers shoving storm debris into long walls lining the curbs and asked, "Are you disappointed that Smoky stole the card?"

Tilman steered onto Highway 19 heading north. "I gave up being disappointed by people years ago. They're too damn good at it."

Twenty quiet minutes later, he turned west. Tawny recognized the causeway leading to the beautiful pink hotel he'd pointed out to her the previous day. When they reached the boulevard in front of the hotel, he slowed down. "Want to check it out?"

She again sensed pressure building from him to get married. He knew she was concerned about him, that she felt bad for his pain. She didn't want to think he was taking advantage of the vulnerability of her soft heart to push her into marriage. But she couldn't stop her doubts—she'd been manipulated too many times. "You don't play fair, Tillman."

"Never claimed to." His smirk admitted her suspicion was right.

Dammit, he'd chosen a romantic setting that was hard to resist.

"I want to go for a walk on the beach," she said.

"It'll be littered with Irma's flotsam and jetsam." Nevertheless, he parked the van. They crossed the street and spotted a front-end loader scraping storm debris from the sand, scooping the trash into its bucket. Farther down the beach, a dump truck waited, its bed already full of palm fronds, driftwood, and broken boat parts.

In front of the hotel, the sand was clean, clear, and white as sugar. As they walked on a pathway amid palm trees, Tillman pointed out the loader and truck. "Hotel probably hired a private contractor to clean up their section of the beach. Not waiting for the city to get around to it."

Tawny scanned the shoreline in either direction. The stretch of sand before them was indeed the only pristine area.

As long as Tillman had brought her here, she meant to take advantage of the opportunity to enjoy the beach. She leaned against a wall, toed her sneakers off then sank her bare feet into warm sand.

It felt soft and fine, not like rocky lake beaches in Montana. As she walked, each step caressed her feet like a massage.

Tillman also ditched his shoes and joined her. She slipped her hand into his and he held on firmly. It felt good after he'd been so distant. They walked in silence that, for once, seemed peaceful instead of tense and strained. It reminded her of the way she and Dwight used to walk, holding hands.

A pair of pelicans waddled in front of them, showing no fear. Gulls wheeled overhead, crying. A white ibis poked its curved beak into the sand, searching for food.

She sighed and leaned into his arm. "This is so beautiful."

He bent to kiss the top of her head. "Why don't we check into the hotel without luggage? Pretend we're sneaking out on our spouses for an afternoon tryst."

His unexpected change of mood surprised and pleased her. "I wouldn't know how to act. I never cheated on Dwight."

"I never cheated on Rochelle either." His tone turned playful. "How else are we going to know what we missed by being faithful?"

She smiled up at him. "You're the craziest lawyer I ever met."

"Well?"

She burrowed her feet deep in the sand. "Let's go wade in the water first. I've never set foot in the ocean." She pulled him toward the lapping waves.

His cell rang and she released his hand so he could answer. She continued to walk, inhaling the fresh smell, and stepped into the bathtub temperature water. She sloshed up to her knees, feeling like a kid.

She turned to call Tillman to join her but he stood still, listening to the phone. The set of his shoulders alerted her.

She hurried back to him. As she drew close, he said, "We'll be there soon." Then disconnected. Hardness had again settled over his expression.

"What is it?"

"That was Parrot, the bartender at X-Isles. Smoky's boat has been found."

Chapter 14 – Emerald Princess

Late afternoon sun slanted through the cypress trees surrounding X-Isles. The murky water in the channel lapped quietly against the wobbly piers. Parrot, the bartender, squatted at the shoreline where a battered aluminum boat had been pulled up on the mud. Dents in the metal looked as if someone had taken a sledgehammer to it. Elaborate scrolling letters on the stern read: *Emerald Princess*. Pretty fancy name, Tawny thought, for a fifteen-foot jon boat.

Parrot straightened at their approach, a rag dangling from his hand. "Fishing buddy of Smoky's found the boat. Towed it back here." He held up the rag, a ripped, stained towel. "This was wedged under the trolling motor on the transom."

Tillman took the towel and held it out with both hands to examine it. "Is that rust or blood?"

"Both," Parrot answered. "Might be fish blood."

Tillman didn't look convinced. "Where's the guy?"

Parrot lifted his chin toward the bar. "Inside, having a beer."

They moved onto the dock and entered X-Isles. Unlike the night when they'd visited previously, the place was now practically empty, only a few drinkers. The power was back on, lighting up neon beer signs.

At the far end of the bar, a man with a mustache watched "Family Feud" on a TV mounted high on the wall.

Parrot whistled. "Hey, Commodore."

Commodore, gaze fixed on the TV, called out, "Suspenders!" then waited until his answer flipped up at number one on the lighted game board. With a satisfied grin, he lumbered toward them.

He was a short man, maybe five-six, well into his seventies with a round belly and chicken legs. He wore a captain's hat with scrambled egg insignia on the visor. A gray braid dangled down his back. "These Smoky's friends?" he asked Parrot.

Tillman extended his hand. "I'm Tillman and this is Tawny."

The elderly man craned his neck up at Tillman. "You're a big 'un, ain't ya?"

Deadpan, Tillman answered, "Air gets pretty thin up here."

A harsh, phlegmy laugh erupted from the old salt. "Good one. They call me Commodore because I ran gun boats up the Mekong Delta all the way to Laos, where we weren't supposed to be."

Tawny's breath caught. "My husband was in the Army in Nam."

Commodore peered at her with watery blue eyes. "Navy, ma'am. But I won't hold your husband's bad judgment against you."

She smiled and shook his calloused hand, knowing the immediate affinity Dwight would have had for a fellow Vietnam veteran. She also remembered the never-ending rivalry between the services. "He'd have said only a real idiot would choose to enlist in that goddamn war."

"Despite my exalted nickname, I only made lieutenant in the reserves, ma'am."

"An officer? Even worse. My husband *worked* for a living—he was a Master Sergeant."

Commodore chuckled. "Parrot, get the Master Sergeant's wife a drink."

They settled at a three-foot-diameter wooden wire spool that had been turned into a table. Tillman's chair looked like a 1970s-era bucket seat salvaged from a VW Bug. He leaned forward to stop its unsteady rocking. "Tell us about Smoky's boat."

Commodore drained his beer and gestured to Parrot for another. "I keep a skiff at a marina in one of the channels on the Anclote. I was headed out fishing in the Gulf when something caught my eye way back in the woods. Irma had knocked down quite a few trees and made some of the little tributaries inaccessible. Had to tie up and hike back through the jungle a ways to get to it but, sure enough, there's Smoky's boat hung up about three feet out of the water in the roots of a fallen tree. When the river flooded, must've lifted the boat and left it hanging. Sorta like the boat out in front here with that high-water-mark sign."

Parrot brought another beer plus a *Cuba Libre* with lots of ice for Tawny and scotch for Tillman.

Commodore went on: "Had a helluva time wrestling it down from the tree. Called back here and a couple guys came to help me. Been tossed around pretty good. Takes some powerful force to dent that aluminum hull." He sipped beer, foam sticking on his mustache. "Parrot said Smoky's gone missing."

131

"Did you see any sign he'd been on the boat?" Tillman asked.

Commodore shook his head. "All the gear he'd normally carry was gone—cooler, battery, poles, tackle. Only thing left was that raggedy old towel he'd wipe his hands on after cleaning fish. No footprints in the mud. Course, all that rain would've washed those away."

"Can you show us where you found the boat?" Tawny said.

"Figured you'd want to see. Enjoy your drinks then we'll head out."

Tillman rose without touching his scotch. "Let's go now."

"Impatient, aren't you?" Commodore said. "Relax, man. The swamp isn't going anywhere." He leaned back and slowly sipped beer, in no hurry to accommodate Tillman's demands.

Tawny's muscles tightened. Telling Tillman to relax was waving a red flag at a bull. She nudged his foot with hers. He read her message then sat again, almost vibrating. He gripped his shot glass and downed the drink in one swallow.

Tawny leaned across the wood spool table, smiled, and laid her hand on the Commodore's hairy arm. "Tell me about your skiff."

His chest puffed. "Suzuki motor, two-hundred-fifty horses, does forty-five knots, stepped hull, faster than the gun boats in Nam and they were pretty damn fast."

"Your boat sounds amazing." She squeezed his arm. "I love to go fast."

He beamed. "Well, Mrs. Master Sergeant, it would be my honor to take you out." He hitched himself out of the chair and made a sweeping motion with his arm toward the exit.

Tawny led the way outside to the dock, smiling over her shoulder at Commodore. Tillman brought up the rear, glowering.

They boarded the skiff while Commodore untied the lines. Tillman bent to whisper in her ear. "'I love to go fast?'"

She whispered back, "Worked, didn't it?"

Commodore sat in the captain's chair and started the burbling engine. Tawny took the seat beside him as he guided the craft out into the channel. Tillman sat behind.

They motored through branching tributaries to the mouth of the river, out into the open turquoise water of the Gulf. Commodore pushed the throttle to the max. In only seconds, Tawny's braid whipped her neck and salty spray cooled her face. He swerved through a few breakneck turns, showing off. As the skiff leapt over the frothy wake, Tawny grabbed the armrests to keep from going airborne.

Commodore shot her a grin. "Fast enough?" he called over the engine noise.

She grinned back, even though her stomach felt like a basketball bouncing inside. She glanced over her shoulder to Tillman whose glare should have melted the back of Commodore's neck. His yellow polo shirt billowed in the wind.

After ten more minutes of showing off, the elderly sailor spun the wheel to port, making a wide circular sweep. At last, he headed toward a different channel and dropped the speed. They entered the tributary which quickly narrowed to twenty feet wide, with vines hanging over the water. Ahead, many trees had snapped in half, blocking the passage.

"Little twister cut a nice swath through here on Irma's tail," Commodore said. "Knocked down those trees and tore off a couple of roofs not far from here."

Tawny asked, "Is this where you found Smoky's boat?"

He thrust his calloused finger toward a tiny inlet littered with fallen debris. "Over yonder." He nosed the boat close to shore and tied it to a half-submerged tree trunk. He scrambled out onto the log then extended both hands to help Tawny climb out of the boat. Tillman clambered up without help.

They carefully balanced along the slippery trunk until they reached land and hopped down into spongy dirt. Commodore led them about fifty feet through the storm wreckage to a giant root ball sticking out of the ground, caked with mud. A red bandanna was tied to a protruding stick.

"Marked where I found the boat," he said. "I checked around but couldn't find Smoky's missing gear. Tornado likely carried away whatever wasn't screwed onto the boat. Kinda surprised the motor didn't get ripped off the transom, too."

Tillman explored the area, poking into hollows, climbing over limbs.

Tawny scanned the dense forest. "We really don't have any idea if Smoky was in the boat. Could it have broken loose from where he usually moored it and the storm carried it here?"

Commodore shook his head. "Two different channels half a mile apart. My best guess is he was heading out in the Gulf but the boat got blown into this inlet."

"I don't understand why he'd go out in the middle of a hurricane."

He regarded her. "You know Smoky very well?"

She shook her head. "Tillman does but I just met him the day he disappeared."

Commodore folded his arms. "Been out on the water a lot with him. Way the hell and gone where no one's around, just the sun and the sky and the sea. A man gets to talking about stuff he wouldn't normally mention."

"Like?"

His brows drew together in a frown. "Killing himself. He said he'd caught and eaten enough fish. Now it was time for the fish to eat him."

Tawny had half-suspected suicide but to hear the possibility voiced out loud still gave her a chill despite the mugginess. She checked where Tillman had gone exploring, far out of earshot. "Why now?"

"The leg, I think. He got around pretty good on that fake one but he still had a lot of pain. Gave me the willies when he'd pull that appliance off. God, his stump looked like a raw, bloody ulcer. He liked to sit on the diving platform on my boat and dangle the stump in the water. Said the sea was healing." He shuddered. "Jesus, I couldn't live the way he had to."

She thought back on the night Irma had hit, how it almost felt like the old coach was saying goodbye.

"There was the money thing, too," Commodore went on. "He'd run up a lot of debts. Course nobody held a gun to his head and made him place those bets. But still..."

"Do you know who he owed money to?"

"He ran with some damn strange people. He'd tell me he was going to Dubai or Singapore or Johannesburg to meet wealthy collectors. Never knew if he was bullshitting me. I like sports OK but who in their right mind pays half a million bucks for a dirty, sweaty, old baseball?"

"Do you know Gabriel?"

"Is that the slick dude who's so impressed with himself? Met him one time but that's it."

"How about Smoky's girlfriend?"

Commodore cracked a smile. "Which one? For a one-legged gimp, that boy sure got around. He spent most of the time with this gorgeous black woman. Real classy. He'd bring her to X-Isles when a good band was playing."

"Nyala?"

"Yeah, that's right. She had friends who used to be pro athletes. Some of 'em have big yachts, forty, sixty footers. They'd invite her for a cruise and she'd take Smoky along, down to the Keys, the Bahamas, Cuba."

"Was he good with a boat? Knew what to do in high seas?"

A one-shouldered shrug. "Not like me but pretty fair."

"Would *you* have tried to go out the night Irma hit?"

He wagged his head. "Not on your life. Back in my Navy days, I was on the Bonnie Dick—y'know, the *Bonne Homme Richard*— during a typhoon. Scared the living crap out of me. Thirty-thousand-ton aircraft carrier bouncing around like a ping-pong ball in a bathtub when a two-year-old's throwing a tantrum."

The sun was dropping low. Soon, darkness would end their ability to search. In the deepening shadows, she caught a glimpse of Tillman's yellow shirt through the jungle and asked the question she didn't want him to hear. "Do you think Smoky meant to commit suicide?"

Commodore blinked as if his watery eyes were burning. "Honest to God, I don't know. He was a gambler. He could have been making a break for it, trying to outrun his creditors. But sometimes he'd get despondent, talking about how bad he'd screwed up his life, the chances he'd blown, the great jobs he'd pissed away. Didn't even know his own daughter's name. Pretty damn pitiful." He studied Tawny. "You think he's dead, don't you?"

"I'm afraid so. And I'm worried about how Tillman will react. They were close."

He gave a slight jerk. "Yeah. Smoky was always talking about this kid he wished had been his son. Couple weeks ago, he told me he hadn't seen the guy in years and wanted to get together one last time. Didn't pay much attention at the time. But, now, looking back, I think he wanted to say goodbye."

Another chill ran up Tawny's neck when Commodore echoed her thought of only moments before. She'd been praying the leg bones wouldn't match Smoky's DNA but had a sick sense they were going to.

Thrashing sounds came from deep in the woods. She caught a glimpse of yellow, Tillman plowing through brush like an angry grizzly. Heavy footfalls pounded the trail. Then he burst out of the vines near Tawny.

He held a metal rod with a flexible sleeve on one end, a plastic foot on the other. In black marker on the sleeve, a single word was printed: *Annalise*.

Chapter 15 – Heavy Bag

Tawny called five Tampa prosthetists the next morning before she tracked down the clinic that had built the device Tillman found. They drove to the office adjacent to a hospital on Martin Luther King Boulevard.

In the laboratory, a young woman patient walked on a treadmill, testing her new leg. At a worktable, a technician sculpted fiberglass into a socket to hold an artificial arm.

The owner was a Hispanic man in his mid-fifties named Fernandez, himself an amputee. He sat on a tall stool before a computer, using a modeling program to move around three-dimensional diagrams of arms and legs.

Tillman handed the prosthetic to Fernandez and explained the circumstances.

Fernandez examined the metal shaft and cracked plastic foot. "Held up pretty well for being bashed around in a hurricane," he said. "I remember building this, two or three years ago. If I recall, the man had lost his leg in a boating accident. That's why it stuck in my mind because I'm a sailor myself." He gestured to a framed picture on the wall. "Took the Bronze in the ninety-six Paralympic Games." The photo showed him standing on a sailboat, wearing cargo shorts, his prosthetic leg visible.

Beside Tawny, Tillman clenched his fists and shifted from one foot to the other. She slipped her hand into his and squeezed, hoping his impatience wouldn't put off Fernandez. Tillman attempted to still his fidgeting.

The prosthetist tapped on his computer. "Yes, I remember him now. Smoky Lido. I built several devices for him. This was the first. Always interesting how patients react to losing a limb. He named the device *Annalise,* like it was human." He shook his head. "Because of the configuration of his stump, he had difficulty getting a tight fit. I worked through quite a few adaptations. Fitting requires a lot of trial and error. He finally gave up and said he'd just live with the pain. I was concerned when he didn't come back because he had problems with blistering and infection that could lead to necrosis. I would've kept trying but I can't chase the man down and drag him in here."

Tillman leaned forward. "You're positive this is his?"

Fernandez answered, "Absolutely. Each device is as unique as a fingerprint. Besides the name *Annaliese*, see, here's the serial number on the foot portion. No doubt at all."

＊

The DNA testing center was only a few miles away from the prosthetic lab. During the drive there, Smoky's artificial limb lay on the back seat, the elephant in Raul's van.

"Should we turn the leg over to the sheriff?" Tawny asked.

Tillman looked scornful. "You've got to be kidding. That place is a cluster."

"Except, isn't this evidence?"

"That they'd misplace before they ever got around to checking out the missing person report. Better to beg forgiveness..."

Right, she thought, as if Tillman Rosenbaum had ever begged for anything in his whole life. "You're not worried about losing your license?"

"My only concern right now is Smoky."

Tillman understood more about the law than Tawny could ever hope to. His knowledge intimidated her, mostly because he was so casual about it, as if any slob could graduate *magna cum laude* with a Stanford law degree. Dyslexia had almost made her flunk out of high school and she still remained in awe of education. But if he wasn't worried, why should she?

When they entered Rupert Jefferson's clinic, the doctor was talking to a client in the waiting room. As soon as he saw them, he quickly excused himself from the client and escorted them into his office. "I was just going to call you. Please, have a seat."

Tawny sat in front of the desk, knowing from the doctor's somber expression that the news was bad. Tillman knew it, too. He remained standing, as if his defiance would change the results. She took his cold hand in both of hers.

Jefferson's voice was soft and gentle. "The known specimens, the hairbrush and tissues, match both the blood on the shirt and the bone fragments. All samples belong to the same person. I'm sorry."

138

Tillman's hand stiffened in hers. He pulled free, fist clenched. For a second, she thought he might punch the wall. Instead, he asked, "Where's your restroom?"

Jefferson said, "Just outside on the right."

Tillman left the office, the door banging shut behind him.

Tawny's eyes filled with acid tears, feeling his anguish. The faint hope they'd been clinging to, that Smoky was simply missing—not dead—just evaporated. She placed her elbows on the desk and let her head drop into her hands.

The doctor came from behind the desk and set a box of tissues in front of her. He gently patted her shoulder. "I am sorry. Will Mr. Rosenbaum be all right?"

"I don't know. Smoky is the worst loss since his mother."

"I hope he'll allow himself to grieve."

She looked up at the kind face, the crinkled brow and wise eyes. "He's been shutting himself off pretty tight since Smoky went missing."

"Does he have a sport?"

Jefferson's question raised her curiosity. "Baseball, when he was in high school. Now, mostly weights and running. Why?"

"Does he box?"

She remembered the punching bag in his home gym. "A little, I guess."

He opened his desk drawer and pulled out a card. "My father has a training center only a few blocks from here. Maybe pounding a heavy bag for a while is what he needs."

She accepted the card and smiled through tears. "Doctor, that sounds like a very good idea."

"Tell my dad I sent you." He picked up stapled pages from his desk and gave them to her. "These are the DNA results."

"Thank you…very much."

When they shook hands, his grasp was warm. "He's a fortunate man to have someone who cares about him the way you do."

She left his office, sad but grateful.

In the hall, the restroom was vacant, light off. No Tillman. She checked with the receptionist who said he'd paid the bill and left. "He didn't even wait for his change," the receptionist added, handing the money to Tawny.

In the parking lot, she found him in the driver's seat of the van. She opened his door and put her arms around him, burying her face in his shoulder. "I'm so sorry," she whispered.

Again, he felt like a marble statue.

She wanted to share the heavy burden of his pain, help him carry the loss. But she knew from past experience that he would wall himself in, like a wounded wild animal crawling into a cave to escape enemies that threatened to finish it off in its weakened state.

After a minute, he still had not responded so she backed away. "Move over and let me drive."

He transferred to the passenger seat without a word.

She drove three blocks to the storefront facility and stopped.

"What's this?" he asked.

"Dr. Jefferson's dad owns this gym. This is a free pass for a workout." She handed him the card.

While Tillman studied it, Tawny got out, walked to the glass door, and held it open, waiting for him. A moment later, he followed.

Inside, the rhythmic *thud-whump* of punching bags and the grunts of men doing pullups echoed off the high, warehouse-style ceiling. The smell of sweat, leather, and menthol sports cream hung in the muggy air.

In the center of the open room was a boxing ring, surrounded by a group of middle-school kids wearing padded helmets and boxing gloves that looked impossibly large on their thin arms. They gathered around an elderly black coach who gave them instructions in a voice nearly as deep and throaty as Tillman's. He tapped the shoulders of two kids. They climbed into the ring and started clumsy sparring. The stooped coach raised his left fist in front of his face, demonstrating how to protect themselves.

At the front counter, Tillman presented the card and rented a pair of gloves. He stripped off his polo shirt, handed it to Tawny, and wrapped his hands with tape. The clerk fastened the straps on the gloves and Tillman approached a heavy bag suspended in one corner.

She stood to the side and watched as he tried out a couple of jabs. Then harder. And harder, until the bag jerked on the thick chain that fastened it to metal eyebolts in the ceiling and floor.

He pounded the bag over and over, not pausing for breath. He bounced from one side to the other on his toes, hitting from different angles. Soon, sweat drenched his hair and skin, droplets flung into the air by the force of his smacks. Still, he pounded, relentless.

Several men who'd been working out stopped to stare at the angry giant pummeling the leather bag. Tawny heard someone say, "That dude's big as Klitschko." She recalled the name of the Ukrainian heavyweight, back from when her husband and son used to watch boxing on TV.

She sat on a wood bench beside the wall, marveling that Dr. Jefferson had known exactly the right release Tillman needed for his sorrow over Smoky's death.

The elderly coach approached and sat beside her. "My son called. Said your man is in a powerful world of hurt."

"That was kind of him." She leaned against the wall. "He had a coach who was like a father to him. We just found out he's dead."

The man ran a hand over his sparse hair. "I'm ninety-one years old. My wife's gone, two of my children, and all the friends I grew up with. My past is nothing but dead people."

Tawny remembered the Agent Orange deaths of her husband's Army buddies, one by one, how each loss had eaten away another part of Dwight's heart until cancer finally killed him, too. "Hard to be the last man standing," she murmured.

He peered at her through rheumy eyes. "You're a wise young lady."

She grimaced. "Not so young."

A small, hoarse chuckle. "Come back and see me in about forty years. *Then* we'll talk about how *old* you are."

She smiled. "Your son is a good man, Mr. Jefferson."

"In *spite* of his daddy, not *because* of him."

"Somehow, I don't believe that."

With a wink, the old man planted his hands on his thighs and slowly rose. Each movement made his tired joints click and snap. He nodded toward Tillman, still pummeling the heavy bag. "He'll get by. Give it time." He limped toward the center ring, back to the boys he'd been coaching.

***

Two hours later, at Smoky's house, Tillman filled the kitchen sink with ice cubes and water. He plunged his swollen, bruised hands into it, lower teeth biting his upper lip.

At the gym, when he'd unwrapped the bloody tape under the boxing gloves, Tawny had been horrified at his mangled, pulpy hands.

"Do you want some ibuprofen?" she asked.

A single shake of his head. "Does Smoky have any scotch around here?"

She opened cupboards, vaguely remembering a pint on a back shelf, one of the few bottles that hadn't been broken when Gabriel's men searched the house. She retrieved it, filled a tumbler mostly full, and held it to Tillman's mouth. He tipped his chin up, gulping greedily. She kept tilting the glass until he'd drained it. Probably the equivalent of five shots.

A couple of inches remained in the bottom of the bottle. "Might as well finish it off," he said.

Tawny poured the rest into his glass, maybe another four shots.

In the past, she'd worried his drinking might turn into trouble, like her dad. But, given his size, his tolerance was high. Besides, he'd backed off a lot since his daughter, Arielle, at only fifteen, showed signs of developing her own booze problem.

But Smoky's death justified Tillman drinking himself into a stupor if he wanted to.

After five minutes, he lifted his puffy hands out of the ice water, shook them, and examined the purplish fingers and raw, split knuckles. Then he gingerly picked up the glass and moved toward the bedroom. "Going to take a nap." The door closed.

Three hours later, his snores still roared.

Tawny barbecued chicken they'd picked up at the supermarket the day before. When the aroma didn't bring him out, she ate by herself. As the sun set, she watched TV. Clicking on a lamp gave her a little surge of pleasure after the long darkness.

Two hours later, she spotted a line of light under the bedroom door and peeked in.

Tillman was naked, sitting up, propped against the headboard, swiping his laptop, half-glasses down his nose.

Tawny went in and curled beside him on the bed. "Whatcha doing?"

"Finding a local attorney. Have to get Smoky legally declared dead. I'm executor of his estate but I don't have a Florida law license. I need someone here to file with the court."

Tawny's worry eased a little, reassured he felt up to taking care of business. "Find anyone?"

"A woman I went to Stanford with practices in St. Pete. Except for getting him declared dead, the will is straightforward. I'm the sole heir." He swept his long arm around the room. "Someday, all this will be mine. Too bad I'm not a fan of Hawaiian shirts."

The return to his normal sarcasm made her feel even better. "Why not? I think you'd look good in them."

He stared down his nose at her. "In Montana, an attorney can get away with wearing cowboy boots in court but flowered shirts? Never."

She smiled and stroked his thigh. "What will you do with his stuff?"

"Donate it to charity. His biggest asset is a waterlogged car."

Tawny thought for a moment. "What about the Honus Wagner card?"

"I think we can safely assume since Smoky's gone, the card went down with him. Three million bucks in the bottom of the swamp. Tough luck for Gabriel." He didn't sound the least bit sorry.

She studied his hands, still swollen and discolored. They had to hurt. "Want me to type for you?" She reached for his laptop.

He moved it away with a sly smile. "By the time Google figures out what you're trying to spell, we'll be back in Montana." He often teased her about her poor reading and worse spelling because of dyslexia, claiming he needed to hire a cryptographer to decipher her reports.

She folded her arms. "OK, mister, who convinced the Commodore to take us to Smoky's boat?"

"I never said you weren't smart, just that you can't spell." He took off his glasses and set the laptop on the bedside table. "You earned your pay today."

She tucked into his side and ran her hand over his muscular chest and belly. Despite his banter, he felt tight, tense. She watched, knowing he was ready to detonate.

Pain contorted his mouth. His eyes squeezed shut. One bruised hand balled into a fist.

"I failed Smoky." His deep voice cracked. He cleared his throat but the huskiness remained. "I should have nailed him down sooner, forced him to tell me the problem. When I asked him what the hell was up with all his hiding-under-the-radar shit, he blew it off as gambling debts. And, dammit, that had happened so often, I took him at his word."

Tawny rubbed his tight shoulders, wondering how much she should say.

His swollen hands fisted again. "I could've gotten that damn Honus Wagner card back from him and settled the squabble with Gabriel. He didn't have to take off and get himself killed in the hurricane."

She summoned her courage to break more bad news. "I didn't want to tell you before but maybe he didn't leave only because of Gabriel. I think he meant to commit suicide. That's what his buddy Commodore thinks, too. He said Smoky was in a lot of pain from the amputation and he'd hinted about killing himself. But..." She caressed Tillman's cheek. "Smoky didn't want to go without saying goodbye to you. You're the son he wished he'd had."

Tillman pondered, staring far beyond the bedroom walls. Tawny knew he had to be thinking of his other loved ones who'd tried to kill themselves. His mother had succeeded. His sister tried and ended up in an institution, forever impaired. Most recently, Tawny had saved his oldest daughter, Mimi, from an overdose, and she was still in treatment. Guilt and frustration dogged him that he couldn't solve their problems, that he couldn't prevent their despair.

The silence stretched into several moments. At last, he said, "Smoky talked me out of killing my old man."

Tawny straightened. She knew Tillman's relationship with his father was troubled but she hadn't heard this part before. "What happened?"

"It was the second time my mom tried to kill herself. First time, I was a little kid."

Tawny flashed back on the heartbreaking story he'd once told her of finding his mom unconscious and giving her CPR, even though he was only ten years old. That was when, despite her intense dislike for him, he'd cracked open Tawny's heart.

"Second time," he went on, "I was sixteen, almost as big as I am now, pissed off and boiling over with testosterone. My mom found out about yet another girlfriend and took pills. She was in the psych lockdown. I knew if the old man didn't stop philandering, she'd try again and eventually succeed. But he wouldn't quit. I decided to off him so he couldn't hurt her anymore."

Tawny's heart ached. She ran fingers over his stomach, skin taut as a drum.

One side of his mouth twitched. "I had it all worked out. I'd been tailing him and knew what time he'd leave for his girlfriend's house. I'd jump him in the dark, slice his throat open, take his Rolex and wallet. Make it look like a robbery gone bad. Had rubber gloves and a rain slicker to keep blood spatter off me."

Tawny held her breath, trying to hide her shock. But Tillman wasn't looking at her.

He continued: "Had my alibi planned, too. That night, I was down in Hardin, supposed to pitch in a varsity game, fifty miles from home. Claimed I'd strained my shoulder and went to the locker room to ice it. I'd allowed enough time to race home to Billings, kill him, then get back to Hardin before the game was over. But Smoky sensed something was up. He caught me in the parking lot.

"He sat with me in my car for two hours, ignored the whole rest of the game. Any time the other coaches came looking for him, he'd yell out to handle it themselves. He wasn't going to leave me alone until he'd talked me out of doing a crazy thing that he said would ruin my whole future." He heaved a sigh. "My miserable old man doesn't know he has Smoky to thank for his long life."

They sat in silence, leaning together, until Tawny felt a spasm shake him. His face contorted in a mask of anguish. Wounded animal sounds choked in his throat.

She clambered to her knees on the mattress and embraced him, pulling his face into her breast. He shook in her arms, his body wrenching. She held him tight even when he tried to pull away. "It's OK," she murmured into his black curls. "Let it out."

Chapter 16 – Tracking Number

The next morning, Tawny rose quietly and picked up Tillman's laptop, leaving him snoring in bed. In the kitchen, she made coffee then sat at the table with Smoky's wallet. In the middle of the restless night, between the moans of Tillman's nightmares, an idea had occurred to her. The wallet might hold a clue to the coach's intentions.

She opened the leather billfold, removed the driver's license and fishing license. Nyala's photo was still damp. Although the woman's dazzling smile was seductive, even playful, an air of mystery clung to her, as if she always kept a secret, like an African Mona Lisa.

Next, Tawny pulled a wad of papers from an inner compartment and carefully spread them on the table to dry. Some had started to dissolve from being wet, the folded edges tearing. With ink smeared, several were unreadable. She found a business card for the lab that had made Smoky's prosthetic leg.

Another card was from Sports of Yesteryear with only a phone number, no address. The subheading read: *Memorabilia for the Discerning Collector.*

One scrap of paper looked like a postal receipt. Through her readers, she squinted to make out the tiny, faint print—dated in August, over a month before, and sent from a post office branch in St. Petersburg. A postal code for a destination address was too blurred to read. She recognized a long string of numbers as the tracking code.

She opened Tillman's laptop, logged into USPS.com, and typed the numbers into the search bar.

The result showed an item mailed on August 7 from the branch on First Street North in St. Petersburg. The destination was Panama, arrival confirmed on August 14 to general delivery in a town called Puerto Armuelles.

Who did Smoky know in Panama? What did he send there?

If he saved the receipt, it must be important.

Recollections clicked quickly in her brain. Gabriel had told Tawny and Tillman that the Honus Wagner card disappeared from his safe about a month before. Smoky might have mailed it to someone in Panama.

Nyala said she met Smoky three years ago on an airline flight from Panama, shortly after the amputation of his leg.

Yet Gabriel said Smoky had been working for him for many years.

Brother and sister knew Smoky well. Nyala had an ongoing sexual relationship with him. Gabriel trusted him enough to share his safe combination. Yet Nyala claimed she hadn't met Smoky until three years ago. Their stories didn't mesh, meaning one or both of them was lying.

Tawny wondered if Nyala knew Smoky had stolen the Honus Wagner card from her brother. The woman apparently didn't approve of the beating Gabriel's thugs had given Smoky yet otherwise she seemed ambivalent. Gabriel claimed his sister wasn't involved in his business yet her name appeared as the registered agent for Sports of Yesteryear.

What was the relationship among the three of them?

Tawny sensed if she uncovered the truth about their connection, that might hold the key to solving the mystery of Smoky's death.

Tillman suspected Smoky intended to disappear to escape from Gabriel but the attempt had gone awry during the hurricane. If his plan had worked, Smoky might have resurfaced in Panama to begin a new life, using the Honus Wagner card to finance his fresh start.

But, to succeed, Smoky would need help—help to escape during the hurricane, help from an accomplice in Panama to keep the three-million-dollar baseball card safe for him.

Smoky had admitted to Tawny that his circle of friends was small, most driven away by his gambling addiction. His former girlfriends no longer wanted to be associated with him.

His buddy, Commodore, believed Smoky went out in the hurricane to commit suicide. Or maybe he told that to Tawny to back up Smoky's motive for disappearing. As she reviewed their conversation, she decided Commodore seemed transparent and truthful, not deceptive, unlike Nyala and Gabriel.

The X-Isles bartender, Parrot, had said if a man wanted to disappear, that was his own business. Parrot might have helped Smoky.

Tawny pondered what had happened during the final few hours of Smoky's life.

Maybe he hiked to his boat on the far end of the lake then ventured out in the storm, perhaps planning to meet up with a trusted friend.

Somehow, that theory seemed unlikely. In the violent wind and rain, too many things could go wrong to count on a rendezvous by boat.

Unless the Commodore was right about suicide and Smoky deliberately motored into the hurricane, intending to die at sea.

Tawny's head spun with confusing possibilities as she poured another cup of coffee. Then the bedroom door opened.

Tillman emerged from the hallway, naked, haggard, with bloodshot eyes and lines of strain between his brows. Barefoot, he crossed the kitchen, took the mug from her hand, and drank.

"Rough night." His voice was gravelly. His knuckles remained swollen and discolored.

She rose on tiptoes to kiss him. "You were having nightmares."

"Not surprising." He pinched his forehead. "Hangover."

"Want some breakfast?"

"No." He drank more coffee. "Going to see the attorney in St. Pete."

"The one you went to law school with?"

"Yeah. I texted her. Appointment's at eleven."

"Today? She's going to meet you on a *Sunday*?"

He gave an offhand shrug. Even hungover, the man could be amazingly persuasive.

"OK, I'll get ready." She turned toward the bathroom.

His heavy hand grasped her shoulder. "Some rotten vacation."

She tipped her head sideways. "Sure hasn't been boring."

He scowled. "I figured we'd spend half a day, tops, sorting out Smoky's problem then laze around Clearwater Beach the rest of the time. Sorry it didn't work out that way."

"Irma kinda put a dent in the plans."

He stroked the back of her neck. Although his fingers were bruised, they still gave off sensuous electricity. "Through all this, you've been amazing."

She rested her head against his chest. "Thank you."

He pulled her close, his warmth surrounding her. "I got us a reservation at the Hyatt Regency. They've been jammed with hurricane refugees and out-of-town contractors here to repair the damage. But a suite just opened up with a whirlpool tub. We can finally get out of this dump."

She nestled against him, savoring his feel, his smell. "Nice."

"I also scored a rental rig, only one available in central Florida. I was on the phone with reservations when a contractor turned in a pickup. You don't mind renting a truck, do you?"

"I'm a Montana girl. I was practically born in a truck."

He squeezed her waist, making her wish they had time to go back to bed. "We'll drive Smoky's T-bird to the hotel. The rental lot's not far from there. I already booked you a massage in the spa. While I talk with the attorney, you can relax and be pampered. When I finish in St. Pete, we'll start this vacation for real."

She leaned back and gazed up at him. "For a guy with a hangover, you've been busy."

"Gotta make it up to you for putting up with my shit."

She nibbled his bristly chin. "That all sounds wonderful." Then she remembered the items on the table. She pulled free and retrieved the paper. "Look what I found in Smoky's wallet. It's a post office receipt. Smoky mailed something to Panama more than a month ago. I wonder if it could have been the baseball card."

Tillman glanced at the damp scrap but shook his head. "I don't care if it is. I'm not busting my ass to get Gabriel's card back for him. As far as we're concerned, Honus went to the bottom of the swamp with Smoky. My only job now is to have him declared dead and settle the estate."

Unanswered questions chafed at Tawny. "Are you sure?"

"Damn sure. Now let's pack and blow this joint."

***

While Tillman went next door to enlist Raul's help to remove the T-bird hardtop, Tawny packed. When she rolled their carryon bags out to the carport, Raul, Jessica, and her dog Churro were there to say goodbye.

As the men shook hands, Tawny hugged the girl. "Thank you for all your help."

Jessica clung to Tawny's arm. "I wish you were staying so you could meet Mama. Uncle finally found her in Puerto Rico. Papi's sending her money to come home."

"That's wonderful. I know she's missed you." Tawny produced a baggie full of leftover barbecued chicken. Churro plunked his butt on the ground as his nose twitched at the scent of food. She handed him several bites which he gently took. Then she gave the rest to Jessica. "Churro's treat for later."

The dog leaned against Tawny's leg, tail wagging. She scratched his ears.

"I'm going to keep training him to be a search dog," Jessica said. "Next time, I want the person to be alive." Tears glistened in her brown eyes.

Tawny kissed the girl's hair. "It's sad that Smoky's dead but at least we know, thanks to Churro."

Tillman shook hands with the girl, who still looked up at him with awe bordering on fear. Churro thrust his nose into Tillman's crotch. "Shit!" He jerked backward.

Tawny suppressed a smile and took his arm. "We better go or you'll be late to your appointment." She winked over her shoulder at Jessica, who giggled soundlessly.

In the T-bird, Tillman grunted as he backed out of the carport. "Damn dog's fixated on my manhood."

Tawny chuckled. "At least that gives you something in common."

He rolled his eyes.

"Did you give back the keys to Raul's van?"

"Yeah. And when he wasn't looking, I stuck five hundred cash in the visor. He'll need that to bribe officials to get his wife out of Puerto Rico."

Tawny squeezed his arm. "I don't care what everybody says— you're not an asshole."

"Yes, I am, and shut up."

They drove south on Highway 19 in bright morning light. Tawny's earlier sunburn had peeled away. She raised her face to the pleasant warmth, inhaling the sea breeze, anticipating romantic walks on the beach and rolling around in the whirlpool tub with Tillman. But the workaholic lawyer couldn't stay away from his practice much longer.

As if reading her mind, he said, "Talked with Esther this morning. She got continuances on a couple of hearings. But I have to be back in Billings by next Thursday." He shot her a sideways glance. "Still gives us enough time to get married at the hotel. I checked. The Sky Terrace is available."

Her jaw clenched in anticipation of another argument. "Not going to happen, Tillman. If it does, I want our children with us. Neal would need time to get leave and fly home from wherever the hell the Army has him posted. It's going to mean a big fight with Emma. You know how she feels about you. And I can't get married without my best friend. Virgie has to be my matron of honor."

She'd carefully lined out her arguments. Now she waited for the rebuttals she knew he would launch. But they didn't come.

Instead, his smirk grew broader.

"What's so funny?" she demanded.

"You are."

"Why?"

He turned onto the Highway 60 causeway. "Because we're finally getting down to earnest negotiations."

She glared at him. "You make it sound like a settlement conference in some lawsuit."

"Isn't it?"

She folded her arms. "Tillman, you're the most exasperating man I've ever met. Why would I want to marry you?"

"Because we're good together."

Yes, they were. But Tawny wasn't about to admit that. She hunched in the seat. "Can't we just enjoy the time we have left here?"

Sun sparkled on the placid turquoise Gulf and palm trees swayed in a gentle breeze but Tillman refused to drop the subject. "At least, pick out a ring. I checked a website for a custom jeweler in St. Pete. Nice designs you might like. When I called him, he said he can cut off your old ring."

Horrified, she covered her left hand. "I don't want to cut off my ring."

"Why? You're not married anymore."

She massaged her knuckle, broken several years before. Permanent swelling ensured she could never slip off the worn gold band. And that was fine with her. "Maybe you tossed your wedding ring when you got divorced but mine is precious to me."

"Fine, be sentimental. I'll still buy you a better one."

"Don't you understand? It's not how fancy the ring is. It's what it represents. Thirty-two years with a good man. It took a lot of building by both Dwight and me."

She twirled her ring, while a growing pain pulsed in her temples. Arguments with Tillman wore her out and happened too often. She loved so much about him, his tenderness toward his children, his brilliance and dedication, how he never gave up, no matter how impossible the task. And his sensuous ways in bed thrummed in a constant undercurrent she couldn't ignore.

But Dwight would never have lashed out at her as Tillman did last spring during the crisis with his daughter, Mimi.

How could she explain? "Tillman, if I marry again, I don't want it to blow apart. I don't know if you're capable of building a marriage that will last."

His already-dark eyes deepened into bottomless caves. "I'm not the man Dwight was."

She shook her head. "That's not it. You're both good men but you're different."

He turned into the portico of the pink hotel and braked in front of the uniformed valet. "And you don't think I can live up to *Saint* Dwight."

The resonant boom of Tillman's voice often startled people, even if he wasn't shouting.

The valet stepped back in alarm.

Tawny's face grew hot with embarrassment. "Let's not talk about this here. Please." Not in front of strangers who shouldn't know their deeply personal business.

He got out of the car and stared down at her, an unreadable expression in his nearly-black eyes. She couldn't identify if it was anger, sorrow, or pain. Now he did raise his voice to a shout: "Decide if you want to stay married to a dead man or have a live one."

He pulled his phone from his pocket and flashed a confirmation code at the valet for their reservation.

The man briefly checked the screen but quickly homed in on Tillman's split knuckles and swollen hands. He sneaked a sideways glance at Tawny, as if looking for corresponding bruises.

Tears started down her face. She quickly wiped them away but they kept flowing.

Tillman shoved a five in the valet's hand. To Tawny, he snapped, "Going to pick up the rental car." He strode away from the hotel entrance out to the sidewalk, long legs scissoring.

Tawny hugged herself, struggling to hold back sobs. How could he be so hateful about Dwight? She'd tried to explain but he took everything wrong.

"*Señora?*" The young Hispanic valet had come around to her passenger door, brows furrowed in concern. "May I be of service?"

She shook her head and wiped her eyes again before facing him. "*Gracias.* It's all right. The bags are in the trunk."

He opened her door and offered his hand. She clasped it and was grateful for the support because her legs felt wobbly.

He beckoned the bellman who hurried to the trunk. The pair exchanged a few words in Spanish, unsuccessfully trying to hide their curiosity about the tearful woman and her huge, angry boyfriend with bruised knuckles. An older, silver-haired couple stood at the entrance and stared.

Great, now four strangers were witness to her humiliation.

She forced herself to stand tall and walked past the couple into the lobby, trailed by the bellman wheeling their bags.

Chapter 17 – Gentleman Thief

Tawny lay face down on the horseshoe pillow and moaned as the masseuse dug deep into her painful, knotted muscles. Soft flute music played in the background, belying the confused thoughts twisting in her brain. The fragrant, silk-sheet luxury of the spa would have been delicious if she hadn't been so upset.

Tillman's ultimatum stung. The third anniversary of Dwight's death a few months before had hit her like a scar freshly torn open. Yet Tillman expected her to simply discard her love and memories.

His own and his parents' marriages had both been terrible. He had no frame of reference how to build a relationship that worked for the long haul.

He was a good man but a bad risk.

Yet, despite his temper and volatility, he would do anything for her. Anything.

Except, be patient.

The expression in his eyes came back to her, the meaning now clear: he was hurt. He'd allowed her inside his hard shell, opening himself to her, but she'd rejected him.

A further realization unfolded.

Tillman, the cynical, logical, rational attorney, was jealous.

Of Dwight.

Competition from a living rival wouldn't have fazed Tillman. But he couldn't obliterate a man whose memories were embedded forever in Tawny's heart. And that pissed him off.

The conclusions settled her mind. She couldn't change Tillman's feelings but now she understood more what she was dealing with.

The argument had wrung her out but the two-hour-long massage soothed her spasms and partially calmed her anguish. When it ended, she wanted to drift off to sleep on the padded table but had to rouse herself to dress. She planned to nap in the hotel room until Tillman returned from seeing the attorney. Then, maybe, they could settle their squabble.

When she left the private massage room and went out to the reception area, she heard a familiar voice coming from the adjacent nail salon.

Nyala.

The woman wore tight denim capris and a sleeveless hot pink halter. A wide scarf held her dark curly hair back from her face. She tapped her phone while talking to a manicurist, her fresh nails the same hot pink as her halter. "Two weeks from today," she said. "But one-thirty works better for me. Are you available then?" She finished setting up her appointment and turned to face Tawny. "Hello."

Tawny knew this couldn't be a coincidence. "What a surprise."

Nyala tucked her phone into a straw bag. "Do you have time for a drink?"

Why? Tawny wondered. Then again, why not? Maybe she could learn more about Smoky and the Panama connection. Not that it mattered now except to satisfy her own curiosity. "All right."

"There's a nice little bar on the beach a few blocks away. We can walk."

Tawny noticed the woman wore blue moccasin-style deck shoes instead of high-heeled sandals. "What are you doing here? Besides getting a manicure?"

"I'm meeting a friend later. His yacht is at a marina not far from here. We're going to cruise over to Caladesi and Honeymoon Island. Have dinner aboard and enjoy the sunset."

Tawny recalled Commodore's description of trips Smoky had taken with Nyala on yachts that belonged to her friends. Perhaps one of the boat owners was the person Smoky planned to rendezvous with on the night he disappeared. An unexpected opportunity presented itself to question Nyala more. Tawny had to seize the chance.

She had a strong intuition that Nyala knew more about Smoky's fate than she'd admitted. Maybe she also knew the person in Panama that Smoky had mailed the package to. But Tawny couldn't ask without revealing a key detail that might help Gabriel find the missing baseball card. She had to watch what she said to his sister.

"Nyala, what are you *really* doing here?"

The woman's lovely face remained impassive. "Actually, it's no accident. I called Raul this morning because he's been helping

155

me locate a contractor to repair Smoky's carport. He mentioned you and Mr. Rosenbaum were spending the rest of your vacation at the Hyatt Regency. I have my nails done here anyway so I just waited until you came out of your massage. I wanted to talk to you about Smoky."

Tawny's throat tensed. "He's dead."

Nyala didn't react. No shock, no surprise. Had Gabriel told her?

Tawny envied her ability to mask her reactions and feelings, something Tawny could never do.

They left the hotel and crossed the street to the beachfront promenade. During the several-block walk, Nyala kept up idle chit-chat about the best places to shop and eat. She didn't say one word about Smoky.

They entered a waterfront bar that was almost empty. "The town's pretty quiet since Irma," Nyala said. "Tourists haven't come back yet and the locals are still busy digging out from storm damage."

She led the way across a concrete deck, enclosed by a railing, elevated about fifteen feet above the beach. Palm trees with basketweave trunks grew through open holes cut in the concrete. Driftwood and Irma's scraps still littered the sand below.

Steel drum music played through speakers, Jimmy Buffett lamenting his lost salt shaker. A line of white rocking chairs faced the water. Nyala sat in a rocker and neatly crossed her shapely legs.

Tawny sat in the next rocker, a table between them, in the shade of an umbrella. The positioning of the chairs was ideal for enjoying the view but awkward for conversation. She couldn't gauge Nyala's expression without being obvious about watching her. She wondered if that's why Nyala had chosen this bar.

A server took their orders, zinfandel for Nyala and a frozen Margarita for Tawny. One drink only, she decided. No matter how tempting, getting wasted in Margaritaville wouldn't help her learn more from Nyala.

The woman gazed far out into the bay and finally asked, "Do you have proof that Smoky's dead?"

"Yes," Tawny answered. "Tillman is meeting an attorney now to have him declared dead because of DNA and other evidence found."

"Evidence?"

"I can't say more."

"I understand."

The conversation felt strange, neither of them looking at each other but instead staring at the expanse of turquoise water.

Their drinks arrived and, for a brief instant, when they clinked glasses, their eyes locked. Nyala's calm demeanor hid many secrets. If she already knew about Smoky's death, Tawny wondered how she had found out.

"You don't seem surprised," Tawny said.

"No."

"Why not?"

Nyala reached into her straw bag and withdrew a pair of sunglasses. She put them on and rocked gently in the chair. "Smoky was always full of surprises."

The Margarita had a delicious tart tang and the icy glass cooled Tawny's hand. The lull of rocking soothed her. She was now officially on vacation and should no longer care but Nyala's strange non-answers bothered her. She decided on a different tack. "You said you first met Smoky in Panama not long after his accident."

"Actually, that's not quite accurate. I've known Smoky for a number of years because he worked for my brother. At one point, we were...very close. When he got hurt, he called me to fly down and help him travel back."

"Why didn't you say that before?"

"I try to be circumspect where Smoky's concerned. That version best suited his privacy concerns so that's the one I told."

"What about your brother?"

"He knew Smoky's past, the debts, and that people were hunting for him. He made sure Smoky earned enough to keep his creditors satisfied. Sometimes he even acted as a go-between, a buffer, to prevent the creditor from—shall we say—collecting an extra penalty. Gabriel was very protective of Smoky."

"Until the Honus Wagner card disappeared."

Nyala shifted sideways in her chair with a brief glance at Tawny. "That breach of trust deeply hurt Gabriel. Far more than the actual theft."

"Why do you think Smoky took it?"

She lifted one shoulder. "His circumstances changed. He had different priorities."

"What priorities?"

"He was getting older. He looked back on his life and found it full of regrets. He wanted to leave behind a better legacy."

"By stealing?"

"I don't think he saw it that way."

Tawny faced the woman. "What other way is there to see it?"

Nyala's head swiveled toward Tawny but the dark lenses obscured her eyes. "As his last chance." She sipped her wine and re-crossed her legs.

"So, you knew he'd stolen the card?"

"He told me, after the fact. He knew Gabriel would be enraged and he didn't want me stuck in the middle. He was a gentleman that way."

A gentleman thief, Tawny thought, but said nothing. "How did he plan to sell the card?"

"I don't know. I stay completely detached from that business. I have my investments, my rental properties, all legitimate. I pay taxes. I don't want trouble."

"Gabriel handles his business a little differently than you do?"

"Some people take risks. I don't care to." She smoothed an imaginary wrinkle in her tight capris. "As you know, I was once the registered agent for my brother's company but I ended that affiliation several years ago."

"You were concerned about getting in trouble?"

"I've worked hard to build my portfolio and I protect it. I never want to be beholden to or dependent on anyone's performance except mine."

"You're your own woman."

"Exactly."

A slight buzz made Tawny aware of how easily the Margarita was going down, a lime snow cone with a tequila kick on an empty stomach. She needed to be careful how she worded her questions. "What do you think happened the night of the hurricane?"

"To Smoky? I couldn't know."

"Do you think he wanted to commit suicide?"

Now Nyala shook her head. "I'm certain he didn't."

Smoky's fishing buddy Commodore thought differently. Tawny wondered which one— Commodore or Nyala—knew the old coach better. "What makes you say that?"

"He had regrets but he was also full of optimism."

"Because he had a three-million-dollar baseball card to give him a fresh start?"

"Perhaps." She raked pink fingernails through her curls. "Did you ever see the card?"

"Only the photo your brother showed us."

"Ugly thing. Drab colors. I don't understand its appeal."

The rest of the Margarita slid down Tawny's throat. She spotted a dolphin lazing in the crystal water. She pointed. "Oh, look."

Nyala leaned forward in her rocker and raised the sunglasses to her forehead. "Have you ever swum with dolphins?"

"No."

"You and Mr. Rosenbaum should try it. Lovely experience. So very Florida." Nyala finished her wine and stood. "I need to go. I have to meet my friend at the marina." She held out her elegant hand.

They shook as Nyala added, "Oh, if I might make another recommendation for the true Florida experience. There's a wonderful seafood place with oysters on the half shell that are so fresh you still taste the ocean. You and Mr. Rosenbaum might like to try it. But you need reservations. Even the hurricane didn't slow down their business. It's very popular with locals."

"What's the name?"

"Barnacles. It's just a quick walk. Down those stairs and across the parking lot and you're there. You might still be early enough to make reservations for dinner tonight."

"OK." Tawny had nothing better to do while waiting for Tillman to return.

"What a shame you received such an unfavorable impression of Florida, between the hurricane and Smoky's death. If you come again, please call me and I'll arrange my nicest rental for you." She waved toward their empty glasses. "I'll settle the bill on the way out. Goodbye."

Nyala threaded between empty tables toward an enclosed area of the bar, graceful hips swaying. Inside, she paused to speak to the bartender then disappeared toward the street exit.

Tawny leaned her elbows on the rail, reviewing the conversation. Nyala played a great Ms. Florida Chamber of Commerce but she had not given a single straight answer about Smoky's death. Why had she sought out Tawny?

The server delivered another frozen Margarita. "Compliments of Ms. Obregon."

Tawny thanked him, still pondering Nyala's motives.

In the shimmering water, the dolphin circled and dipped then moved farther out into the Gulf. Tawny squinted until it disappeared from sight.

She could stay and enjoy the drink, listening to the cries of seagulls, and watching the sun fall lower into the Gulf. Tempting, but it was almost three-thirty. Tillman should be back or have called by now but she'd left her phone upstairs in the hotel suite during her massage.

His mood would probably depend on the answers he'd received from the attorney. She wondered if the evidence they had was really enough to declare Smoky dead without a waiting period.

Most of all, she dreaded a continuation of their fight. After a few hours to cool down, she hoped he might be ready to apologize or at least listen. She took a sip of the second Margarita but set it down. She *should* return to the hotel. The showdown had to happen eventually. Suck it up, buttercup.

A soft breeze wafted delicious aromas from the restaurant Nyala had recommended. Tawny's stomach growled. She hadn't eaten all day. No wonder the drink was hitting her. If she walked to the restaurant to make dinner reservations, she could also pick up a quick snack to tide her over.

She left a tip then clipped down the stairs to the deserted parking lot. The lower level of the building had a roll-up warehouse-style door. An older white delivery van parked near the open door. Two uniformed men in ball caps leaned on hand trucks, facing the delivery entrance and smoking. They had parked close to the bottom of the stairs, forcing Tawny to sidle past.

"Oh, excuse me, ma'am," one man said. "Should've left more room."

She kept up her brisk walk.

The second man moved out of her sight for an instant.

Suddenly a cloth hood dropped over her head. From behind, muscular arms gripped her in a bear hug.

She screamed and stomped at the man's feet. The attacker's vise grip on her arms prevented her from jabbing with her elbows. She whipped her head straight back, hoping to smash the man's nose with her skull, but the blow wasn't solid.

The second man grabbed her legs. Together, they lifted her off the ground and dragged her inside the van. Despite her desperate kicking, she felt straps tightening around her legs. Then more straps looped around her arms, securing them to her sides.

She screamed again, hoping against hope that someone would hear her.

The edge of the hood lifted and a rag was stuffed in her mouth. A chemical smell filled her nostrils.

She couldn't see, couldn't move, couldn't breathe.

Her last thoughts before she passed out: *Nyala set me up and I walked straight into the trap.*

Chapter 18 – Gone

Tillman slid the key card into the slot and opened the door to the suite. Their two roller bags sat in the entry. Otherwise, empty. "Tawny?"

He checked the living room, bedroom, and bath. No one. The place was as sterile and undisturbed as if housekeeping had just made up the room. No hint of the citrus fragrance of Tawny's shampoo.

He dropped his laptop case on the sofa, pulled out his cell, and tapped her number. A rattling noise from the desk caught his attention. On the wood surface, her phone wobbled on vibrate mode. He picked it up. The only new text was from him, an hour ago, when he left St. Pete.

She hadn't read his apology.

I'm an asshole. Why didn't you smack me across the mouth? I'll make it up to you.

Where was she?

He used the room phone for a direct connection to the spa. "Is Tawny Lindholm still there?"

"No, sir. Her massage finished a little after two-thirty."

"Did she say where she was going?"

"No."

He left the suite and took the elevator up to the pool area. Not there. Then down to the lobby. He pulled up her photo on his phone to show the bartender and restaurant host but neither had seen her.

Then to the spa.

He loomed over the reception counter. The woman in her twenties wore a heavy mask of makeup with black-red lipstick. Perfumed air gagged him. "I'm looking for Tawny Lindholm. You said she left here about two-thirty. I need to know where she went."

The receptionist's eyes flicked back and forth under thick lash extensions.

Tillman pulled a ten from his wallet.

"She left with a client who's a regular." She took the bill.

"Who?"

"Our client list is confidential. I could get fired."

He pulled another ten from his wallet.

She quickly scanned the spa but no one else was there. "Her name is Nyala Obregon."

A fist tightened in Tillman's chest.

The receptionist went on: "She comes in every couple of weeks for her mani and pedi. I think she was waiting around until Ms. Lindholm's massage was finished, like they were planning to meet."

"Did their conversation seem friendly?"

She flicked at her acrylic thumbnail, black-red like her lipstick. "I guess. They chatted for a minute then walked out together."

"What direction?"

"I don't know. Another client came in and I was busy with her. I didn't pay attention."

Tillman headed for the manager's office.

Twenty dollars had bought information that made his blood run cold.

***

In the security office, the duty manager, the head of security, and Tillman watched as video replayed from various cameras around the hotel. Tillman pointed at the screen. "There. Stop it now."

The shot captured Tawny walking out the front entrance with Nyala Obregon. Another feed in the parking lot showed the two women from the rear, strolling on the sidewalk. The final shot caught the edge of them crossing the street toward the beach. The security man flicked through different cameras and angles but they had moved out of range.

Nothing in Tawny's stance or behavior indicated duress or trouble. Was she still investigating Smoky's death? She refused to let unanswered questions drop. She kept digging until she uncovered the truth—one of many reasons why she was so good at her job. Since she'd started working for him, Tillman couldn't imagine being without her help.

But, even more, without her presence.

Their days apart, when she was at her Kalispell home and he was in Billings, made him hollow. The emptiness of waking up without her beside him had grown unendurable. That had to change. He had to convince her to marry him.

Outside, he found Smoky's T-bird still parked in the valet lot. That meant she was likely on foot, unless she'd left in Nyala's car. He flicked through his contact list to Nyala's number and tapped it.

She answered on the fourth ring. "Mr. Rosenbaum."

"Ms. Nyala, where is Tawny?"

"We had a drink together at the Sandspur. I left her there about an hour ago because I had an appointment."

"Where are you now?"

"Cruising on a friend's yacht. I'm a little surprised there's cell reception this far from shore."

"Was she alone when you left her?"

"Yes. The bar was practically deserted. We sat outside on the deck overlooking the Gulf. Maybe she's still there. It's a lovely view. She seemed quite entranced with a dolphin frolicking in the water."

"Where is the Sandspur?"

"A few blocks south of your hotel. I suggested you might take her to swim with dolphins. It's a delightful experience. Unfortunately, there's not a facility in Tampa Bay but Orlando is an hour—"

The call dropped. He redialed. No answer.

The yacht she was on must have sailed out of range. Or Nyala broke the connection deliberately. From her breezy tone, he couldn't judge if she was telling the truth.

Just as well. Tillman didn't give a shit about dolphins.

He only cared about finding Tawny.

Tillman drove the truck south to the Sandspur and hurried into the bar. A quick scan of the deck area confirmed she wasn't there. He showed his phone photo to the bartender.

The man sliced a lime into wedges. "I just came on duty about fifteen minutes ago. Haven't seen her. But I think Manuel, the server, might still be in the kitchen."

Tillman barged through the swinging doors. Three workers were prepping food. He shouted, "Manuel!"

Heads jerked up. A man wearing a chef's toque approached Tillman. "Hey, you can't be in here."

Tillman stood his ground. "Where's Manuel?"

A man emerged from a storeroom. "I'm Manuel."

Tillman pushed past the chef and held up his phone with Tawny's photo. "Did you see this woman?"

"Yeah, served her a couple of Margaritas. Another lady with her. Zinfandel."

"The other woman—was she tall, black, gorgeous?"

An appreciative smile spread across Manuel's face. "Oh, yeah, man, she was sweet. They both were. Ladies like that make it worth coming to work."

In his peripheral vision, Tillman caught the chef moving behind a prep table. "Did they leave together?"

"No, the black lady left first. She ordered another drink for the redhead on her way out."

"Did the redhead say anything?"

"Just thanked me. And she left me an extra five."

Yeah, that would be Tawny. "When did she leave?"

"Don't know. Maybe an hour or so ago. I was here in the kitchen for a while. When I went back outside, she was gone. Left most of her second drink."

"Which way did she go?"

He splayed both palms. "Like I told you, man, I was inside. Didn't even see her leave."

Tillman slapped a ten in Manuel's hand, along with this business card. "If you remember anything or see her again, call me right away."

"Sure, man."

The chef had moved forward, closer to Tillman, face flushed, squinty eyes angry. Tillman asked him, "You got surveillance cams?"

The chef whipped a carving knife from behind his back. "Who the hell are you?"

Tillman snatched the man's wrist, bent it backward, and kept pressing until the chef dropped the knife. It clattered to the floor. Tillman kicked it under the prep table, out of reach. A little more pressure forced the man to his knees. "I'm the guy who wants to look at your video footage."

The chef's anger gave way to teeth gritted in pain. His words sputtered out in breathless gasps. "Ain't none. Irma exploded a transformer. Burned up the electronics. Surveillance is down all around here."

Tillman looked to Manuel for confirmation. The server nodded.

"Goddammit." He released the chef's hand and strode outside to his truck.

He called 911. "I need to report my fiancée is missing."

***

An hour later, two officers knocked at the door of the hotel suite. Tillman explained he'd been in St. Pete while Tawny had a massage downstairs. She then went to the Sandspur with Nyala Obregon and disappeared.

He recognized from the set of their mouths that they thought he was overreacting, even though they didn't say so. One cop left to watch the hotel security video while the other stayed in the suite to question Tillman. Could Tawny have gone shopping or for a walk on the beach?

Tillman shook his head. "She wouldn't go without calling or leaving a message. But she left her phone here in the room."

"May I see it?"

Tillman handed the device over.

The cop noticed Tillman's abraded knuckles. "What happened to your hands, sir?"

Shit. He suspected Tillman had hit Tawny. "Heavy bag at the gym. Overdid it."

"You sure did. Bust any bones?"

"No." Goddammit.

The cop read the text and Tillman caught the slight side movement of his eyes.

I'm an asshole. Why didn't you smack me across the mouth? I'll make it up to you.

"Sir, was this message from you?"

"Yes."

"Sounds like you two had a disagreement?"

"Minor."

He again studied Tillman's discolored hands. "You know how the ladies are. You and I think it's minor but, to them, it's the apocalypse."

"No chance." The jerk thought Tawny had walked out in a huff. But Tillman knew she wouldn't. Not like that. If she wanted to end it—and, dammit, he'd given her enough reasons—she'd say it to his face.

No. Something was wrong.

They took the elevator to the lobby and met the second officer, who gestured with his chin to his partner. The two cops stepped out of earshot for a moment to confer then both approached Tillman.

"Mr. Rosenbaum," the first cop said, "you already confirmed with me that you and Ms. Lindholm had a disagreement, right?"

"Yeah, but that's not—"

Cop Two broke in: "Sir, when you arrived at the hotel this morning, the valet and bellman said you were visibly angry and Ms. Lindholm was crying. Two other witnesses said the same thing and security video confirms that."

"She's missing!" Tillman roared. "Something's happened to her."

"Mr. Rosenbaum, we have to go on witness reports and video surveillance. Nothing appears suspicious in Ms. Lindholm's activity. She left the hotel voluntarily in good condition under her own power. We can't file a missing person report based on that."

Cop One leaned closer. "Sir, we understand you're concerned but, based on experience, chances are she just went someplace to blow off steam. If she's like *my* wife, she took your credit card and she's probably charging up a storm. Most likely, she'll be back soon and everything will be fine."

Tillman fought to control his anger. The cops had been ineffective in Smoky's disappearance and now were equally useless for Tawny. He had to think of another way to find her. "You logged my call, right? It's on record that I'm asserting she's missing."

"Yes, sir. If she isn't back in forty-eight hours, you can file a formal report then." Cop One made a point of staring at Tillman's knuckles again. "And, if she does remain missing, *you* will be the first person we talk to. Understand?"

To keep from clocking the asshole, Tillman stalked out of the lobby toward the parking lot.

Of course, that was their obvious conclusion. The spouse was always the first suspect in disappearance cases. If it would kick the lazy dimwits into searching for Tawny, he'd get himself arrested this minute. But that wouldn't help. They'd spend hours sweating him instead of looking for her.

He strode to his truck, brain racing. Why had Tawny met with Nyala? If Nyala was operating on behalf of her brother, Gabriel, Tawny was in danger. The prick must think Tillman had the Honus Wagner card. Had he abducted Tawny to trade for the card?

If so, that meant a ransom call would come soon. Tillman had to figure out a bluff on Gabriel.

And find Tawny.

Chapter 19 – The Ship Has Sailed

A rocking movement woke Tawny, along with the slapping noise of water against a hull. She smelled diesel fumes and the slight residue of whatever chemical that had knocked her out. Her head pounded. Her sleeveless tank and shorts stank of cigarette smoke. The hood had been removed but her vision remained blurry. She blinked to clear her cloudy eyes and took stock.

She was lying on a bunk below decks on a boat. Woven nylon tie-down straps bound her arms and legs. One strap was looped through a wooden railing on the bulkhead to prevent her from getting out of the bunk.

Opposite from where she lay, the sun shone through a narrow window above a dinette with built-in bench seats. From the angle of light, she guessed seven-thirty, close to sunset. She must have been out for almost four hours.

The lack of engine thrum indicated the boat was drifting or lying at anchor.

Footsteps sounded on the deck above her head. A hatch opened and a man came down the ladder into the cabin.

She recognized Gabriel's thug—the bulky guy she'd first seen kicking in Smoky's ribs, then later when the men searched Smoky's house.

The smell of cigarette smoke drifted in with him. He peered at her. "Want some water?"

Her lips cracked from dryness. "Yes."

He reached into an under-counter refrigerator adjacent to the dinette and took out a bottle of water. When he grasped her shoulder to pull her to a sitting position, she smelled rum heavy on his breath, even stronger than cigarette smoke. He cracked open the cap and put the bottle to her lips. She gulped greedily, downing half.

What kind of tough guy worried about the thirst of his captive? Maybe he had a human side. If she could get him talking…

She tipped her head away. "Thanks."

He looked a little surprised at her gratitude then recapped the bottle and set it on the table.

She studied him, committing his features to memory. Mid- to late-forties, six feet, broad chest and shoulders, flabby midsection. A gray-streaked brown beard tried unsuccessfully to mask a double chin. A jock gone to seed but still powerful.

"Why am I here?" she asked.

He was expressionless, blasé, as if kidnapping was an everyday occurrence. "Waiting for your boyfriend to cough up Honus Wagner."

"He doesn't have it. We don't know where it is. It probably went down with Smoky when he drowned."

"We'll see."

"Kidnapping me is a stupid stunt. You'll go to prison for life. And for nothing. We don't have the card."

"I do what my boss tells me."

Change the tack. "What's your name?"

"Wally," he answered.

"Wally, how much is Gabriel paying you to take this chance?"

"That ship has already sailed." He grinned. An eye tooth was missing. "Get it? Ship has sailed?"

A bad comedian. "Where are we?"

"Past the twelve-mile limit."

Damn. They were in international waters. Even if Tawny escaped, she couldn't swim twelve miles through sharks and God only knew what other dangers. She was screwed. "Is Gabriel on board?" Maybe she could convince him that they didn't have the card. Would he risk a kidnapping rap for a fortune he couldn't collect?

"Nah," Wally answered.

"Where is he?"

"He doesn't give me his schedule."

"How does he get in touch with you? Ship-to-shore radio?"

Wally ducked to peer out through the window at the setting sun. "He won't need to. I already have my orders." His gap-tooth grin turned sinister.

The stark meaning of his words sunk in.

He climbed the ladder to the deck and closed the hatch.

It didn't matter whether or not Gabriel got the baseball card.

Wally intended to dump her at sea.

Either way, her body would be feeding the fishes, like Smoky.

Chapter 20 – Point Last Seen

Raul and Jessica stood in the living room of the hotel suite while Tillman searched through Tawny's roller bag that he'd placed on the desk. He pulled out her clean, folded clothes, looking for something she'd already worn for Churro to use as a scent article. The dog sniffed around the room, tail waving, excited to have a job.

"How about these?" Tillman started to grab a pair of used panties.

Jessica cried, "Don't touch them! We need Tawny's scent, not yours." Using a baggie, she scooped the panties inside it then tugged Churro's lead to bring him close. She held the baggie open for the dog. He buried his nose deep, snuffling the silky material. "That's Tawny, Churro. Go find Tawny."

Tillman had called Raul out of frantic desperation, unable to think of any other way to track where Tawny had gone. He'd already canvassed businesses for blocks around, seeking security cam footage. Except for the hotel, which had a backup system, all were non-op from hurricane damage, as the chef at Sandspur had said.

Her fate rested in the nose of a badly-behaved, adolescent dog. The thought strangled Tillman like a noose. But he had no other options.

The dog pulled them out of the suite, down the hall, and stopped in front of the second of three elevators. When the doors opened, he smelled the floor and climbed on. They followed and descended to the lobby. There, Churro sniffed the air, trotted to the spa entrance, and raised his paw to scratch the door.

When Tillman opened it, Churro pushed through, moving to a closed interior door. He sat in front of it.

The black-lipped receptionist called, "You can't bring a dog in here."

"Official business," Tillman snarled. "Search and rescue."

"Oh." She squinted suspiciously at Churro. "Isn't that dog supposed to wear a vest or something?" Then she noticed Jessica, gripping the lead. "She doesn't look like a handler, either."

Tillman moved to where Churro sat and tried the door handle. Locked.

"Hey!" The receptionist jumped up from her stool and hurried to him. "Don't open that door. There's a client in there."

"Is this the room where Tawny Lindholm had her massage?"

"Yes."

Tillman's glare backed her off. She retreated to her desk. He grasped Jessica's shoulder. "OK, this is good. It's verification he's following her."

The girl beamed.

He wondered how the dog sorted out Tawny's scent hidden in the stifling cloud of spa perfume.

They started to leave but Churro pulled Jessica sideways to a small alcove with shelves full of folded sheets and towels. A laundry hamper sat on the floor. The dog zeroed in on that, running his nose up and down the woven wicker basket.

The receptionist forgot her protests and now appeared interested in the dog's work. "That's where the used linen goes. He must be smelling the sheet she laid on."

Maybe, Tillman decided, the irritating, crotch-sniffing dog knew what he was doing, after all. He held the spa door open as Churro tugged Jessica at a brisk walk, across the lobby, out to the street.

There, the dog hesitated, wavering.

"He's getting confused," Jessica said. "The sun, the wind, people walking, cars driving by—they're all stirring up the air and diffusing the scent." She squatted beside the dog. "Find Tawny, Churro."

At last, Churro crossed the boulevard toward the sidewalk beside the beach. That matched Tawny's path as shown on the hotel security video.

The dog wandered back and forth on the promenade, checking out a still-wet glob of spit, a discarded sandwich wrapper, bird droppings, and the place where another dog had marked the wall.

Shit, Tillman thought, now the damn goofy dog was sightseeing. The brief hope he'd felt evaporated. After several minutes watching Churro's aimless sniffing, Tillman growled, "Why is he messing around? How come he isn't following her trail?"

"He's trying to filter out the distractions," Jessica explained. "Just give him a minute."

Soon, the dog committed to moving south, toward the Sandspur Bar.

Tillman and Raul trailed behind Jessica and the dog.

Raul said, "Jessica, she study many books about search dogs. She feels very bad that she did not find Smoky alive. She's determined to find Tawny. Very nice lady, very kind to my daughter."

Tillman ground his teeth, fear rising. Tawny *had* to be alive. The possibility that she wasn't sent razors through his insides. If she died, he was responsible for dragging her into Smoky's problems.

Earlier that afternoon, foreboding had weighed on him when he returned from the appointment with the attorney in St. Pete. He suspected Tawny might tell him they were finished, that she'd had enough of his bullshit.

Now, he knew his sense of dread stemmed from a much worse cause.

Churro continued in a straight shot for the next three blocks then veered toward the Sandspur. When they entered the bar, the bartender looked up at Tillman, nodded in recognition, but said nothing about the dog.

Churro snuffled the floor, moving back and forth, then tugged Jessica toward the outside deck.

The swinging doors of the kitchen burst open. The chef came through. "What the hell do you think you're doing? You can't bring a dog in here."

Tillman blocked the man's path. "Let's make peace, buddy. Will twenty convince you to go back to work in the kitchen?"

The chef grumbled but no longer showed signs of his earlier aggression. "If the health department shows up, I'm in deep shit."

Tillman took a twenty from his wallet. "With the contamination Irma left behind, you really think they have time to run restaurant inspections?"

The man took the bill, glowered at the dog, then retreated behind the swinging doors.

Outside on the deck, Tillman found Churro sniffing the seat of a rocking chair shaded by an umbrella table. The dog whined.

Jessica looked up at Tillman. "Tawny was sitting here."

"OK, honey." He squatted beside her. "This is where the search gets tricky. Nobody saw her leave. It's important to find out where she went next."

"Search and rescue calls this the *point last seen*," Jessica said.

Tillman's diaphragm contracted at the ominous sound of those words. "Do it."

Jessica patted Churro's back. "Find Tawny."

The dog's tail wagged. He headed across the deck toward a stairway, yanking the girl behind him. He trotted down the steps. At the bottom, he paused, head turning back and forth. He zigzagged around the parking lot, panting and snorting.

His demeanor had changed. Before, except for a couple of distractions, he'd seemed mostly confident in the trail. Now, confusion flustered him. He sniffed the air and the ground, circling and whining. Finally, he sat and stared at Jessica.

"What is it, Churro?" the girl asked. She frowned at Tillman, worry in her brown eyes. "Something's wrong. He's lost the scent."

He scanned the empty parking lot. "What if Tawny got in a car and it drove away? Could he still smell her?"

Jessica shook her head. "I don't think so."

Ice solidified through Tillman. Tawny had gotten into or been forced into a vehicle.

The trail ended here.

Chapter 21 – Tie-downs

Tawny's calves and feet cramped from the effort of inching the nylon straps down her legs. The strap finally went slack around her ankles. One foot at a time, she slipped free. She flexed and stretched her knees, trying to ease the pain from the arduous struggle.

Perspiration poured down her face, burning her eyes, but with bound arms, she couldn't wipe it away. She kicked aside a blanket that Wally had earlier covered her with. If he intended to kill her, why did he care if she was warm or cold? He'd given her water when she was thirsty. She hoped enough human instinct hid inside his hulking body to spare her life.

The straps binding her arms proved a tougher problem than her legs. Tight loops squeezed her elbows to her torso and held her wrists and hands fast to her hips. No matter how she tried to rearrange the loops—inhaling deeply to make her waist smaller, wiggling her elbows—she couldn't budge the stubborn strap.

Dwight used to have similar tie-downs to secure his four-wheeler to a trailer. They were rated at five thousand pounds breaking strength. No way to snap them.

The metal clamp that cinched down the straps worked like an airplane seatbelt. The buckle dug into her back. She tried to flip open the clamp but couldn't reach it with her numb hands.

She tugged hard on the strap looped through the wood grab rail, hoping to pull the rail out of the bulkhead. But the screws held fast.

Her tongue felt thick and dry. She craved the rest of the bottle of water Wally had left on the table but she couldn't reach it.

Was Wally alone on the boat? She'd only heard one set of footsteps above her. Where was the second phony deliveryman who'd grabbed her in the parking lot? She prayed he wasn't aboard, also. She might get lucky against one assailant but not two.

Lucky, hell. She'd need way more than luck.

Chapter 22 – Couldn't Hurt, Might Help

Tillman paced the suite. Ever since Churro lost Tawny's trail, a surreal nightmare had taken over his brain. His heart thudded with sledgehammer blows. In past months, he'd unwittingly put Tawny at risk while working on his cases but he hadn't learned about those dangers until after the fact, after she was safe. Guilt over the previous episodes already tormented him.

But, now, she was in jeopardy real-time. Rage, frustration, and helplessness built inside him, ready to explode.

Raul and Jessica sat at the dining table and ate the room service dinner Tillman had ordered. Churro lay under the table, hoping for dropped scraps.

No ransom demand yet. Why not?

Tillman tried Nyala's number again but it didn't answer.

He debated whether to call Gabriel. The longer the delay, the more time Tawny was in danger. Yet, the longer the delay, the more time he had to form a strategy.

So far, his strategy sucked.

He didn't have three million in cash. He could borrow against real estate and stocks but loans took time.

He always advised clients: *never pay a blackmailer or a ransom*. Yet, here he was, panicked enough to consider it.

Kidnapping guaranteed a life sentence for the abductors. Too often, they killed their victims so they couldn't testify.

Was Gabriel that rash? Tillman reviewed conversations with the man, his courtly manners and smiling green eyes that masked a ruthless calmness.

Yes, Gabriel was that rash.

Tillman's stomach twisted into harder knots.

His best P.I. back in Montana had put him in touch with a local private detective. Tillman had given the investigator every detail he'd scraped from the internet about Gabriel Marquez Garcia, Nyala Obregon, and Sports of Yesteryear. The P.I. was now contacting personal sources he knew, in search of a home address for Gabriel.

Tillman needed a hostage to exchange for Tawny.

Nyala.

Except he couldn't locate her on a boat at sea.

If the detective dug up a home address for Gabriel, Tillman would take Gabriel's wife and children instead.

Until Tawny was safe, the man's whole family was fair game. Consequences be damned.

His cell rang.

"*Señor* Rosenbaum?"

"Yeah. Who's this?"

"Manuel from the Sandspur Bar."

A possible lead. "What's happening, Manuel?"

"Me and my friend, we like the way you make *el jefe* kneel. That *maricón* is always threatening us with a knife but we can't do nothing. We need our jobs."

"Someday, someone's going to take that knife away and use it on him." Tillman had had to resist the temptation himself. "What do you know?"

"My friend says today there is a van outside the delivery door. But nobody brings nothing in. We know the regular guys. These aren't the regulars. He says these two just hang around and smoke by the door. This was happening about the time your lady left."

Tillman's pulse quickened. "Where were they parked?"

"In the lot that's at the bottom of the stairs from the outdoor bar."

The stairs the dog had led them down until he lost Tawny's scent in the parking lot. "What'd the van look like?"

"White Ford, maybe late nineties. No signs, no windows."

"What about the men?"

"I didn't see them but my friend, he says they are Anglos, gray uniforms and caps. One is kinda big, like a linebacker. My friend hardly noticed them except they didn't deliver anything." Manuel paused. "Is the lady OK?"

"No, those men dragged her into the van and took her." The words tasted bitter in Tillman's mouth.

"Shit. I'm sorry, man."

Tillman disconnected and called Nyala. No answer. He typed a text: *You will never sleep in peace again.*

Now that he'd verified how the kidnapping happened, he called Gabriel.

177

The smooth voice answered. "Mr. Rosenbaum. I thought I might hear from you."

"Your sister set Tawny up to be kidnapped. Nyala will go down with you. And you *will* go down."

"Mr. Rosenbaum, there's no need for such angry talk. The solution is simple. Deliver the Honus Wagner. Then you and Ms. Lindholm can enjoy the rest of your vacation."

"The card is gone. It went to the bottom of the swamp with Smoky."

"I wish I could believe you but I don't. Smoky trusted you. You are the logical one he'd give the card to."

"If it will convince you, you can do a body cavity search. I do not have the card. I never saw it. I didn't know of its existence until you told me."

"I need my property back, Mr. Rosenbaum."

Goddammit, the truth wasn't working. Tillman needed a different angle. "Your sister is not a criminal. I have to ask—what kind of brother would involve her in a felony that carries a life sentence? The only answer is, a brother with small *cojones*."

Gabriel chuckled. "Your insults against my manhood are desperate and pitiful. Call me when you're ready to deliver Honus." The connection broke.

Fury surged through Tillman. He flung his phone against the sofa cushions. It bounced back hard and dropped to the carpet. Fortunately, it didn't break.

He was losing it. He forced himself to resist the furnace blasting inside his gut. The device was his lifeline to find Tawny. He grabbed it off the floor.

From the table, Raul and Jessica watched him, their eyes wide and worried. "*Señor*," Raul said softly, "your steak is getting cold."

Tillman unclenched his fists and flicked his hand at the untouched plate. "Give it to Churro."

Surprise and a hint of joy replaced the concern on Jessica's face. "Really?"

For brief instant, the girl's expression gave pause to Tillman's frenzied strategizing. She reminded him of his own Arielle. Same gangling awkwardness, eagerness to help, and gutsiness. "Yeah, honey. He earned it."

While Churro wolfed his steak, Tillman stepped outside on the balcony overlooking the Gulf and pondered his next move.

Involving the police would waste precious time. They already harbored doubts about him. Before they'd take action, he'd first have to convince them to eliminate him as a suspect. As he massaged bruised knuckles, he had to admit that their concerns sounded valid.

Twin claws of guilt and regret returned to tear at him.

He'd dragged Tawny into Smoky's problems and now she might die. It was his fault.

He'd pressured her too hard about marriage. If he never saw her again, the last memory of them together would be a stupid fight.

Goddammit, he was an asshole.

A waning crescent moon shimmered on the rippling Gulf. The sight would have made Tawny's face light up.

Tillman hadn't prayed since he was a kid and only then out of respect for his Orthodox grandparents. *Bubbe* always believed Hashem had delivered her from the camps. Tillman went along with her but suspected, if he'd endured the torment that she had at Stutthoff, he would have become an avowed atheist.

Now, he wondered, if there was a God, would he listen to the prayer of a skeptical Jew, begging for the life of the woman he loved?

His grandfather, a practical, down-to-earth wheat farmer used to say, "Couldn't hurt, might help."

Tillman closed his eyes and lowered his head.

A text chirped on his cell. A message from the Florida P.I. read: *G's home*, followed by a St. Pete address.

Tillman raced back inside the suite to his laptop and called up Google Earth. The house was in the Venetian Isles neighborhood. Finger islands were interspersed through canals, connected by narrow roads to the mainland. The street view showed a stone-sided house with a white tile roof, a boat dock off the rear, and a swimming pool inside a screened enclosure.

By an astounding stroke of luck, the house was for sale. Three-point-two million.

He pulled up Zillow. The listing showed a dozen photos of the interior and floorplan, enough to familiarize himself with the layout. That knowledge enabled him to launch an attack on Gabriel's home.

Estimated travel time was an hour. By then, he would have formulated a plan to get inside.

Already, Tillman imagined the satisfying snap as he broke Gabriel's fingers, one by one, until the man screamed out where Tawny was.

Chapter 23 – Trolling for Sharks

At first, Tawny thought she imagined the burbling sound in the distance. But, as it drew closer, she became certain. Another boat was approaching.

At dusk, in international waters, it was too much to hope for the Coast Guard.

Gabriel?

She recalled the postal receipt and again wondered if Smoky had mailed the valuable baseball card to someone in Panama. If she told Gabriel that detail, he might let her go and follow that lead instead.

Maybe.

Except, by kidnapping her, Gabriel had already committed to a course that led straight to prison. Could Tawny convince him to trade her life for a vague chance of recovering Honus Wagner?

The slapping of water grew louder and the boat rocked from increased wake. Several bumps jarred as the two yachts glanced off each other. She heard male voices. The boat dipped—someone climbing aboard. Then, a female voice.

Nyala.

What the hell?

Tawny quickly kicked the blanket over herself to hide that the tie-downs no longer bound her legs. With her arms and hands useless, her feet were her only weapons. She drew her knees up taut and tightened her quadriceps.

The hatch opened and a light clicked on inside the dark cabin. Tawny squinted as her eyes adjusted to the brightness.

Nyala descended the ladder. She pulled the hatch closed then faced Tawny. "Are you all right?"

Tawny didn't answer.

The woman approached the bunk, looking down at Tawny. Her voice was low, urgent. "There isn't much time. Don't talk."

Come a little bit closer.

When Nyala leaned down to pull the blanket aside, Tawny kicked as hard as she could. Both feet caught the woman in the stomach, knocking the wind out of her. She staggered back into the dinette table. Her arms crossed defensively over her middle and she gasped for several seconds. When she caught her breath, she stared daggers at Tawny.

"That was foolish," Nyala hissed. "I'm here to help you."

What? "You set me up," Tawny retorted.

"You can listen to me and let me help you or you can go overboard. Your choice."

Tawny's brain scrambled to change gears. Why was Nyala on the boat? Was she really trying to help?

Without any better options, Tawny had to take the chance. "All right."

Nyala moved closer but with caution. "Don't kick me again. I'm going to untie you." She reached behind Tawny's back and flicked open the metal latch. The strap slackened and fell loose.

Blood rushed into Tawny's numb arms and hands in excruciating, pin-prickling relief. She shoved the tie-downs aside and flexed her elbows and wrists. "What is going on, Nyala?"

The woman sat on the bunk beside Tawny. "I did *not* set you up. Gabriel just asked me to question you to see if you knew where the baseball card was. I didn't know he was going to pull a stupid stunt like kidnapping. I won't be involved in a crime, even for my brother."

"How did you get here?"

"I told you I had a date with a friend on his boat. Ezekiel used to play for the Tampa Bay Buccaneers. So did Wally. They're old teammates. My brother told me you were on Wally's yacht. I convinced Ezekiel we needed to rendezvous for a visit. But he doesn't know anything about what Wally's doing or that you're on board.

"While Ezekiel was busy tying the boats together, I told Wally that my brother sent me to talk to you. He thinks I'm acting for his boss, Gabriel, and he's not going to get in my way."

Tawny's head spun with confusion. "Are you taking me with you?"

Nyala's eyes narrowed. "If you want my help, there are two conditions."

"What?"

"Ezekiel is a man of God. He runs a sports ministry for kids on probation. He won't be involved in anything illegal. He knows my brother and wants no connection with him. Ezekiel can't find out that Gabriel's people kidnapped you. If he knew, he'd go straight to the Coast Guard and my brother would be arrested."

Tawny wanted to say *as he should* but bit her tongue. "What else?"

"Second, Gabriel is a greedy fool. But he *is* my brother, the only family I have left. If he learns I acted against him, it's over." For the first time, Nyala's calm demeanor cracked. Her chin quivered. "He can never know I helped you. *Never*."

Tawny's thoughts tangled, trying to sort out the complicated double play Nyala proposed. Neither her friend nor her brother could know what she was *really* doing. Apparently Nyala wanted to prevent Gabriel from killing Tawny. Yet Nyala also wanted to protect him from the consequences of kidnapping.

It sounded crazy but Tawny had no choice. "OK, how do we do this?"

"I'm going to distract Wally and Ezekiel at the bow of the boat. You'll slip out and over the stern. Ezekiel's boat has a dive platform. You'll hold onto that and stay down in the water, out of sight, and we'll go back to shore."

Fear clenched Tawny's throat. "You mean, tow me behind the boat? The propeller will chop me to pieces."

"It's an inboard motor. You won't be near the prop."

Tawny shook her head. "It's still insane. Wally said we're past the twelve-mile limit."

"You don't have a choice. If your fiancé doesn't deliver the baseball card to Gabriel—and we know he can't—Wally will throw you overboard."

"When Wally finds out I'm gone, he'll tell your brother you helped me."

Nyala tossed her hair. "Wally's a drunk. I brought him a gift, a bottle of Captain Morgan, spiked with roofies. He'll pass out and never know what happened."

Tawny recalled the smell of rum on Wally's breath. That small part of Nyala's plan might work but the rest was suicide. "I can't hold onto a speeding boat that long."

"Fine. Just choose another of your many alternatives." Nyala rose from the bunk and started for the ladder.

"Wait!" Tawny stood on wobbly legs and steadied herself on the dinette. "Why can't I just get on Ezekiel's boat after Wally passes out?"

Nyala whirled, anger flashing in her green eyes. "I *told* you—Ezekiel can't know anything about this." She gripped Tawny's aching forearms. "Take it or leave it. This is your only chance."

The options terrified Tawny: she could die for sure at Wally's hands or she could likely die from drowning. Guaranteed death or near-guaranteed death. "All right."

"'All right' isn't good enough. Do you believe in God?"

What was Nyala getting at? "Yes."

Nyala grasped Tawny's face between her hands and peered deep into her eyes. "You have to swear to your God that you won't tell Ezekiel anything."

She was Tawny's only chance. "I swear."

Nyala held her face for a few more seconds, driving home the promise. Then she released her. "I'll throw a life jacket to you. That will keep you afloat." She picked up the strap. "Use this to tie yourself to the diving platform. I'll ask Ezekiel to go slowly, tell him I'm feeling queasy."

Tawny rubbed hands up and down her sore arms, trying to revive feeling. After being bound for hours, they were weak, flabby noodles. No way could she survive Nyala's insane plan.

Tillman.

She couldn't die with an argument as their last moment together.

"Nyala, if I don't make it, you have to do something for me. I need to write a note."

The woman shuffled through drawers until she found a slip of paper and a pencil. "Hurry."

Tawny gripped the pencil. These might be the last words she'd ever say to Tillman. They had to be right.

She tried to print carefully but her still-numb hand trembled too badly.

I love you, Tillman. Here & now. That's all that matters. No more excuses from me. Forever yours, Tawny.

Without her readers, the words looked blurred. She prayed he could read them.

"I need to go, now," Nyala urged.

Tawny folded the paper and handed it to her. "Please, if I die, give this to Tillman."

She was surprised to recognize empathy in Nyala's green eyes. The cool, impassive woman loved someone, too, as much as Tawny loved Tillman. A flicker of understanding passed between them.

Nyala slipped the note into her cleavage. "I'm going to distract them. As soon as you hear us talking on the bow, go over the side. Stay down."

Tawny looped the nylon straps around her torso. They had been her shackles but were now her lifeline.

Nyala turned out the light and climbed the ladder. "Guys," she called, "Ezekiel has a great idea about getting the old team together for a reunion. Wally, how long has it been since you've seen…" Her voice grew muffled as she moved forward.

Tawny waited a few seconds for the men's voices to join in, as her eyes adjusted to the darkness. She ascended the ladder and peeked out of the hatch that Nyala had left open. A tall flying bridge blocked Tawny's view of the bow but would also block their view of her. She crouched low and tiptoed across the rear deck. She climbed over the railing and down a ladder into the sea.

Unlike glacial Montana lakes, hypothermia wouldn't kill her in the tepid gulf water. Still, after being constantly overheated since she'd been in Florida, the shock made her suck in a breath. She swam several yards to the stern of the adjacent boat, a thirty-foot cabin cruiser a little smaller than Wally's. She looped the strap a couple of times around her waist then wove it through the metal handrail on the dive platform and locked the clamp down.

Crap, she'd never even been water skiing or wakeboarding. She wasn't that good a swimmer. Soon, she'd be dragged behind a boat, trolling for sharks. The only person who knew she was there refused to tell anyone.

The voices from Wally's yacht sounded closer now, but only those of Nyala and Ezekiel. No more from Wally. Tawny hoped he was well on his way to being too drugged to notice her disappearance. She ducked lower, eyes and nose barely out of the water. Her ears filled, muffling all sound except a gurgle around her head.

The boats were tied together with two lines, one fore, one aft. White vinyl fenders hung over the sides to cushion the hulls from banging together, leaving a gap of about eighteen inches. Ezekiel stepped across the space first, causing his boat to sink low. In the darkness, Tawny made out his hulking form, bigger than Wally, not as tall as Tillman but much bulkier. Might have once played offensive lineman. The red starboard running light illuminated the nearly-black skin of his shaved head.

He stretched arms across the gap toward Nyala. She grasped his hands and daintily crossed over. The boat dipped much less under her weight than Ezekiel's. He entered the cockpit and started the engine while Nyala pulled in the fenders.

Her head barely out of the water, Tawny saw the woman quickly glance over her shoulder to make certain Ezekiel wasn't watching. Then she dropped a life jacket off the stern.

Tawny grabbed it and put it on, fastening the plastic clips. It looked light-duty, too flimsy to prevent her from drowning as the boat rolled through the waves.

She ducked out of sight as Ezekiel leaned over the side and untied the two lines securing the boats together. He coiled them neatly and set them on the deck.

Tawny's salvation was simple: open her mouth and call to him for help. Ezekiel would take her onboard, wrap her in a blanket, and head for shore, while summoning the cops to arrest Wally and Gabriel. She'd be safe and the kidnappers would be punished.

But...she'd promised Nyala.

She'd given her word, sworn to God.

But that insane promise was going to kill her.

Dammit, no. She had to live.

She pulled herself onto the diving platform and gripped the handrails of the ladder to climb into the boat and safety. She made it up the first two rungs but the tie-down around her torso caught. With still-shaky hands, she fumbled to release the lock but couldn't see in the dark.

"No! Get out of sight!" Nyala appeared, bending over the stern, head jerking back and forth, watching Tawny then checking to see where Ezekiel was.

Tawny stepped up another rung. "Nyala, I'm not going to die to protect your reputation with your boyfriend."

"You swore," Nyala hissed. She looked toward where Ezekiel had settled in the captain's chair and was adjusting controls. Her mouth twisted as she again faced Tawny. With both hands, she shoved Tawny backwards.

Tawny's butt hit the diving platform. At the same instant, the engine roared and the boat leapt forward.

She lunged to grab the handrail of the metal ladder. As the speed rose, the boat jumped over waves while Tawny bounced on the hard fiberglass platform.

She desperately held onto the rail with both hands. The hammering continued, jouncing her up and down, side to side, like being tumbled in a manic clothes dryer. Her hands were still numb, her grip slipping. Only the tie-down strap that looped through the ladder kept her from falling to drown in the frothing wake.

Pain exploded as her elbow cracked on the unforgiving fiberglass platform. Then her knee, her shoulder, her tailbone. Each blow knocked the wind out of her. She struggled to catch a breath. At any moment, her bones could shatter like dry sticks. The bucking of the boat was slowly beating her to death.

If she released the clamp, she'd be free—free from the relentless agony, free to breathe without the air being slammed out of her lungs.

Free to flounder alone, left behind in deep water until she drowned or was attacked by a shark.

She had to hang on. She looped her elbow around the ladder.

All sense of time and place disappeared, only the slamming of her spine and shoulders into the diving platform.

The faces of her children, Neal and Emma, drifted through a gray fog of pain. Then Tillman's children, Mimi, Arielle, and Judah. They weren't blood but they were as dear as the two she'd given birth to.

She had to survive.

For their children.

For Tillman.

No, she couldn't die.

Just hold on. Just breathe.

Her fuzzy mind chanted, naming each inhalation. *Neal. Emma. Mimi. Arielle. Judah. Tillman.*

She didn't know how many times she repeated the refrain. A hundred? A thousand? Her strength ebbed, beaten out of her by the pummeling.

The boat jumped an extra-large wave. Her head cracked hard against the stern. Stars exploded in her vision. Her grip on the ladder rail slipped, her hands grasping nothing.

The ladder was gone and the platform, too.

She was down in the water, being dragged, the nylon strap now a tow rope. She extended one arm, reaching for it. Her shoulder wrenched with new pain.

Waves of dizziness crested over her.

Keep your head up. Hold onto the strap.

But she couldn't feel her hands anymore. Was she holding on?

A black curtain closed down on her vision, suffocating her thoughts. It wrapped around her, dragging her down.

Down into a long darkness.

Chapter 24 – Exit Strategy

While Raul, Jessica, and Churro finished dinner, Tillman hurriedly changed in the bedroom. Navy-colored sweats were the only dark clothes in his roller bag. He hadn't packed with the expectation of needing camouflage to sneak up on a kidnapper's home. He tucked Smoky's little pistol in the pants pocket. Pitiful but better than nothing.

He hustled Raul, Jessica, and the dog out of the suite, down the elevator, and out to the parking lot. No explanations—he didn't want to implicate them in what he was about to do.

He didn't wait for the parking valet, nor did he want to be remembered, should the police later ask questions. His size made him instantly recognizable in security video but that couldn't be helped.

When they reached Raul's work truck, Tillman barked, "Get in the cab, Jessica."

She jumped, as if he'd raised his fist to her. The dog emitted a warning growl.

Raul looked sideways at him but gave a single nod. "*Ahora*," he said to his daughter. Now.

She clutched Churro's collar and stared up at Tillman, eyes unwavering even though he'd scared her. "Please find Tawny," she murmured. She motioned for the dog to jump up in the cab then clambered in beside him and slammed the door.

Regret stabbed Tillman but he didn't have time to apologize to her. He turned to Raul. "Got tools I can borrow?"

Without hesitation, the man unlocked a side compartment in the truck bed. He understood what Tillman was up to but said nothing.

Tillman rattled through the tool box and grabbed a screwdriver, diagonal cutters, and pliers. With them, he could jimmy a lock, cut electrical wires, and, if need be, convince Gabriel that he'd be better off releasing Tawny than losing his ear or nose.

"*Gracias, amigo*," Tillman called over his shoulder as he ran to the rental truck.

"*Buena suerte, señor*." Good luck.

Right.

Tillman tossed the tools on the passenger seat. The turbocharged engine roared to life. Under the pressure of his heavy foot on the accelerator, the truck lurched forward and sped toward the exit, black exhaust spewing out the rear.

He entered Gabriel's home address in the truck's GPS and raced toward Highway 60, watching the rearview mirror for cops.

***

Violent choking spasms brought Tawny back to consciousness. Her lungs burned as she gagged, hacked, and threw up seawater.

At last, the choking subsided. But when she gulped in a deep breath, that triggered another coughing frenzy so violent she feared she would black out again. Finally, it eased enough that she dared to inhale—shallow, cautious, slow. She gripped the edge of the diving platform and pulled her torso up onto it, legs still dangling in the water.

Arrows of pain shot through her head. Fingertips found a painful knot swelling under her hair.

Then she realized the boat had stopped. The motor now barely burbled, at idle, coasting. Foamy bubbles dissipated around her.

Her foggy thoughts slowly cleared. She'd fallen from the diving platform into the sea. The nylon tie-down still tethered her to the metal ladder. If the boat had continued at speed, with her unconscious, she would have drowned.

The vicious pounding on her body had stopped but nausea churned in her stomach. Another coughing fit seized her. Pain from her ribs exploded inside her body.

After a moment, she again risked shallow breaths. They gave her enough strength to haul herself the rest of the way onto the diving platform. She released the tie-down clamp and the strap fell free. The tender skin under her breasts burned, rubbed raw by the nylon.

Water muffled her hearing. She tipped her head sideways. Wicked spinning overtook her. She vomited as water drizzled out of her ears. When the worst dizziness had passed, she took a couple more breaths, and gripped the hand rail to pull herself to a standing position. She could barely peek over the stern but lacked the strength to climb up the four rungs of the ladder into the boat.

In the distance, a soft glow of lights marked the horizon. Tawny wondered how far from land they were. Overhead, a waning crescent mood shone down on the ripples. Stars sparkled in the black sky. The engine shut down, leaving only the soft lapping of waves against the hull.

On the mast, a white mooring light shone over the yacht. She could see Ezekiel and Nyala, standing in the cockpit, embracing.

"I love spending the night at sea," Nyala purred.

"Oh, yeah, baby."

"How far out are we?"

"At least five miles. No one's going to bother us."

"They better not." She pulled him forward to the bow and down onto the cushioned seats.

Tawny's stomach clenched in a cramp, causing a sudden inhale that triggered more choking.

"What's that noise?" Ezekiel's voice.

"Just a sea lion, baby. Come back down and give me some sugar."

Coughing spasms gripped Tawny. She doubled over and vomited seawater.

"Who's there?" The boat rocked as Ezekiel moved side to side, peering over the gunwales, heading toward the stern.

"Help," Tawny gasped.

Ezekiel shone a flashlight over the side, blinding Tawny. She held up a hand to block the glare. "Help me, please."

"Sweet Jesus in heaven, lady! What are you doing down there?" He grasped under her arms, yanked her up and onto the deck in one smooth movement, as if she weighed less than a toddler. Gently, he set her down on a padded seat.

Coughs contorted her body as she gagged up more water. He thumped her back.

At last, the choking spasms subsided. She panted, catching a few almost-normal breaths.

Ezekiel squatted before her, his huge hand resting on her shoulder. He had a wide mouth with lots of teeth that made him look as if he was always smiling. "Lady, what happened to you?"

Tawny wanted to sob with gratitude but resisted, afraid of triggering another coughing frenzy.

Nyala stood beside him, staring down at Tawny, concern in her eyes. "Did you fall overboard, dear? Those party boats—someone's always falling off and everybody's so drunk no one notices. Is that what happened to you?"

She was feeding Tawny a script. This woman had nearly killed her yet coolly invented an instant excuse to cover her deception.

Tawny wanted to tell Nyala to go screw herself but couldn't muster the strength. Uncontrollable shivers came over her.

"Babe, get her a blanket," Nyala said. "And she needs oxygen, too. Bring a dive tank."

Ezekiel straightened and hurried forward to the bow. Hatches banged as he pulled supplies from storage compartments.

Nyala bent low to Tawny's ear. "Go along with me. Don't talk."

"Call Tillman," Tawny croaked.

Nyala nodded.

Ezekiel returned, carrying a blanket and a scuba tank. He wrapped the blanket around Tawny's shoulders. "OK, don't you worry now. Nyala here is a nurse. She knows what to do."

Yeah, right, Tawny thought as the woman fitted the mask over Tawny's face.

After several minutes of breathing, she felt revived with new strength.

She was finished with this charade. From now on, Nyala had to cover her own ass. Tawny pulled the mask off and opened her mouth to tell Ezekiel the truth, to beg him to take her to a hospital, to Tillman. "I need help—"

Nyala cried, "Please, don't..." Her eyes widened, full of panic.

Ezekiel frowned at Nyala then looked back at Tawny. "What's the matter, lady?"

A single tear rolled down Nyala's cheek. Her lip quivered.

Tawny flashed back on the brief connection that had passed between them when she'd given Nyala the note for Tillman. The meaning of that moment now became clear.

Ezekiel was the man Nyala loved.

If he learned the role she'd played in Tawny's near drowning, he would find out about Nyala's deception. And she would lose his love.

Tawny sagged back against the cushions, overcome with weakness that gave Nyala an undeserved reprieve. The truth would all come out soon enough anyway.

She swallowed hard. "Another blanket, please."

"Sure." Ezekiel hurried forward.

Nyala clasped Tawny's hands. "Thank you," she whispered.

***

Ezekiel helped Tawny below decks to a cabin with a bed. Nyala followed with the scuba tank and sat beside her on the edge of the bunk, holding the mask against Tawny's face.

Ezekiel returned to the cockpit. The engine roared to life and the boat lurched forward at high speed.

The supplemental oxygen had helped but the bouncing yacht jarred Tawny as it skipped through waves, reminding her of the punishment on the dive platform. Every fiber of her body hurt.

"I'm sorry," Nyala said. "I should never have pushed you. I panicked when Ezekiel almost saw you." She swallowed hard. "Afterwards, all I could think of was you being dragged back there, maybe drowning. Then I couldn't stand it any longer. I suggested sex to make him stop the boat. I didn't know if you'd be dead or alive. When I heard you coughing, I thanked Jesus."

Tawny pushed the mask away and licked her salt-caked lips. Through the throbbing in her head, anger swelled for the hell Nyala had put her through. She wanted to say: *If my dead body was dangling off the boat, how would you explain that to Ezekiel and your brother?* But she didn't have the energy.

"Call Tillman," she gasped again.

Nyala scanned the horizon through a porthole. "We might be close enough to land now to catch a signal." She took out her cell and tapped.

Even with the background thrum of the engine, Tawny heard Tillman's roar over the phone's speaker. "Nyala, where the hell is Tawny?"

"She's with me. She's all right. We're on a boat heading for shore." She named a marina.

"Put Tawny on, now."

Nyala handed the phone over.

Tawny grasped it with trembling fingers and croaked, "Tillman."

"Tawny...Tawny," he gasped. "Are you in danger now?"

Tears ran down her face at hearing his voice. "I'm OK." Another coughing fit took hold. When it ended, she said, "Can't talk much."

"Answer yes or no. Can Nyala harm you?"

With Ezekiel nearby, Nyala wouldn't try anything. "No."

"You're really safe?"

Tawny studied the woman who'd nearly drowned her. The normally calm green eyes now brimmed with regret, her mouth pinched in worry.

"I'm OK."

"I'll be there in twenty minutes." Then rage returned to his tone. "Put Nyala back on."

Tawny handed her the phone, closed her salt-burned eyes, and lay back on the bunk. In the background, she heard Tillman questioning Nyala about what had happened.

"I'll tell you when we get to the marina. It's complicated."

What possible spin could the smooth, unflappable Nyala dream up to justify her action? No excuse would matter once Tillman learned the truth.

Then Tawny realized their conversation had ended. She opened her eyes to catch Nyala quickly tapping a text.

To Gabriel? Was she luring Tillman into an ambush?

Tawny grabbed the phone from the woman. Too late. The text had already been sent. The screen read: *Exit strategy. NOW.* "What does this mean?"

Nyala pressed her lips together. "I told my brother to get out of town immediately."

"Tillman's already sent the police after him."

"A man in my brother's business is always prepared at a moment's notice."

Tawny tried to shift to a position that didn't hurt. Whether sitting or lying down, each bounce of the boat was agony. She was in too much pain to care anymore what happened to Gabriel, his henchmen, or his sister. She only wanted Tillman. Nothing else mattered. She curled on her side.

Nyala adjusted the blanket around Tawny. She remaining sitting on the bunk, hands folded neatly in her lap. What rationalizations twisted in the lovely woman's brain, what explanations would she offer the cops, if any? She seemed like someone who knew enough to exercise her right to remain silent.

Tawny turned away from her and closed her eyes.

Maybe ten minutes later, the engine throttled back. Through the porthole, she saw the dock lights of the marina. She raised up on one painful elbow for a better look. On the shoreline, wrecked boats lay jumbled in bunches. Many finger piers had been splintered by Irma. Floating boards still littered the bay.

Ezekiel maneuvered the boat into an undamaged slip, shut down the engine, and tied lines to cleats on the dock. Then he came below to the cabin. Together with Nyala, he helped Tawny up to the deck.

When her legs went liquid, Ezekiel caught her. His arms felt as warm and safe as a loving father's. He gently carried her as he stepped from the boat onto the pier.

High beams flashed across the dock, catching her attention. In the marina parking lot, a vehicle skidded to a stop. Tillman leapt out. He ran down the ramp, each footfall shaking the pier like an earthquake. Overhead flood lights showed panic in his dark eyes. He grabbed her away from Ezekiel.

His fierce grasp around her bruised body hurt but that didn't matter. Nothing mattered except that he was with her.

His hand cradled the back of her head. She winced when he touched the knot. His fingers ran lightly over the lump, examining it. "What happened? Jesus Christ, I thought you were dead."

A sob started her harsh, hacking cough again. More water rose from her stomach, a disgusting mixture of salt and bile. He steadied her as she spat on the wood planks.

Nyala had followed and now stood beside Ezekiel, watching.

Tillman shouted, "What the hell happened to her? She's soaking wet and sick."

Nyala spoke calmly. "Hypothermia and she swallowed some salt water."

"Where's the nearest hospital?"

"Morton Plant. Take Sixty east. You'll see it."

Tillman half-walked, half-carried Tawny up the ramp to the parking lot. He lifted her into the truck then studied her again under the dome light. "They did this to you?"

"Yes. No." It was too hard to explain.

"The cops are on the way. They'll arrest them."

"No." She coughed. "Not Ezekiel. He helped me. He's innocent."

"They'll sort it out." Tillman's mouth looked as if he were chewing gristle. He closed the passenger door, got in the driver's side, and started the engine with a roar. He tore out of the parking lot onto a street, swerving to pass slower cars.

Tawny struggled for words. "Two thugs grabbed me, threw me in a van." The effort started another strangling spell.

"Don't talk. This can wait."

"No. It's important." She had to put together a coherent account, make him understand. "I was on a boat...not that one, a different one. Belongs to Gabriel's thug, Wally." She paused. "If Gabriel didn't get Honus, Wally was going to throw me overboard."

Tillman grunted as if bayonetted and grasped her hand tightly.

In short, breathy sentences, Tawny explained the complex double play Nyala had concocted, deceiving both her friend, Ezekiel, and her brother, to cover Tawny's escape. A plan that had nearly drowned her when Nyala shoved her over the side.

"Motherfucker!" The truck swerved, almost jumping a curb. Tillman quickly corrected, straightening the wheel. "She's going down, along with her goddamned brother."

"Too late." Tawny sighed. "She texted him to disappear."

Tillman shook his head. "The FBI will find him. Gabriel can't hide forever. He's wealthy but he won't walk away from his family and his three-million-dollar house."

"How do you know?"

He veered into the emergency room portico, stomped the brakes, and faced her. "I tracked down a home address for Gabriel. When Nyala called, I was on my way there." For an instant, his dark eyes showed a window into hell. "She saved her brother from a much uglier fate than the criminal justice system."

Chapter 25 – Binding Contract

During four hours in the ER, Tawny underwent a battery of tests. The CT scan showed a concussion but no intercranial bleeding. Amazingly, X-rays didn't turn up any broken bones but massive contusions covered her body. The doctor warned of the possibility of pulmonary edema or pneumonia and released her with strict instructions to Tillman to bring her back immediately if her symptoms worsened or she showed signs of a brain bleed.

Tillman drove them to the hotel suite, bathed her in the whirlpool tub, and put her to bed. She fell asleep in a haze of pain medicine, her head pillowed on his thigh, comforted by his soothing strokes on her forehead.

The next day, her back and butt were mottled with magenta, blue, and purple bruises. The tie-down strap had left raw, chafed abrasions around her ribs and under her breasts. Her shoulders felt as if they had been dislocated multiple times. But she was able to breathe better.

In the suite, police detectives and FBI agents took Tawny's statement under Tillman's hawk-like supervision. When she struggled for breath, he stopped the questioning and enforced frequent rest breaks.

The FBI had raided Gabriel's home but he'd disappeared. His wife claimed she didn't know where he was. Nyala was in custody and being interrogated. Ezekiel was temporarily detained but released after Tawny insisted that he was innocent of any wrongdoing and had saved her life. Search aircraft spotted Wally's yacht adrift in the Gulf and the Coast Guard was on the way.

***

After three days of rest in the hotel suite, Tawny awoke to morning light, at last feeling stronger. She emerged from the bedroom to find Tillman working at the living room desk, paging through a thick sheaf of papers. A rolling cart held the remains of breakfast and a carafe of coffee.

She padded barefoot across the carpet to his chair.

Tillman looked up over his half glasses and gently looped an arm around her waist, careful to avoid the worst bruises and scrapes. "How are you feeling?"

"Almost human. Muscles still pretty sore."

"Want the masseuse to come up again?"

She smiled. "I could get used to these daily massages."

He lifted her t-shirt and kissed her belly. "Three times a day if you want."

She sat on his lap and nestled her head in the warm crook of his neck.

He rocked her gently, his cheek against her forehead. "I cancelled the plane tickets and told Esther to get continuances. We're staying here until you're up to flying."

She peered at the papers. "Whatcha doin' with this stuff?"

"The attorney in St. Pete messengered these over. It's Smoky's estate work. The statement of death without recovery of a body."

"Lots of pages."

"Yeah."

"Want me to help?"

He frowned. "You need rest."

She unwound from his arms, rose, and went to the table where she poured thick, black Cuban coffee. The rich, sweet brew promised a quick caffeine jolt. "As soon as this wakes me up, I'm ready to work."

"You don't have to."

She sipped coffee. "I know. But it'll feel good to do something normal, for a change." She fetched extra readers from her roller bag and carried the cup to the desk. She leaned into his shoulder. "Come on, give me part of the pile."

He studied her for several seconds, shook his head in resignation, and handed over a stack of papers. "Make sure everything appears complete, the DNA report, the inventory of recovered evidence."

She sat in a nearby chair, enjoyed the coffee, and scanned inventory pages.

Material, 100% cotton measuring approximately 15 centimeters by approximately 33 centimeters, color pink with orange hibiscus pattern. Blood stains consistent with known DNA from subject.

Tooled leather billfold, color brown, containing Florida driver's license, Florida saltwater fishing license, $37 in cash.

Remains of a damaged partial tibia and fibula of the right leg, approximately 28 centimeters long, with partial ankle bone. DNA consistent with known samples from subject.

One below-the-knee prosthesis with attached right foot, serial number...

She stared at the words. Something sounded wrong. She reread the page several times.

"Tillman, which side was Smoky's prosthesis?"

"Right."

"That means he lost his *right* leg in the accident three years ago on the boat."

"Yeah?"

"Shouldn't these recovered bones be his *left* leg? It says here the ones Churro found are the right leg."

Tillman leaned toward her and peered at the report. "What?"

"If his right leg was amputated three years before he disappeared," she murmured, "how can that be?"

Tillman's voice rumbled low. "Jesus Christ."

They stared at each other, frowning.

"That night before he went missing," Tawny said, "he told me this crazy story about losing his leg. Said some butcher from Argentina amputated it. Claimed the guy was so drunk, he thought if he saved the leg, it could be reattached. He wrapped it in plastic and threw it in the hold with the frozen fish. I though Smoky was bullshitting me. But...what if he *kept* the leg?"

Tillman's mouth pulled to the side. "Pretty whacked if that was his idea of a memento."

Tawny's mind sped ahead. "With his gambling problem, maybe he figured someday he'd need to fake his own death." Her pulse fluttered with excitement. "Tillman, he didn't lock the Honus Wagner card in his freezer. It was his *leg*. That's why he was so peculiar about us looking inside."

"Tawny, you know what this means?"

Her breath caught. "Maybe he's not dead?"

Tillman's cell rang. He picked it up and frowned, showing Tawny the screen. *Nyala*. He tapped the speaker button. "Ms. Nyala."

"Mr. Rosenbaum, I have something for you. Would it be possible for you and Tawny to come to my condo this morning?"

Tillman raised an eyebrow at Tawny. "I'm surprised you're not in custody."

A long pause. Finally, she said, "I retain excellent counsel, Mr. Rosenbaum. Almost as good as you. Now, will you come?"

"What do you have?"

"I prefer not to discuss it on the phone."

He mouthed to Tawny: *You OK to go?*

She nodded.

He answered, "We'll be there in about an hour."

"Thank you." She disconnected.

"What's that all about?" Tawny asked.

"Damned if I know. She ought to be in jail unless she's cut a deal to testify against her brother." He sprang to his feet and paced the living room, seething all over again. "I can't believe she has the balls to call me. She must know I'm ready to kill her because she almost drowned you." During the past three days, he'd alternated between unbelievable tenderness while caring for her to epithet-filled rages at Gabriel and Nyala.

On his next agitated pass, Tawny caught his hand. "I agree. It was a crazy risk. But if she hadn't come for me, I *would* be dead, for sure."

He dropped to his knees beside her chair. For the first time since her brush with death, his depthless eyes filled. She pulled him close. His breath huffed in her ear, coming in husky sobs as his tears ran down her cheek and dampened her t-shirt.

***

Inside Nyala's condo, Tawny and Tillman sat on a wicker couch with lime green and turquoise cushions that was a twin to the one in Smoky's house. Tawny wondered if she'd gotten a buy-one-get-one-free deal, furnishing both homes at the same time.

Nyala wore a yellow pareo and sat opposite them on the matching chair. Her bare legs peeked through the split in the dress. A house arrest monitor was fastened around one ankle.

Tillman noticed it, too, and exchanged a silent message with Tawny: *that's why she's not in jail.*

Tawny's bag had disappeared when she was abducted but now it sat on the glass top of the wicker coffee table, along with a small, padded envelope.

"I recovered your purse when I came aboard Wally's boat," Nyala said, with a glance at Tawny. "You know how men are. They can't tell one woman's purse from another. Neither Wally nor Ezekiel even noticed when I took it. They both thought it was mine." She pushed the bag closer to Tawny. "Your ID, money, credit cards are all there. I wanted to spare you the nuisance of having to redo that."

Tillman's eyes narrowed. "No, what you're saying is you took it to remove evidence of the crime you perpetrated against Tawny."

Nyala said nothing for a long moment. At last, she lifted her chin high. "What people think of me doesn't matter. But I did want to keep Ezekiel's good opinion. Unfortunately, when the police and FBI questioned him, he learned what my brother is accused of and the part I played." She folded her hands and stared down at her graceful fingers. "He's a fine man. I regret he was dragged into this." Wistful sadness flickered in her green eyes. "I had hopes…for a future."

The elegant woman's duplicity, while trying to protect her brother, had cost her the man she loved and probably her freedom.

Tillman didn't care. He leaned forward, his tone harsh and commanding. "Where's Gabriel?"

Nyala swallowed, a movement that appeared painful. "I'm sure he's left the country. I don't know if I'll ever see my brother again."

"Not our problem," Tillman growled. "He should be in prison."

She pressed her lips together. "I know what he is. But he is my brother." Her reserved façade returned. "Wally's boat was found adrift yesterday with several empty liquor bottles. He was not on it. The Coast Guard suspects he was drunk, fell overboard, and drowned."

Tillman's muscles tightened against Tawny's arm. "He deserves his fate," he said.

Nyala's wordless gaze flicked between them.

All three of them knew Wally's disappearance was no accident and that Nyala was ultimately responsible.

She picked up the envelope from the coffee table.

"That wouldn't be the Honus Wagner card, would it?" Tillman asked.

She shook her head, opened the flap, and tipped out a small package wrapped in tissue paper. She handed it to Tawny. "I believe this is meant for you."

Puzzled, Tawny unwrapped the tissue. Inside was a single emerald stud earring. She gasped. "Smoky's?"

Nyala removed a folded paper from the envelope and offered it.

Tawny and Tillman put on their glasses and read the scrawled handwriting.

Tell Tillman to have this set in a nice ring with diamonds around it. He can afford it. Green looks good with your red hair. Sorry to miss the wedding.

Tawny clasped the emerald in her hand. "Is he alive?"

"Yes," Nyala answered.

Tillman's voice reverberated low. "You knew all along."

She nodded. "He called the night Irma hit and asked me to pick him up. He'd already planted most of the evidence by then. He'd cut his boat loose in the channel to blow free, threw his extra prosthetic out into the jungle, and left his wallet and shirt in the lake."

"The leg?" Tawny asked.

Nyala's smile was tight, grim. "He'd saved his amputated leg. The reason he called me three years ago to bring him back from Panama was because he figured, as a flight attendant, I'd know how to handle it so it wouldn't be inspected." She shuddered. "It was repulsive but I helped him. He called it his insurance policy. He knew someday he'd need to stage his death."

"He kept it in his freezer?" Tawny said.

Another shudder. "He'd offer to cook dinner for me but, knowing about it, I could never stand to eat there. We always went out."

Tillman frowned. "Why did he steal the Honus Wagner *now*?"

Nyala sighed. "Ten years ago, he was married to a nurse in Panama. When she divorced him, she didn't tell him she was pregnant. After his accident, he got himself admitted to the hospital where she worked, hoping she'd give him another chance. She refused but she let it slip about his daughter."

Tawny remembered her conversation with Smoky, his regret that he didn't even know the little girl's name or her birthday.

Nyala went on: "He said his ex-wife was proud and stubborn, damned if she'd take a penny from him. Six weeks ago, she died from ovarian cancer. The girl's grandparents reached out to him. They will care for the child but they need money. The only way he could provide for her was to steal the baseball card. He mailed it to them in Panama."

Tillman grasped Tawny's knee. "That postal tracking number you found."

Nyala continued: "Smoky knew he'd have to disappear or my brother would kill him. The hurricane was his opportunity. When he called, I picked him up and hid him out here until he could scrounge passage out of the country."

"The day we came to see you," Tillman said, "he was here?"

"Yes."

Tillman shot to his feet, fists pounding his thighs. "That motherfucker put us through all this grief, letting us think he was dead. Goddamn him!" He paced the small living room, covering the length in two steps.

Tawny caught his hand on the return. "Tillman," she said softly, "we need to hear the rest."

Bringing his fury under control, he again sat beside her, letting her cradle his tense hand between both of hers.

Nyala remained calm in the face of his explosion and rubbed her calf, as if the ankle bracelet was chafing. "Smoky could have escaped earlier but he wouldn't leave until he saw you, Mr. Rosenbaum. When I picked him up that night, he was weeping. Not a side I'd ever seen of him." She studied Tillman for a long moment. Finally, she continued: "When he left from here, he flew partway on a small plane, then caught a boat and made it to Puerto Armuelles. Now he's gone someplace in Asia. I guess there are insane, wealthy, baseball memorabilia collectors there. He'll sell it and have money for his daughter."

Tillman planted elbows on his knees and let his head drop in his hands. "That crazy sonofabitch." Between his sneakers, a tear splashed on the tile floor. Tawny touched his bent-over back.

"You think I'm a terrible person and perhaps I am," Nyala murmured. "I'm guilty of loyalty to my brother but Smoky is my friend and I do care."

Tillman ran a hand across his eyes, raised his head, and stared at her. "Ms. Nyala, I believe you." He stood to leave.

Tawny gathered her bag and the package containing the emerald. She opened the front door and stepped out onto the porch. But Tillman didn't follow.

She looked back inside.

He and Nyala were facing each other. Tillman loomed above the beautiful woman and extended his hand. "Notwithstanding what you put Tawny through, I thank you for helping my friend, Smoky."

They shook. Nyala said something low that Tawny couldn't hear. Tillman's wide shoulders blocked her view for several seconds. Then he joined her on the porch.

For an hour, they drove in silence toward Clearwater Beach.

As they approached the Highway 60 causeway, Tillman pulled off the road and parked at a beach access. "Are you up to a walk?"

The long ride had stiffened her injuries. She needed to stretch. "Sure."

They got out and together moved from the pavement into soft, warm sand. Seabirds sailed overhead, cawing and clamoring. Across the inlet, power saws screeched as carpenters repaired docks damaged by Irma.

Revelations about Smoky still tumbled in Tawny's mind. She wondered what Tillman was thinking. He was rarely quiet this long. After a few minutes of walking, she said, "I'm glad Smoky's alive."

He glanced down at her. "If he and Gabriel ever cross paths again, he won't be. And if *I* ever see him again, I'll kick his goddamn ass into next week." But a faint smile flitted across his mouth.

They passed a makeshift graveyard of damaged, abandoned boats, battered into scrap by the hurricane, now piled high, waiting to be hauled away. A bent mast stuck up, broken pulleys with frayed lines running through them, personal floatation devices, torn seat cushions, a shattered galley countertop, a cracked portion of a sink.

And a twisted metal ladder similar to the one Tawny had desperately clung to on Ezekiel's yacht. The memory caused a sharp inhale, followed by a brief coughing spell.

Tillman watched her, waiting for the spasm to end, worry creasing his brow.

She recovered and sipped small breaths.

"You OK?" he asked.

She swallowed. "ER doc said my lungs might be touchy for a while."

His stare bored through her. "I can't believe you're alive."

"Me either." She rested her hand on his solid chest, feeling the thud of his heart. "You know what kept me hanging on?"

His long fingers played with her braid. "Hmm?"

"I kept repeating your name and the kids' names, over and over."

He let go of her braid, put on his half glasses, and pulled a slip of paper from his pocket.

She recognized it. Nyala must have given it to him as they left.

He unfolded it and read aloud what Tawny believed would be her last words to him. "*I love you, Tillman. Here and now. That's all that matters. No more excuses from me. Forever yours, Tawny.*" He took off his glasses and refolded the paper, studying her.

She let her hand drop from his chest to her side and lowered her eyes, embarrassed. "Nyala wasn't supposed to give that to you unless I died."

"But you didn't, thank God." A long pause. "Do you still mean what you wrote?"

After nearly drowning, marriage to Tillman no longer felt as terrifying. She whispered, "Yes." Then she looked up at him and said more loudly, "Yes, I do."

His dark eyes crinkled with tease. He held the paper up as if presenting it as evidence in court. "In that case, my considered legal opinion is you have proffered an open offer that is awaiting my acceptance. Once I accept—and I do—this document constitutes a valid binding contract."

She slid both hands across the muscular contours of his chest, over his wide shoulders, coming to rest on his hard biceps.

No longer did she feel as if she stood on either side of an earthquake fault, the ground ready to shift without warning under her feet.

Her footing finally felt steady, in bedrock.

His mouth curved into the crooked smile that brought back memories of the first night they'd made love. He tilted his head sideways. "Do we have a deal?"

She stepped closer, into his arms. "Deal."

THE END

Dead Man's Bluff

A Note From Debbie

Readers and book clubs are the lifeblood of an author. I'd love to hear from you and meet with your book club. Please visit my website to share your thoughts and questions or to arrange an appearance.

debbieburkewriter.com

If you enjoyed *Dead Man's Bluff*, I'd greatly appreciate your taking the time to write a short review on Amazon or Goodreads.

Many thanks!

About the Author

In addition to Tawny Lindholm Thrillers With A Heart, Debbie Burke writes articles for many print and online publications. She is a regular contributor to the award-winning crime writing website, The Kill Zone.

debbieburkewriter@gmail.com